SAILORS DELIGHT

By Malcolm Torres

Books by Malcolm Torres

Novels
  Sailors Take Warning
  Sailors Delight

Stories in the Sea Adventure Collection
  Sixty-Four Days
  The Pirate
  Shark Tooth Rosary
  Back to the Philippines
  Making Peace with Japan

Subscribe to the iTunes podcast:

Lost at Sea with Malcolm Torres

For more information:

www.malcolmtorres.com

Copyright © 2016 MT Press
All Rights Reserved
ISBN: 978-1500786366

This book is dedicated to all the sailors
who served aboard the USS Enterprise CVN-65.

Table of Contents

Red skies at night

Sailors delight

Red skies at morning

Sailors take warning

An old nautical saying

SAILORS DELIGHT

PART I

Chapter 1: USS Enterprise

The Northern Pacific Ocean ran rough beneath a blue sky.

Gusty winds tore the tops off the whitecaps, splashing spray in the troughs between the waves.

Big brass propellers churned beneath the great gray ship, pushing her bow forward, cutting a tattered wake on the gray-blue sea.

Several plane captains—young men in brown helmets, brown jerseys and flotation vests—clambered from a watertight door in the side of the hull and tromped along a catwalk of welded metal grates and railings alongside the flight deck high above the churning ocean. Each young man carried three tie-down chains slung over each shoulder. Their dirty hands, in fingerless gloves, clutched the chainhooks and turnbuckles to their chests.

In a few minutes, several A-7 Corsair jets would land and each young man would scramble across the deck, weaving between blasting jet engines and spinning propellers to secure their aircraft to the deck. They would fasten one end of each chain to the jet's landing gear and the other end to a padeye in the steel.

For the moment, though, they hung their chains by the hook-ends to the scupper, a steel rain gutter that runs along the entire edge of the flight deck, and they stood in the catwalk waiting for their jets to land.

An F-14 Tomcat fighter jet, with its dual engines shrieking like 4th-of-July rockets, flew out of the sky behind the ship, its extended wheels slamming the deck as its tailhook grabbed an arresting cable. The plane captains watched the Tomcat as it was yanked to a stop. They stayed put in the catwalk, waiting for their Corsairs to land. Next an E-2 Hawkeye, with its big propellers spinning so fast you couldn't see them, swooped out of the sky behind the ship and it too grabbed one of the thick, greasy arresting cables in the landing area and was yanked to a stop. An A-6 Intruder, with engines rumbling like thunder in a bowling alley, landed next. And, finally, the first A-7 Corsair howled in, accelerating toward the back of the ship.

A man's voice, crisp with amplified intelligence, rose above the roar of a dozen engines now running on the 4-acres of steel. The voice spoke from deck-edge loud speakers mounted in the catwalks all around the flight deck. "CORSAIR NEXT!   STAND BY TO LAND AIRCRAFT!"

The Hawkeye, a big aircraft with an enormous propeller on each wing, was right then being backed into its parking spot on the deck directly above the catwalk where the young men stood waiting.

The hurricane gale thrown back by the Hawkeye's whirling propellers pressed Larry Tynan's goggles flat on his face. Steven Oaks, Angelo and Martin Weary were there gripping their greasy knuckles white on the scupper, holding fast as the gale-force wind off the Hawkeye's propellers blasted their boyish faces. The tremendous HURRRRRR and WHIRRRRRR of the Hawkeye's engines whet their senses.

A few feet in front of them and above them, the Hawkeye rolled slowly, precariously backward several inches with each burst of power applied to its engines by the pilot in the cockpit at the throttles. The weight of the Hawkeye's fuselage and the folded-back wings compressed the stout hydraulic landing gear and weighed heavily on its fat black rubber tires.

A flight deck director, a man in a gold jersey, helmet and goggles, gave hand signals to the Hawkeye's pilot who looked out through the cockpit window. The pilot kept the Hawkeye going backward until its tires were just a few feet from the scupper. Blasting stronger than a gale wind, air came off the Hawkeye's starboard side propeller and hit the young deckhands hard in their faces.

It was Larry Tynan's A-7 Corsair that touched down in the landing area, so Christopher Marlow helped Larry swing three chains over each shoulder. Larry smiled to say thanks because talking on deck is useless when engines are roaring. Larry climbed the ladder and started to scramble onto the flight deck, but one of his chains got stuck on the scupper. He stopped and looked back, frustrated.

The chains always were too heavy for him. Although he had big shoulders and staunch legs, he'd never lost his baby fat. You could see it in his pink cheeks. Larry's blue eyes, framed in black rubber goggles, looked at Christopher Marlow, his best friend—a cry for help.

Larry knelt but he couldn't reach to unjam the chain from the scupper, because both his hands held the chains and turnbuckles to his chest. If he reached out to unstick the chain, all his chains would slide off his shoulders and fall into a tangle around his ankles.

Chis knew the look—a frustrated request for help—because he had looked at others the same way in the same spot when one of his chains had gotten stuck on the scupper.

Chris unhooked the chain and smiled at Larry but Larry was gone, throwing himself forward in frustration.

The night before, Larry had received a letter from his girlfriend back in Detroit, and since he was out of the country for nine or ten months again, she was going to date some other guy for a while.

Maybe that thought was stuck in Larry's mind when his chain snagged on the scupper—nobody would ever know.

Larry threw himself forward with the palm of his baby-fat hand on the front of his helmet and his other arm across his chest, holding the chains and turnbuckles. Instead of walking outboard from the Hawkeye's landing gear, Larry lurched forward next to the fuselage and the propeller caught him as it arced around.

When the prop is spinning, it's a blur, almost invisible.

It might've only knocked Larry's arm off but the chains tangled on the propeller, killing him instantly.

Horrified, the flight deck director ran in close to the spinning propeller, his arms extended, fingers clutching at the air as if he wanted to grab Larry and pull him out of that awful machine.

The propeller spun, its vortex instantly vaporizing Larry into a gory mist that splattered everywhere. Chain links busted apart and flew like bullets. One beaned Steven Oaks' so hard it shattered his helmet.

Martin Weary, Angelo and Christopher Marlow looked on in shock.

An explosion of gore, shreds of Larry's clothing and lengths of chain hit the Hawkeye's fuselage, splattered on the deck.

A red plume blew over the side of the ship.

Blood painted the loudspeaker on the catwalk railing red.

Christopher Marlow and Larry's other friends in the catwalk ducked in fear of being pummeled by busted lengths of chain and the detritus that had, a fraction of a second ago, been Larry Tynan's body.

Angelo yelled, "Oh my fucking God!" so loud it distorted his voice.

Christopher Marlow closed his eyes so tight the tears would never escape.

Two years later . . .

Chapter 2: Land Ho!

Along the edge of the USS Enterprise's flight deck, Sailors in dress white uniforms stand arms-length apart facing the sea. A salty breeze flutters their black neckerchiefs and ruffles the cuffs of their white pants.

The breeze threatens to blow the white hats off their heads.

The ship moves at a moderate pace, barely rocking on the calm sea.

Wind and sunrise disperse morning mist, revealing Diamond Head Crater, a jagged volcanic ridgeline a few miles away on the coast of the Hawaiian Island of Oahu.

Many sailors are fidgeting and whispering to each other. They are excited to see land for the first time in over eight weeks.

"Land ho," Christopher Marlow whispers when he catches sight of the island. To his right and left stand men he's never seen before; their skin is white from working below. They haven't seen the sun since leaving San Francisco eight weeks ago.

But working on the flight deck every day turned Christopher Marlow's face and shoulders a leathery-tan. His fingertips still tingle though, from handling steel tie-down chains in subzero winds up north on the Bering Sea. At twenty, Christopher has been a deckhand aboard the Enterprise for several years. And he's been carrying chains, drums of aircraft cleaner and dragging fuel hoses across the black steel as it pitched and rolled on oceans around the world. All that and strong-backing bombs under jet wings has roughened his hands and broadened his shoulders.

Christopher's polished shoes, his white jumper and a Dixie cup hat crimped over his freshly trimmed crew cut make him look squared away, but the truth is he feels horrible. He's been going to sick call a couple times a week but the ship's doctors haven't been able to tell him what's wrong.

The hotels on Waikiki Beach are getting bigger as the ship nears Pearl Harbor.

Christopher Marlow thinks about all the times he's been on an examination table at sick call with a corpsman looking at him. He remembers pointing to his chest, near his heart, and saying, "I finished the pills you gave me last but it still hurts right here."

They hardly look at him while they hold a pen in one hand and his medical record in the other, scribble the same old thing: "Changed patient's meds, fit for full duty." Then they move on to the next sailor in the long line at sick call. And Chris adds another vial of antacids, muscle relaxers or painkillers to the collection in his locker.

And now he's standing on the edge of the deck with the tips of his polished shoes against the scupper, looking down at the catwalk. He thinks about Larry Tynan but quickly looks away at the horizon where green mountains loom over the hotels on the beach. He takes a deep breath of fresh sea air and feels the anxiety in his chest ease. He listens to the soothing sounds of the ship's bow cutting through the water.

Seagulls ride the breeze, flapping their wings, swooping and cawing.

Chris listens to the gulls. They've flown out to greet the ship.

In the water, beams of sunlight penetrate the green-blue depths. For several minutes he listens to the steady hush of the ship's keel pushing aside the water, cutting like a knife through the breakers close to land.

And suddenly the sandy bottom is visible through the transparent blue water.

Land ho!

He hasn't seen dirt or trees in over eight weeks, never mind houses, cars or women. He lifts his gaze and sees a beach a couple hundred feet away. The palm trees are so green and vibrant they burn his retinas like a bright light shining in his eyes.

Sailors standing along the edge of the flight deck blink at the brightness, and on the black backs of their eyelids they see blurry green ghosts shaped like palm fronds. There's a row of little houses with cars in the driveways. A woman holding a baby standing in the street waves at the sailors aboard the big ship entering the channel to Pearl Harbor.

A stiff breeze comes across the deck and dozens of white hats take flight to leeward. Men put their hands on their heads and feel their hair.

Surprised looks appeared on their faces as their hats twirl on the breeze and fall eighty feet to the water where the mighty ship plows them under its frothy white spume.

"Attench hut!" a voice snaps from the deckedge loudspeakers. A line of marines standing on the bow and sailors all along the deckedge snap to attention.

Tugboats come alongside.

On the water's surface, cement memorials like floating tombstones appear. Chris reads the old battleship names painted in neat navy-blue letters: USS California, USS Tennessee, USS West Virginia, USS Maryland, USS Oklahoma, and USS Nevada. These mark the ships sunk on Battleship Row when the Japanese pulled a sneak attack on Pearl Harbor back in December of 1941.

As the Enterprise comes alongside the Arizona Memorial, a voice crackles from the loudspeakers. "Hand salute!"

There below the surface all behold the hull of the once mighty battleship, now sunk in the mud on the floor of the harbor. Her superstructure and stacks cut away. All the holes torn in her hull by Japanese torpedoes, welded over with steel plate patches. And there built over the sunken hull, the white memorial seems to float on the water—a memorial to all who lost their lives that day.

Forward on the Enterprise's bow, a marine barks a series of commands. Bolts slide and triggers click and rifle fire pierces the morning air. Three times a marine gives the command and three times seven rifles fire, rendering a 21-gun-salute in tribute to our shipmates lost so long ago on that day that lives in infamy.

A stroke of rainbow rises from the plush green mountain and a light rain begins to fall. "To," bangs from the loudspeakers, and everyone drops the salute. The sun slips behind a cloud, a thrusting cat's paw caresses the deck, and Chris's Dixie cup hat flies away like a wingless gull. With one hand on his freshly clipped crew cut, he watches his hat spinning towards the water along with many others. For a moment he sees his hat floating like a tiny, empty life raft and he imagines himself in miniature sitting in it, holding on for dear life, helpless before the ship, a gray wall of steel bearing down on him.

Lightning splits the sky and thunder rumbles over the green hills. Big cool raindrops fall, soaking through the shoulders of Chris's white crackerjack blouse. The wind blows more hats over the side. Sailors fidget and hold their hats on their heads as gusting winds sweep the harbor.

A shrill whistle blows and the formation breaks.

Sailors scramble between the jets on the deck to find their way to hatches leading into the ship.

Chris walks aft between the fighters and bombers, helicopters and ground support equipment. He lifts his feet over tie-down chains securing aircraft to the deck.

Far aft, he pauses at the edge of the flight deck before jumping over the scupper and landing several feet below in the catwalk. Through the metal mesh under his feet, he sees 80-feet to the water below, and then he hops down the steps down a ladder welded against the hull and goes through a watertight door into the ship.

*   *   *

Upon entering the living compartment someone yells, "Get out of the way, Marlow!"

Chris's head is blocking the TV, where a show never seen at sea appears on the screen. He looks at the TV and sees a beautiful woman in a white bikini performing deep knee bends. Blooming flower gardens surround her and a tall white hotel towers in the background. What captivates Chris isn't her flat tummy or her firm thighs but her sweet voice counting, "and two and three and four." He hasn't heard a woman's voice since leaving San Francisco eight weeks ago. Sure, he'd heard women on the television, talking in movies, but this show reminds him that today he's going ashore where he'll definitely meet some girls.

"Marlow! Get out of the way of the TV, man!"

Chris pushes through the crowd, into the compartment's center aisle. Every few feet to the right and left are cubicles packed tight with bunks and lockers and men in every stage of dress, every phase of conversation. Eighty aircraft mechanics live in the compartment. Forty work nights and forty work days, but today the ship is pulling in for three days of liberty, so no one is at work. Everyone is in the compartment. Cigarette smoke and cologne are overpowering. Men talk excitedly about going out in Honolulu as they pull on jeans, shirts, tennis shoes.

Chris shakes a Marlboro from his pack and lights up as he enters his cubicle. His friend, Steven Oaks, stands in the florescent shine of the overhead lights.

"You manned the rail." Steven is a 20-year-old from Boston. He wears blue rubber sandals and tighty-whitey underwear. He has square shoulders and a chiseled chest. He's dragging a comb through his brown hair. With his free hand he plucks the cigarette from Chris's fingers.

"Our hats blew over the side." Chris kicks off his shoes and climbs into his bunk, the middle in the tier of three on the left side of the cube.

Chris rests his head on his pillow and glances across at the bunk above Steven's. It's Larry Tynan's old bunk. The mattress is stripped and folded over. The locker emptied and the curtains removed. It's been well over a year but nobody has moved into Stanley's bunk. That would have been bad mojo.

"We ought to go see the Arizona Memorial," Chris says. "I mean, we've been here like six times but we've never been."

"Maybe tomorrow," Steven says.

"Did you know there are a thousand guys buried inside the sunken hull?"

"No shit?" Steven says.

"After forty years it still leaks oil."

"Right," Steven says. "I bet maintenance guys row out there at night and top it off with oil." He wraps a towel around his waist, locks his locker and grabs his mesh bag of toiletries.

"We really ought to go see the Arizona on Sunday," Chris says.

"You going to that Army hospital today?"

"Yeah, what are you doing?" Chris says.

"Me and Angelo are going to Waikiki." Steven says. "First I was thinking we'd get some steaks and a pitcher of cold beer—"

Chris is still thinking about going to see the Arizona.

"—and for dessert I'm gonna order a big bowl of vanilla ice cream and a jigger of cream de mint." Steven smacks his lips savoring the thought of his first meal ashore. "Then we're gonna get a pint of Johnny Walker, that one with the special black label, and a case of Molson Golden Ale." He puts a finger on his chin and a look of deep contemplation comes over his handsome face. "Or Grolsch, yeah maybe Grolsch, I gotta make up my mind! I kind of like the doohickey top on those Grolsch beers." Steven hands the cigarette back.

Chris takes a drag.

"We'll find a grove of palm trees and a couple lounge chairs," Steven says, "and we're gonna spend the afternoon getting stoned, you know, a good old liquor picnic. You want to meet us?"

"Sure," Chris says without conviction.

"Tonight Angelo wants to go to that nightclub the Wave," Steven says.

Chris imagines doing something adventurous, like taking a windsurfing lesson or going out on a charter boat for some deep-sea fishing. So many things are possible when the ship enters port, but when a gang of sailors go ashore, he knows too well, they reduce their options to the least common denominator which means they end up in a bar talking shit, getting drunk, trying to meet girls.

"Let's meet at the Wave around eight," Steven says as he leaves to go take a shower. "Hey," he turns back, "how long until the gangway is down?"

"Any minute, we're alongside the pier now." Chris clamps the cigarette between his teeth and swings his legs out of his bunk. He opens his locker and takes a last drag before snuffing the butt in an ashtray.

From his locker he takes a cellophane packet of Mylanta tablets and pops two into his mouth. He crunches them into frothy foam.

Leaning back, looking at Larry Tynan's empty bunk, Chris recalls the guys who came with the bolt cutters and snipped Larry's padlock. They tossed Larry's shit—his uniforms, toiletries, shoes, paperback books and letters from home—into an evidence bag. And then they left without saying a word.

Larry was dead.

Chris swallows the frothy goop and figures Steven is right—a steak and a pitcher of cold beer is going to make him feel a whole lot better than this shitty Mylanta.

Chapter 3: The Doctor's Eyes

Sailors in civilian clothes flow down the gangway from the Enterprise to the pier. Smiles beam on their faces. After two months at sea they are happy to be on land.

On the pier, amidst the hurly-burly of stevedores and officers, cranes are hoisting nets full of cargo, forklifts belch smoke between the clattering, grinding of their gears. Pallets piled with bails of green bananas, burlap sacks, crates, drums of aircraft cleaner and grease are stacked shoulder-high.

Across the pier from the Enterprise, tugboats guide the USS Sacramento into her berth. Atop the Sacramento's superstructure, a streamer of colorful signal flags flaps in the breeze.

Smoke erupts from a tugboat's stack as it churns up mud from the bottom of the harbor. The stout boat's horn bellows and its engines rev so powerfully a vibration passes through the air and through every person on the pier.

A loud POP slashes the commotion as a man fires a rifle and shoots a ball of twine up to a sailor on the Sacramento's main deck. He scrambles after the ball and grabs it and pulls with gloved hands to hoist up one of the six-inch hemp lines used to tie the ship to the pier.

On the periphery of this commotion First Class Petty Officer Redburn lays couchant, sunning himself on a pile of dunnage. His rotund belly bulges his dress white jumper, and his fingers, interlocked behind his head, push the Dixie cup hat forward over his eyes. Emulating the pose but not so well endowed with girth or shaveable whiskers, Airman Christopher Marlow lays beside his superior officer. A third patient, a marine in camouflage pants and rubber sandals, sits in a wheelchair extruding a low moan of pain. In order to accommodate his inflamed left shoulder, the marine cranes his neck at an odd angle.

"Tell us, marine," Redburn says, "what catastrophe has befallen you?"

"Befallen?" the marine asks.

"What happened to you?" Chris says.

"A forklift dropped a crate on me while I was sleeping on the hangar."

"You don't seem to be in much pain," Redburn says without opening his eyes. "Is anything broken?"

"My collarbone," the marine says. Even with his head bent to one side, appearing disjointed, he looks courageous and strong. His head is shaved in a tight crew cut. A bulldog tattoo on his forearm sneers sharp fangs.

"Hurts when you move, you say?"

"Yeah."

"Does it hurt real bad?" Redburn persists.

"Only when I move." The marine winces.

"Sit still then. A van will be here any minute to take us to the hospital."

"How far is the hospital?" The marine grits his teeth.

"Actually, you could see it from here but I don't advise you move your head. It's that pink edifice nestled in the foothills. Can you see it, Marlow?"

"Sure can."

A Ford Econoline 15-passenger van pulls up, brakes squealing as it comes to a stop. The driver hops out and says, "I'm here to take you guys to the hospital."

As the driver wheels the marine toward the van, Chris reads the nametag pinned to her shirt, "D. Stone." She's the first woman he's seen in two months and he can't take his eyes off her, captivated by the shape of her cheekbones and her eyes. Living on the ship with 5,000 men and now here's this pretty girl, a petty officer he realizes, noticing a chevron on the sleeve of her white blouse.

She asks, "You okay climbing up there, marine?"

"My collarbone hurts if I get jostled," he tells her. "If you would ma'am, take it easy on the bumps."

They pile into the van and she drives slowly across the Navy base. Chris's eyes strain after having seen only vast expanses of ocean and steel bulkheads and men for so long, the palm trees, cars and pedestrians are amazing. The colors and sounds are so bright and vivid he thinks about finding a dimly lit bar, a cold beer, maybe a shot of Wild Turkey or Tequila. It would be nice to shoot some pool, maybe meet a girl.

He sits back and inhales long and slow through his nose, and when his lungs are full, he exhales slowly through pursed lips. All the while he imagines the tension leaving him with the exhaled air.

Driving out of Pearl Harbor's main gate, D. Stone makes eye contact with Chris in the rearview mirror, and he thinks he sees a smile in her gaze. He wonders if he's overthinking it, but then she slams on the brakes to avoid hitting a pedestrian.

The marine yelps like a whipped dog.

"I'm so sorry," she says. "This van has sticky brakes."

Then she glares at Chris as if to say, "Stop distracting me!"

She drives slowly all the way up the mountain to the hospital, easing gently on the brakes and taking the turns wide. But it doesn't matter, every time she stops at a light or curves along the road, the marine whimpers.

Chris puts his hand out and the marine clenches it, squeezing tighter each time the pain rises.

In the corner of his eye, Chris sees the marine's jaw tensing and tears running down his cheek.

Through the trees Tripler Army Hospital appears. The towering pink Art Deco building looks more like a luxury hotel than an Army Hospital, with balconies covered by blue awnings on its upper floors. Surrounded by parking lots and smaller buildings painted the same soothing color, all nestled in the green mountains and white clouds overlooking Honolulu.

Chris figures the Army painted the buildings Pepto-Bismol pink to calm the soldiers and sailors arriving wounded from across the Pacific.

Redburn helps the marine out of the van and the driver wheels him inside.

Chris tries to make eye contact, but she gives him an expressionless glance when he says, "Thanks for the ride."

Redburn and Chris walk through miles of hallways and ask for directions a couple times, before taking an elevator up a few floors to the gastroenterology clinic.

When they check in, the receptionist tells them to wait because the doctor is away performing emergency surgery. Chris scans the covers of Time and Newsweek strewn across a table in the waiting area and the world rushes back at him. Ronald Reagan, AIDS, Cocaine, MTV and starving African children. He flips through an issue of People and glossy shots of Def Leppard, Mr. T, Stephen King and Valley Girls pop off the pages.

After a while, the receptionist tells Redburn that Doctor Burkham will see him.

Chris goes outside onto a balcony to smoke.

Honolulu International Airport is just out of view behind a mountain ridge, and every few seconds a jet airliner circles down out of the sky. Chris watches one of the gigantic metal birds and imagines the tourists belted snugly into their cushioned seats.

He loathes the tourists because he knows they see Oahu through the windows of air-conditioned tour busses, rental cars and from the balconies of their luxury hotel rooms, but he knows he's no better for having seen Hawaii several times through the bottom of a cocktail glass. The fact he's been eight weeks on the Pacific coming over from San Francisco, working twelve hours every day of the passage prevents him from thinking of himself as a tourist. Without hotel or rental car reservations, he knows he's not a tourist. Arriving on land thirsty for cold beer and longing for female companionship, he doesn't know quite what he is, a sailor he figures, certainly not a tourist.

Redburn sticks his head out onto the balcony and says, "Hey, kid, Major Burkham wants to see you." Chris pitches his cigarette into a tin can on the floor and goes inside. "Down the hall, room three," Redburn says.

Major Burkham has a touch of gray in her short brown hair, sharp eyes and a determined jaw. Her runner-lean body stands Army-straight in an impeccable light green shirt. Gold oak leaves shine on her collar points. Her piercing gaze and confident tone make Chris straighten up and throw his shoulders back.

"Tell me what's going on with you," she says.

Something between dread and optimism shoots through his belly. His mind splits in a schism. On one side a mass of worries, fretting over the possibility he's a hypochondriac—Am I making this up? But these thoughts square off against the regrettable fact that he does feel pain in his chest. Somewhere in the middle of his mixed up head, he thinks maybe this doctor can actually tell him what's wrong and set him up with a cure.

"Well Ma'am, uh, Major," he picks his words carefully. "It hurts right here," pointing to the left side of his chest. "Sometimes after eating or when I wake up in the middle of the night or in the morning," he pauses. Unlike the ship's doctors who always read his medical record while he spoke, Major Burkham looks him in the eyes. "When it hurts it isn't too bad, sometimes it goes away in an hour." Her concern catches him off guard, and he has an urge to downplay the pain, to buck up and be tough. Rub some dirt on it and walk it off. But he tells the truth. "There's times it hurts pretty bad for a few days and then it's hard to breathe."

"What kind of pain is it?"

He's seen a whole bunch of doctors on the ship, and what they do is write prescriptions for painkillers and antacids, but she's different. She wants to get beyond the symptoms.

"If it lasts a short time it's piercing like something is jabbing me right in the heart, but when it lasts a few days my chest feels tight and my left arm starts to hurt."

She looks in his eyes, examining his voice and expression for sincerity. "Remove your shirt and sit on the table," she says. "What's it like on your ship?"

"What do you mean?" he asks, because life aboard ship is a completely alien experience compared to day-to-day life on land.

"The food, work, things like that."

"They serve a lot of stew, vegetables and potatoes in the main galley. On the speed line I eat hamburgers and pizza."

"How long between the time you eat and the time you go to sleep?" She knows young men often eat a big meal, barely chew their food and go to sleep right after.

"About an hour or so, I guess," Chris says. "I usually eat dinner and then lift weights before going to sleep."

"That might be part of your problem," she tells him. "Food like that, gravy and fatty meats, can sit in your stomach for several hours after you fall asleep. What kind of work do you do?"

"I'm a plane captain on the flight deck. I have an airplane, an A-7 Corsair, and after it lands I chain it to the deck. I top it off with fuel and work with the mechanics and bomb loaders."

"Tell me about these chains."

"They're six-foot long tie-down chains. I carry three over each shoulder, all together about seventy pounds."

She walks behind him, and the cool disk of her stethoscope contacts his skin. She listens at several spots. Then she prods his shoulders and his spine while explaining how the chains might be pinching a nerve.

The second she touches him, a load of stress and tension rolls off. With the exception of a few high fives and handshakes, it's been months since another person has touched his skin.

*   *   *

Back in the 1960s, Janet Burkham graduated from college and entered the US Army with the rank of second lieutenant and the title of medical doctor. She was assigned to the hospital ship USS Sanctuary off the coast of Vietnam, where she performed surgery over two thousand times. She did amputations to finish the work started by land mines. She put stomachs and intestines back together after bullets and grenades exposed and burned them. After Vietnam, she worked in the emergency room at a veteran's hospital in San Francisco through most of the 1970s, and now in the 80s—here in paradise, on Oahu where living is easy—she sees how young military men behave, when there isn't a war on. A steady stream of soldiers and sailors sit on her examination table with hernias, ulcers, sexually transmitted diseases, PTSD, cracked vertebra. Her patients are typically young men with early signs of cardiovascular disease, cirrhosis of the liver, cancer and all manner of psychological problems.

Airman Marlow's heartbeat sounds a little too heavy and the muscles in his neck and back are tight like ropes.

"I'm sending you for x-rays, and I want you back in two days," she says.

While pulling on his shirt he says, "Thank you, Ma'am."

*   *   *

Chris is wearing a thin cotton robe that hangs open in the back.

A technician takes him to a room and tells him to stand on an X on the floor. Another technician hands him a tiny cup of crystals the size of kosher salt, and a large cup filled with a white liquid. "That's Barium," the technician says.

They fold a metal arm down from the ceiling and attach a drum with what looks like a camera lens pointed at him.

"Turn around," a technician says from behind a green-tinted

window. "Stand up straight and lean your head forward."

Chris complies and feels a draft blowing on his exposed butt.

Mechanical clicking behind him, the machine snapping x-rays of his spine and skull.

"Okay, now turn around."

Chris does as he's told.

"You're going to toss the crystals in the small cup to the back of your mouth and then drink the Barium.   Got it?"

"Sure," Chris says.

"Okay, go ahead."

The crystals hit his tongue and start crackling. Several pop out of his mouth and shoot across the room. He gulps the Barium. It's the consistency of watery pancake batter, tastes like chalk.

He feels his stomach stretching as it fills with the crackling crystals and Barium. The camera clicks, capturing the turgid activity on x-ray.

*   *   *

Sitting in front of the hospital waiting for the bus, Chris wonders about Redburn, but the two men never see each other again. That's how it is with sailors. Shipmates know each other for an hour or a year, and then they're gone forever.

Outside hot and he thinks it would be nice if that pretty driver, D. Stone, arrived to give him a lift back to the base. He imagines sitting across from her at a small table with a round of slushy drinks between them.   He'd make eye contact with her like they did in the van's rearview mirror, but he feels awkward because he wouldn't know what to say. She won't be interested in his rough stories about living on a ship, and if he told her the truth about what he did in foreign ports she probably wouldn't like him at all.

He regrets his sailor lifestyle, exciting as it is.

He wonders what the D stands for. Probably Diane or Debbie or Dolores—one of those fine traditional names. She didn't look like a Daphne or a Darlene, but who knows. Probably never see her again anyway. The thought of people he's never going to see again brings to mind Larry Tynan, his former best friend.

They'd gone ashore together in ports around the world.

But Larry's dead. Torn to bits.

The bus arrives and Chris asks the driver if she goes to Pearl Harbor. "Sure do," she replies. "Navy Exchange, Arizona Memorial, Makalapa gate, main gate and the shipyard."

"Thanks," Chris says wondering where he should get off, but he knows it won't be hard to find the ship. After all the USS Enterprise has a gigantic number 65 painted on the side. He's been in ports all over the world and had wandered around many a waterfront searching until he saw that number and the long gray hull tied to a pier or anchored in the harbor.

*   *   *

Back aboard the Enterprise, Chris puts on shorts, wiggles his toes into sandals. He buttons a floral print luau shirt. The loose-fitting clothes are an extreme change from his flight deck gear. After wearing steel-toe boots, greasy canvas pants, a long-sleeve turtleneck and a cranial helmet make his civilian attire feel wispy.

He splashes on cologne and inhales the aroma with a gusto he hasn't felt since San Francisco. He slips two crisp hundred-dollar bills into his wallet and snatches a fresh pack of Marlboro from the carton in his locker.

When Chris glances at Larry Tynan's old bunk and sees the bare, folded mattress, memories flicker in his mind.

He remembers standing in the catwalk on the flight deck, helping Larry heave tie-down chains onto his shoulders. He remembers Larry trudging up the ladder and stopping because one of his chains caught on the scupper. Larry looks Chris in the eyes—a plea for help—and Chris unhooks the stuck chain from the scupper. Chris watches Larry take two steps closer to the Hawkeye's spinning propeller—

He shivers like bugs are crawling on his belly, and he gasps for breath and puts a hand to his chest. But the memory persists. He sees the back of Larry's cranial helmet and the back of his brown flotation vest. The chains dangle over Larry's shoulders and hang down his back. Those chains always were too heavy for him. It's happening right now. Chris wants to reach out and grab Larry, stop him from taking another step—that fatal step.

Chris bolts from the living compartment. The metal door bangs behind him as he runs from the memory of his dead best friend.

Chapter 4: The Wave

At sea a sailor is surrounded by the vast ocean. Overhead, a haze-gray sky. His mind is habituated to celibacy. Long periods at sea inflict sensory deprivation and encrust his vices and lust under a shell of boredom. The steel bulkheads and decks aboard ship trap the seaman's mind, force it into dormancy like a prisoner sentenced to long days of hard labor. But then he comes ashore and it's like waves crashing on coral, animating his life with the vibrant colors of shore leave. The act of walking off a ship in civilian clothes and stepping on dry land fills a sailor with equal parts delight and danger.

When Chris steps off the bus at the corner of Ala Moana Boulevard and Kalia Road, the Hilton Hotel stands on the beach before him, a white concrete escarpment towering into the brilliant blue Hawaiian sky. The Fort DeRussy Hotel, a 14-story rampart of balconies and sliding glass patio doors stands next in a wall of luxury hotels lining Waikiki.

Following the sidewalk between flowering shrubs and palm trees, he arrives on the beach, flips off his sandals and walks across the sand. He realizes he's spent eight weeks on the Pacific Ocean but hasn't felt a drop of it on his skin the entire time and now all he wants to do is soak his tired feet.

Up to his knees in warm blue breakers, he gazes at the sunset burning in the distance.

He walks along, wading in the water, making his way toward Diamond Head Crater. Sand squishes through his toes, and eight weeks of hard labor melts from his muscles and bones.

At the Royal Hawaiian, a pink adobe palace with blue awnings and courtyard gardens full of stunted palms, Chris slips his sandals on.

He walks around the swimming pool and up the steps to the hotel's main entrance just as two women in colorful dresses exit the lobby. He holds the door for them. Their resemblance says mother and daughter, and when the mother turns to him and says, "Thank you, young man," he's unable to utter a reply. He's overwhelmed by the perfection in the way they both have applied red lipstick. Their eyes bright. Their hair held back behind their ears with white and orange orchids. They descend the steps to a waiting limousine, and Chris can only stare after them, stunned by two perfect pairs of bare shoulders.

He's a sailor who has been too long at sea.

The host leads him to a table on a green lawn ringed by palm trees and takes his drink order. Minutes later a waitress brings a Fog Cutter; a slushy concoction with lots of rum and fruit juice. A couple of sips unwind him before a big plate of mahi-mahi, sliced pineapple, asparagus and rice pilaf arrives. For the first time in over 60 days, he chews his food slowly and savors every mouthful.

Muscular men, surfers by day, set up bongos and torches. When the tables around him begin filling for the evening luau, Chris leaves to meet his friends at the Wave.

The rum lights a buzz in his brain, and back on the street, he admires the beautiful people in vacation clothes walking and driving in shiny rental cars and jeeps. Suddenly in the crowd he sees a shipmate, Ordnanceman Goblat, red faced no doubt after being rummied away in a pier bar with cold beer on tap all afternoon.

"Marlow!" Goblat extends a huge hand at the end of a forearm tattooed with a golden anchor, emblazoned with USN. A black-haired hula girl sways her hips each time he flexes the sinewy bulk of his left forearm. Goblat's jaw is hinged like a bear trap beneath a furry red beard. He stands a stalwart five foot five, wearing brown topsiders, white pants and a pink Polo shirt.

"Hello," Chris says.

"Will you join me for dinner?"

"I just ate at the Royal Hawaiian." Chris puts a hand on his satiated belly. "I'm meeting Angelo and Steven Oaks at the Wave in a little while."

"Drinking at the Wave tonight?" Goblat asks.

"Yeah, let's meet up."

"I'll eat my dinner and head over."

"See you later." Chris waves and walks away.

*   *   *

The Wave sits on a busy street beside a drawbridge, across from the

Waikiki Marina. Masts like sparsely lit Christmas trees rise from sailboats moored between the slips. The block-long building completely covered with a gigantic florescent mural of a tidal wave about to crash on the steep slopes of snowcapped Mount Fuji. A mob of tourists dressed for a night of cocktails and dancing moves slowly past three muscular bouncers who check IDs and collect five-dollars a head.

"Christopher Marlow!" someone is shouting.

It's Angelo's voice, but he doesn't see Angelo. Then Angelo appears floating above the crowd. He's waving one hand over his head and shouting, "Christopher Marlow!"

Chris pushes through the crowd to the street and there's a shiny jade-green Suzuki Samurai jeep with a convertible top. Angelo is standing on the passenger seat holding onto the windshield with one hand. Steven Oaks is at the wheel. Chris leaps in and Steve darts into traffic.

"Where we headed?"

"Cruising!" Angelo has dark skin, a tight afro, and he's stocky with a barrel chest.

Steve wears mirrored Ray-Bans. A cigarette between his lips.

"Nice ride huh?" Angelo smacks the console.

"It's fine!" Chris buckles his seatbelt because he feels like he's going to fly out the back as Steve whips around a corner and accelerates onto a highway entrance ramp.

A big sign looms above: Koko Head 8, Kaimuki 4, Pakalolo 1.

The temperature drops a few degrees as they climb into the Koolau Mountains.

Angelo points to a brown bag on the floor and Chris pulls out a bottle of Beck's from the six-pack. Angelo hands him the opener and a second later passes back a bottle of Southern Comfort.

Chris swigs the SoCo—the familiar hot-candy flavor electric in his mouth. He raises the Becks to his lips and glances at the empty seat beside him—Larry's seat. And just as Larry's smiling face materializes in his imagination, Chris chugs the beer, attempting to wash Larry away. But it isn't enough. Larry continues smiling and Chris takes another hit of Southern Comfort. The beer fizzes in his belly and the warmth from the syrupy liquor radiates up through his chest, rising into his neck and his brain. It feels so good he glances over and smiles at his dead best friend. He lights a cigarette, inhales deep and feels himself coming alive.

Now they are on the King Kamehameha Highway traveling along the shore. Black ocean to the right. Steep mountains to the left. Steve slows near a sign that says Wawamalu Beach. He turns onto a sandy trail through a copse of palms, banyans and monkeypods. Bristles of saw grass and taro grow knee high up to the tire tracks. On the crest of a low dune, Steve stops and cuts the engine. With the headlights off, they sit quietly in the dark. No light mars the seamless night. Not even the moon shows it celestial face. A belt of pinprick stars collect themselves across the heavens.

"Let's take a swim!" Angelo shouts, leaping from the jeep.

It's a footrace to the surf with all three men disrobing as they run and dive on the purling waves. They swim out over a sandbar and beyond a reef where the ocean floor falls deep away. They swim out so far the coast is a dark silhouette on the horizon behind them.

The long, hot workdays on the black steel melt away. The high decibel whine of jet engines singing soprano on the fragile follicles of their inner ears dissolves among muffled splashes in the murky water.

Chris plunges under the waves. Pointing his head down, he scissor-kicks powerfully and reaches, cups his hands and pulls his way into the black depths. Muffled sounds quickly fade as he drags himself into silence. Salt water becomes noticeably cooler. He continues kicking and pulling, descending. Chilly thermoclines wash over him, refreshing and brisk, the salty abrasiveness scrubbing his skin.

He opens his eyes to stinging blackness and quickly clamps them shut. He hangs suspended in the water, his arms out, the current sucking him along, to where he doesn't know and doesn't care. Cool wet darkness on every inch of skin.

He sees water blasting from a shiny brass nozzle at the end of a fire hose. It breaks into white foam against flat black steel. He's clutching a rigid hose. He's the lead man on a team working it back and forth, pointing the powerful spray at the black steel, washing away—

There's blood and flesh and broken bones.

And what else?

He doesn't know. He doesn't want to know.

But he does know.

There's a fucking pink tube—

Chris knows it's a length of Larry Tynan's intestine. And it's stuck under the Hawkeye's fat black tire. They point the hose right at the fucking thing but it wouldn't wash away.

It's stuck there, and—

Godammit!

Someone is going to have to touch it. Pick it up and drop it into an evidence bag or toss it over the side—if they can't spray it overboard.

Chris's eyes are shut but he reaches his arms out as far as he can and scratches at the water with his fingers. He's trying to claw his way further into the abyss, but something holds him back.

The need to breath burns under his sternum, preventing him from descending any further. But he doesn't care. He wants all of this cold blackness.

Later, when he finally surfaces, he gasps for air and plunges under again. He swims down, down until his lungs ache and his ears ring. He shivers in the cool water, shivers with fear because he almost remembers what happened after Larry died.

*   *   *

They collect driftwood and build a fire in the dunes.

"Hot nurses at that hospital?" Steven Oakes asks.

"I swallowed Pop Rocks and chugged a bucket of pancake batter while they took x-rays of my stomach."

"What'd the doctor say?"

"I'm going back in two days for results."

"You gonna stay here?" Angelo asks. "They got the best rec' center in the Navy, so you better keep lifting weights you pussy."

"She's won't keep me here," Chris says.

"She!" Angelo squeals. "She! We're in paradise, the best rec' center in the Navy and you got a lady doctor! Oh, man!" Angelo stands and bends his knees. He does a back flip, almost doesn't land it, then says, "Stay here and get some luau booty, Marlow!"

"I don't know." Chris grins. "I kind of have to go to the Persian Gulf."

"Why, when you can stay here?" Angelo is baffled.

"I need money."

"For the college fund?" Steven asks.

"What?" Angelo can't comprehend.

"My dad gave me three thousand dollars to put in the Navy college fund but I spent it," Chris says.

"On what?" Angelo asks.

"Paid off my motorcycle and took a road trip to Vegas."

"Nice." Angelo laughs.

"They give you two dollars for every dollar you put in," Chris says. "My dad will kill me if I go home after I get out and I don't have that money."

"Take the luau booty," Angelo says.

"You can probably catch up with the ship in the Philippines in a month or so," Steven says.

"I can't afford to stay here," Chris says. He'd spent an hour with a calculator and a pencil working numbers on a legal pad, and he concluded that he has to save every paycheck during the Enterprise's upcoming three-month line period on the Persian Gulf. He knows it means working the flight deck every day and saving every dollar he earns for three months, but he has no choice. His Dad gave him three thousand dollars and he'd spent it, and now he knows he has to work his ass off to earn that money and deposit it into the Navy college fund.

"Let's toast to Larry." Steve hoists his beer.

"To Larry fucking Tynan," Angelo says and downs the last of the Southern Comfort. Then he leans his head back and shouts at the stars, "You stupid son of a bitch!"

*   *   *

A block-long mural of a tidal wave about to crash on Mt. Fuji is painted on the side of the club.

Suntanned girls, their beautiful faces like seashells and eyes like pearls, fresh clipped hair and eyeliner captivate the sailors. Myriad lines lead from the club's entrance and clusters of friends stand around talking, smoking, checking out the crowd.

Goblat is close to the door, so they cut in front of some college guys wearing designer jeans and thin ties. The college guys start to protest, but Goblat and Angelo stare them down.

Steven Oakes leers at them and asks, "Fellas, do we have a problem here?"

They don't say a word.

In the club, a hit song is throbbing from the sound system and above the crowd, surfer videos flash on projector screens.

Goblat and Chris part the mob, push through to the bar.

Someone pays for the first round.

A band comes on stage and jams through big-hair metal music and new wave dance hits.

The scene is dark with splashing colored lights. The crowd is packed in tight and the music is loud and electrifying. Chris feels perfect. No pain. He's having a great time with friends. At one point he thinks to himself that dancing at a nightclub is the same things as drinking liquor at an aerobics workout, not that he's ever done aerobics.

They join a group of sorority girls from Kansas and combine their effort to drink the Wave dry. When the band, which has a three-piece horn section, takes a break, the sisters and the sailors gather upstairs where they bend backwards over the bar and have Kamikaze shots mixed right in their mouths.

Several hours of fun are lost in a frenzy of dancing and drinking.

—leading to blindness.

*   *   *

At sunrise the universe gives birth to Christopher Marlow—a painful and hot-bloody birth jolting him from a black paralysis. He's wobbling and struggling to focus on a lamp on a nightstand. The lamp is ringing as loud as an alarm bell aboard ship. He stares at the lamp as pains shoots through his brain. His eyes burn with hot liquid that he knows is blood on fire. He simply cannot understand why the lamp is ringing, but holy shit is it loud!

He sees a telephone on the nightstand next to the lamp but still does not understand that it's the phone ringing—not the lamp.

Confused, he picks up the phone.

"Aloha," a female voice. "This is a friendly wakeup call for Mister Marlow."

Chris's brain refuses to function.

"It's six am. Is Mister Marlow there?"

Chris glances around the dark room. Sleeping bodies strewn about. He remembers a pretty girl insisting that you can run faster in a hotel hallway than anywhere else on earth. She dashed away along the hall and he ran after her, discovering it was true, you can run remarkably fast in a long hotel hallway. They sprinted through the narrow space, carpet and wallpaper, doors and room numbers sliding past in their peripheral vision.

Parties started in random rooms. There were Germans on vacation, Japanese Navy Guys, more girls on break from college.

Chris remembered seeing his face reflected under white lines on a mirror. Purple-haired Hawaiian reefer smoked in a bong had them all laughing at Goblat and an Australian sailor—both stripped to tighty-whities, comparing tattoos.

He liked the Aussie's accent.

A confrontation with hotel security after someone complained about something, he wasn't sure what. A fight maybe?

He remembered being outside in the warm night, on a balcony under the stars, he and the girl from Kansas were kissing. Later in the bed, he unbuttoned her shirt, but she wouldn't let him unclasp her belt even though he tried.

"Is Mister Marlow there?" The woman's voice in the phone.

"This is me," Chris says, not quite sure.

"Have a wonderful day, Mister Marlow."

They hang up.

He pushes aside the curtain and steps outside onto the balcony.

A deserted beach twenty floors below. More memories flashing in his head. A tattoo parlor where a guy with a Camel no-filter hanging between his lips, breathing smoke as he buzzed the big flank of Goblat's deltoid with a tat' gun. A ferocious orange and black-striped tiger breaking through foliage with sharp claws. And one of the sorority girls got the Egyptian Eye of Ra on her scapula.

What a night, he thinks and slips back into the room. He almost steps on Goblat who is sleeping with his face planted in the carpet, shirtless, a bandage over his new tattoo. Steve and Angelo are in the other bed, under a sheet, spooning a girl between them.

Alone on the other mattress sleeps the shirtless sorority girl, a little snore whistling in one nostril. Brunette locks across her face, her body covered by a blanket. Chris is remembering her great boobs but reality snaps back when he pulls out his wallet and finds a single dollar; not nearly enough for a cab.

He's got to get to his duty section muster on the ship in an hour, at seven.

"Wake up." He shakes Steven's shoulder.

"Dude?" Steven groans.

"Can I have some money for a cab?"

"Take twenty." Steven points at his wallet on the nightstand.

In the hall, Chris waits for the elevator and wonders what hotel he's in. When it arrives, a loud DING hammers like a nail into his brain. The door clatters open.

The elevator descends and his stomach rises about half way up his throat. He swallows hard trying to keep the barf down. He's all woozy like a chubby ballerina is doing a pirouette between his ears. It's hopeless. His stomach bucks alcohol and acid into the back of his mouth. He presses a hand to the wall, sinks to his knees and vomits hard twice.

The bell clangs again and the doors slide open.

There's a mom and dad with a nine-year old girl standing there. The girl has a snorkel mask on her forehead, a bikini and flip flop sandals. "I want to push the button," she squeals and darts into the elevator.

The mom grabs the girl by the arm and yanks her back, shielding her eyes, but it's too late.

Chris hears the girl ask, "What's a matter with that man?"

Chris stays down on all fours, feeling like an animal in a cage at the zoo. The mom is shocked, but the dad smirks and shakes his head.

The door closes and the elevator descends. Chris stands up and wipes the back of his hand across his mouth. Something gnaws beneath his ribs like a hungry rodent inside his stomach trying to chew its way out.

Walking across the shiny marble lobby and out onto the early morning street, he wonders about the exact meaning of the word lousy.

Chapter 5: Hallucinating on Duty

"Airman Marlow!" the watch officer hollers over his clipboard.

"Here, sir," Chris shouts.

"You've got the twenty-four to zero-four security watch up on the flight deck, Airman."

"Aye aye," Chris replies.

"Petty Officer Russell," the watch officer shouts the next name on his list.

"Right here."

"You've got supernumerary, Russell."

"Aye aye, sir."

Martin Weary leans over in ranks and whispers, "Hey, Marlow, how'd it go last night?

Chris feels like he's been dowsed in gas and set ablaze. Every cell in his body accuses him of arson. "Shhhhh," he hisses at Martin Weary.

"All I said was how'd it go last night, you don't have to get your panties in a bunch—"

"Airman Marlow," the watch officer snarls over his clipboard, "cut out the grab assing!"

"Aye aye, sir," Chris glares at Martin then turns his gaze out the oblong opening in the side of the ship's hangar and takes in the green vegetation carpeting the Koolau Mountains. Blue water ripples on Pearl Harbor and palm trees sway in the breeze. He wonders how it's even possible to drink all night and wake up thirsty. He figures the smoke from all the cigarettes had dried him out.

When the watch officer shouts, "Fall out!" the formation breaks and Chris walks across the hangar, picking his way through aircraft chained to the deck, stacks of wooden crates and 55-gallon drums to a watertight door in the gray steel bulkhead. He steps over the knee knocker into a narrow ladderwell and climbs below to the galley for some chow.

A mile-long line of guys waiting to eat goes back through the eight-foot-wide main deck passageway, continues into a dark living compartment, down a ladder to the deck below and into the ship's laundry where washers and dryers the size of garbage trucks clank and growl steadily.

He waits 45-minutes for powdered eggs, hash browns, chipped beef on toast and pineapple chunks, and sits at a small stainless steel table.

A second later, Martin Weary, who must have been a few guys behind him in line, sits across from him.

"Fucking Marlow," Weary says as he shakes pepper on his eggs then plucks the Tabasco from the table.

"What's up Weary?"

"I'll tell you what's up," he says. "I was golfing with a pal of mine on the flying squad yesterday and you'll never guess what that cocksucker told me."

"What'd he tell you, Weary?" Chris asks as he squirts ketchup on his eggs.

"You know what the flying squad is, right?"

Chris knows. "No, Weary, what's the flying squad?" He folds a forkful of chipped beef inside a piece of toast.

"How long you been on this boat, Marlow?" Weary asks.

"Three years," Chris says around a mouthful of food.

"Three fucking years, and you don't know what the flying squad is, damn, I had no idea you were still such a fucking nugget after all this time!" Weary shakes more pepper over his eggs. Apparently, he likes them spicy. "It's the ship's emergency response team, numb nuts! Every time you hear that ear splittin' buzzer," Weary says "buzza" because he's from Boston. "You know those guys who run through the passageways like a fucking stampede, all wearing red jerseys and yelling shit like 'gangway' and 'make a hole!' Marlow, you never heard of them?"

There's a tremendous amount of clattering trays, chairs scraping across the deck, cutlery clicking at the metal tables all around them and a roar of conversation, causing a terrific headache to grind away inside Chris's head.

"So what did your friend say?" Chris chugs a glass of water, attempting to extinguish the peptic ember smoldering at the base of his esophagus.

"You remember that fire we had the first night out of San Francisco," Weary speaks around a mouthful of food, "the one in the

Marine living compartment."

"Sure." Chris remembers the alarms going off.

For several days afterwards, stories went among the crew about the fire. Apparently, there was some welding and the heat from a torch penetrated a bulkhead and ignited the paint on the other side. It turned out that a half-dozen old coats of paint had built up on the bulkhead and the welder's torch ignited them. There was a fire watch posted, like there was supposed to be, but when the paint started bubbling and smoking, the watch squeezed the lever on his CO-2 fire extinguisher and nothing came out because the old fire-bottle was empty. Within seconds, the paint was bubbling off the bulkhead like wallpaper in hell and smoke as black as the backs of your eyelids filled the compartment. The temperature shot up over 300 degrees. The alarm for general quarters was sounded and the entire crew went to battle stations. Before the Flying Squad put out the blaze, it incinerated the entire marine living compartment, torched their mattresses, burned all their uniforms and melted their TV. The entire compartment was reduced to an old, broken barbecue grill, leaving the marines homeless. For the next eight weeks, all the way from San Francisco to Hawaii, the marines slept on the aircraft hangar and worked shifts around the clock. The night before pulling into Pearl Harbor the captain announced that the marines had completely restored their living compartment.

"Well, check this shit out," Weary says. "My buddy on the flying squad tells me the blaze was a whole lot worse than what everyone was led to believe."

Chris pauses with a forkful of scrambled eggs in front of his face and thinks it might be a bad idea to eat such a big tray of food, because he feels like someone wearing steel-toe boots kicked him in the gut, but he decides he's hungry and continues shoveling chow into his mouth.

"Below the compartment where the Marines live, there's a large weapons magazine," Weary says.

"Oh shit, that's right." Chris realizes why the captain put the crew at general quarters that night. He remembers the klaxon blaring and an announcement from speakers throughout the ship telling all hands to man their battle stations. In over three years aboard that was the only time he'd ever heard "man your battle stations" followed by "this is not a drill."

"The whole reason the marines live right on top of that magazine,"

Weary says, "is because that's where they store nuclear warheads."

"No shit!" Chris doesn't want to believe it but he knows it's true.

"That blaze burned through into the magazine and lit off two heat seekin' missiles." Weary says. "But that ain't half of it, Marlow. What you ain't gonna believe is the part about the marine guard and the two cats on the flying squad."

"They get burned in the fire?"

"Worse," Weary says. "The marine guarding the magazine heard the alarm and smelled smoke and freaked out. When the first guy from the flying squad came through the watertight hatch into the area outside the magazine, the fucking marine shot him in the fucking chest."

"Shot him?"

"Right through the heart, man." Weary makes his hand into a pistol and points it at Chris. "Pow!" he says. "The marine thought it was a security breach or something. Then two missiles exploded inside the magazine, which is basically a gigantic bank vault full of high explosives, and the marine shot the next flying squad guy who came through the hatch."

"Shot two fucking guys!"

"That fire was blazing out of control in a magazine full of bombs for twenty minutes before the head of the Marine detachment finally deprogrammed the fucking guy so the flying squad could get in there to flood the magazine and put out the fire."

"That's insane," Chris says. "We're a few decks above on the flight deck and we never heard about any of that!"

Weary shovels chip beef into his mouth. "But the worst part is, one of them nuclear bombs got melted and that plutonium shit came out all over the deck!"

"No fucking way!" Chris says.

"Yeah—way," Weary says, "seriously."

*   *   *

He wakes up around ten that night and it feels like a madman ran a hot poker through his torso. In his locker, in one of the compartments, he keeps a collection of the wonder drugs dispensed by the ship's pharmacy over the years. He has Mylanta liquid and chewable tablets, Tagamet, Alka-Seltzer, Tylenol-3, a few Percocet and a stash of

Amobarbital. He shakes a blue Amobarb' into his palm and washes it down with a swig of cherry flavored Mylanta.

He sits in the lounge alone smoking. It's quiet in the dim red glow of a battle lantern. The AC is cranked all the way up. He's practically shivering it's so cold while he waits for the pill to do its thing.

He looks at the battle lantern glowing inside a plastic globe on the bulkhead. It casts eerie shadows around the lounge. Sections of newspaper, empty pop cans and flattened cigarette butts are strewn on the deck. A faint hum reverberates through the steel all around him from motors and air-circulating units. Chris flips through a newspaper section. He smokes a cigarette, filling his lungs with smoke and exhaling through his nose. The Amobarbital, which at its peak produces mild hallucinations, has numbed the burning sensation in his chest, but he hasn't yet begun to experience the salad of visual and auditory sensations he knows are moments away. His spine feels like a hollow tube with a cool breeze blowing through it and his hands feel as if they are rotating around backwards on his wrists. These are the typical feelings he experiences just before the Amobarb' really kicks in.

In the newspaper, her reads:

> Majority leader Patrick Fitzwater filed charges yesterday in the Dallas Supreme Court against the US Department of Defense, Grumman Aerospace Corporation and several presidential aides after Turkish officials seized 75 crates full of US-made aerospace equipment bound for Tehran, Iran.
>
> Documents showing the crates went from the US to Israel triggered a Turkish official's suspicion. Turkish Customs seized the crates at Istanbul International Airport while US Air Force personnel were loading them onto an Air Force C-5 Galaxy cargo plane. (We hate Iran, Chris whispers, why's the Air Force delivering equipment to those guys?) "It looked shady to me," a Turkish official said. "Had there been only aircraft parts in the shipment we might not have questioned it, but there were many crates full of missiles."
>
> "In the past," Fitzwater said yesterday in Dallas "it has always been defense contractors who have been caught delivering weapons to America's so-called enemies, but now we have the crew of an Air Force plane and several White House insiders caught red handed shipping arms to Iran. Stand back while my colleagues and I blow the whistle on the administration and its

Iran connection." Fitzwater did not reveal names, but alleged
that this shipment is a small part of a much larger secret deal
between Iran and the White House.

   Three years of war with Iraq has left the Iranian Air Force, an
estimated 300 Grumman F-14 Tomcat fighter jets in 1979, in
disrepair. CIA sources revealed several months ago that more
than 200 of those F-14s were grounded due to a shortage of
replacement parts, and those parts are available only from the
United States. "This looks like a deal where the President's
senior personnel are trading weapons for hostages," Fitzwater
said—

Chris lowers the paper and takes a drag off his cigarette.

He notices the red fire light is glowing brighter and he imagines the
electrical power must be surging throughout the ship, but then he laughs
when he realizes the light hasn't gotten any brighter.

It's the Amobarb' playing tricks on him.

Reading the newspaper article makes him think about Larry,
because Larry once told him about Iranian pilots who were trained to
fly Tomcat fighter jets by the US Navy at the Top Gun fighter base in
Miramar, California. Larry was up on all the political intrigue. He was
one of the few military people who knew why wars were being fought
and where the US supposedly stood on the issues. "Back in the
seventies," Larry told Chris one time, "the Navy set up a squadron to
train Iranian pilots and mechanics to fly and maintain the F-14 Tomcat
fighter. The Iranians purchased hundreds of American-made supersonic
fighter jets along with missiles and spare parts and it was all on the up
and up with the US government because the US and Iran were friendly
back then. That is, until the Shah fell and mobs of Iranian students
overran the US embassy and took hostages."

"Do you think the Iranians could fly out and take a shot at us?" Chris
asks aloud but realizes he's alone in the lounge. The breeze in his spine
blows a little cooler. He looks around, thinking he might see Larry
there, but he's alone.

Shadows shrink into the corners as the red light suddenly brightens.
The newspaper pages slide off his lap and separate, fanning out across
the floor. He clutches the edge of the hard plastic chair and exhales
smoke, making an eerie red swirl in the air.

The humming noise from below seems to be getting louder.

Larry told Chris not to worry. "The Iranians don't have anything that can penetrate the Enterprise's defense perimeter. Their only chance against us is to fly an old Tomcat in low to the water and shoot a rocket at us. They'd probably put a hole in the ship but it wouldn't sink us."

The air-circulating unit quiets and the red nightlight dims.

"Shame on those greedy politicians," Larry says, "making a profit on the backs of dead soldiers and sailors."

Chris looks through the cigarette smoke swirling in the red light and sees Larry sitting across from him in the shadows.

"Those scumbags got no morals. They'd sell their grandma to make a buck."

Chris listens to Larry's ruminations as they mix with the newspaper article he'd just read. It's hard to follow, but the sound of his friend's voice soothes him anyway.

"Besides," Larry consoles him, "if the Iranians start shooting, we'll scramble a few fighters and blow 'em out of the sky."

"Yeah, that'd be cool," Chris agrees.

"Navy jets shoot down Libyans over the Med' all the time, who gives a shit about some fuckin' Iranians!"

"Fucking Iranians," Chris whispers.

"Blow them up before they blow us up," Larry says. "Shit, we don't want to end up dead do we?" Larry asks,

Martin Weary appears and starts shaking Chris's shoulder, demanding, "Who the fuck are you talking to, Marlow?"

Chris giggles.

"What the fuck are you laughing at?" Martin Weary demands.

Chris puts the cigarette to his lips, but it's burned to the filter and gone out. He drops the butt on the deck and stands up. "I'll talk to you later, Weary," Chris says. "Right now, I gotta go on watch up on the flight deck."

Chapter 6: End of the Rainbow

On the balcony outside the gastroenterology clinic, Chris sits on a lounge chair smoking, enjoying the view. Fluffy white clouds are stacked up on the ocean and a rainsquall is pouring down from one of them. Gradually the rain dissipates until a vaporous, misty downpour remains. The clouds drift a little on the wind and a golden shaft of sunlight shoots through the last of the falling rain causing a brushstroke of red, orange and yellow across the sky. It's a glimpse of heaven, so beautiful, Chris imagines winged horses and angels flying out of the clouds and God, like Abe Lincoln on his white throne, appearing up there in the sky, hovering over the big hotels on Waikiki. Chris takes another drag off his cigarette, and the taste of smoke in his mouth breaks his daydream. He holds the cigarette up and studies it, turning it in his fingers, reading the brand name—Marlboro—the lettering all too familiar. The brown filter flecked with tan specks. Cowboy Killer, he thinks. Coffin Nail. Cancer Stick. That dog-shit flavor of cigarette smoke in the back of his mouth. He flicks the butt into a tin can and goes inside.

*   *   *

"Ma'am."

"Who's there?"

"Airman Marlow, Ma'am."

"Ah, yes, here you are." Doctor Burkham shuffles paperwork on her desk and pulls out his thick medical record and a large, floppy brown envelope. She opens his file and reads the radiology report.

She knows that a percentage of men who retire after a 20 or 30-year stint in the Navy drop dead within three years after taking off the uniform. It's not the culture shock of finally getting to know the wife they'd always gone to sea to get away from. It's the glycerides clogging their arteries and the heavy tar in their lungs that kills them. She'd seen many stressed-out sailors come to Tripler from ships at Pearl Harbor over the years. She'd seen the look in Chris's eyes when he pointed to his chest and described the dull ache. She'd heard the faint wheeze in his lungs and she'd seen the hernia on his x-ray—warning signs of a sailor's unhealthy lifestyle.

She decides to order a series of tests and give him a couple weeks of rest and relaxation on Oahu while she checks to see if there is anything more serious going on with him—asthma or heart disease perhaps. She'll tell him to quit smoking, quit drinking alcohol, quit gorging at meals. She knows there's no pill to cure him, no operation to correct the ailments brought on by his seafaring life.

Walking out from behind her desk, she turns on a light-box on the wall and hangs his x-rays. With a pencil, she points to the area where Barium dyed his esophagus and stomach. "You have a hiatal hernia," she says.

"What's that, ma'am?"

"It occurs when the stomach pushes up through the diaphragm."

"Is it serious?"

"We need to conduct additional tests. When is your ship leaving?"

"Tomorrow morning." He gulps, alarmed at the thought of his Navy College Fund with a zero balance.

"I'm keeping you here on medical hold." She shuts off the light shining through his x-ray and asks, "Did you say it's hard to breathe sometimes?"

"Yes, ma'am," he admits.

"That's not a good sign." She picks up the phone and dials. "This is Major Burkham, connect me with the annex at Pearl." Then to Chris, she says, "Take a seat in the hall, Marlow."

A storm of worry brews inside him. He's known all along that he's government property, and now he sees this Army Major in a new light, her steel gray hair and impeccable uniform. There's no disputing her orders.

He sits on a hard wooden bench outside her office noticing the freshly waxed floors and the faint smell of clean sheets. He realizes that he might never see the Enterprise or his shipmates again once the ship leaves him behind.

A bell dings and he looks up.

Directly across the hall, an elevator slides open and Chris wants to turn away but he can't.

An old man propped on a pile of pillows, lays in the folds of a white sheet. Cheeks caved in and eyes sunk in the sockets tell of a losing battle with a serious illness. A solemn orderly, dressed in white, pushes the bed out of the elevator. A nurse in a starched white uniform wheels an oxygen cylinder strapped to a handcart. A hose from the cylinder leads to the guy's face where a breathing mask covers his mouth. Tubes descending from IV bags are taped in the crook of his elbow. Beneath the cloud-white institutional pajamas, his chest heaves and deflates laboriously. His blank stare suddenly locks on Chris and refuses to let go. Their eyes meet and Chris experiences an intense fear of death deep down in his soul. In the second it takes to roll past, the old man turns his head slightly to keep eye contact with Chris. And Chris gets the message loud and clear: Get out of here! Run for your life! Find a girl and take her dancing or go out with the guys for a steak dinner and a cold beer! Do anything! Just get the fuck out of here, and stay away from doctors because all they do is find something wrong with you. And most important, never lay down in a hospital bed. When you do they'll stick tubes in your veins and attach wires to your heart, and then, kid, it's game over!

They roll the old guy along the corridor, past a black sign engraved, "Cardiology."

Chris puts a hand to his chest and feels his heartbeat. Fear creeps along his bones because he knows that bed, and the plastic tubes and the oxygen mask, they're waiting somewhere in his future, maybe not weeks or months ahead, but somewhere out there that bed is waiting for him. And he knows that smoking and drinking and taking drugs are sweeping him along toward that bed a little faster every day.

"Airman Marlow!"

"Yes, ma'am." He walks back into Doctor Burkham's office.

"You will report to the administrative desk at the Pearl Harbor medical annex. They will communicate with your ship and make arrangements for you to stay at the Pearl Harbor Naval Base while you are diagnosed here."

"Do I need an operation?" Chris asks.

"I do not foresee an operation in your case, but as a first course of therapy I order you to quit smoking immediately. You must also eat less meat and less fried foods. No tomatoes, chocolate, carbonated beverages or anything particularly spicy. Try eating more vegetables and fruit."

"Yes, ma'am."

"No alcohol either and get plenty of rest."

"Yes, ma'am."

"See the corpsman in the gastroenterology clinic tomorrow morning for scheduling. I'm sending you for a full workup at neurology and cardiology."

"Yes, ma'am, thank you, ma'am." Chris turns to leave but Doctor Burkham steps from behind her desk and blocks his path.

"Ma'am?" He says as she steps close enough for him to smell her breath.

She stares in his eyes and says, "Airman Marlow."

"Yes, ma'am."

"You must quit smoking. You know that don't you?"

*   *   *

At the Pearl Harbor medical annex, a sanitized brick building with a big lobby and hallways leading to doctor's offices and exam rooms, Chris plays it cool at the reception counter as he hands the papers Doctor Burkham gave him to D. Stone.

Barely giving him a second look, Stone explains, "These are two week temporary orders." She puts a new page in his record, stamps it and writes the time and date.

"What's two week temporary mean?" His mind goes to the look they exchanged in the van's rearview mirror—when she almost ran over a pedestrian and made the marine yelp in pain.

"If you're cured in two weeks they'll send you back to your ship—" she glances at his record, "the USS Enterprise."

And there's that smile in her eyes again, but he tells himself to quit thinking like such a horn dog. She's not making a sexual advance, he tells himself. Don't be such an idiot. She's being nice because it's her job to be nice to sick people.

"You need to go to your ship, get your gear, and come back here," she says.

"One question, Petty Officer Stone," Chris says.

"Sure, what's that?" She rolls her chair back and swings one knee over the other. Leaning back she runs her hands through her hair and points her brilliant smile at him. She crackles with a wild kind of energy, like she drank a pot of coffee and the caffeine is pulsing through her limbs the way she swivels her chair this way and that.

"What happens if the doctor doesn't give me a clean bill of health in two weeks?"

"Depends on what's wrong with you," she tells him. "Most people are here less than a week, others have an operation and stay until they've recovered, and some are discharged from the Navy if they have a chronic condition."

He remembers the connection when their eyes met in the rearview mirror and thinks to himself, you could be my chronic condition.

*   *   *

Aboard ship, Chris rustles Chief Hicks out of his bunk. In the dim light of the living compartment, Hicks signs Chris's orders.

"Thanks, Chief." Chris folds the papers.

"Will you be back, Marlow?" Hicks grabs Chris's elbow in a heavy paw and pulls him close to the girth of his belly. "We'll need you on deck when we get out on the Persian Gulf."

"They'll just do some tests and send me back." Chris remembers the old man on the rolling bed and decides he isn't going to let anyone put tubes or wires in him.

"These are two week orders," Hicks' voice still heavy from sleep. "After that you won't be able to come back. So, if it's a bit of vacation you're after," he says, and in the dark a star twinkles in his eye, "don't stay more than two weeks. You can catch a flight and meet us in the Philippines in a few weeks."

"Aye, aye, chief," Chris says.

Steve and Angelo are on the beach so Chris has no chance to say good-bye. He glances over his shoulder at Larry's bunk several times while packing his seabag and feels that sinister energy coming from inside the folded-over mattress where Larry used to sleep. It's not the first time he's felt something in there, or maybe it's in his memories of Larry, but whatever it is, he hears it snickering at him, because it knows it has pushed him off the ship. And it's weird to think that what happened to Larry is causing him to leave the ship. He knows it's nonsense, but sure enough he's packing his seabag and leaving. For what, he asks himself, a little ache in my chest? What is this all about, he wonders as he heaves the heavy green canvas seabag onto his back and stares at Larry's bunk.

He easily recalls his friend's smiling face and the sound of his voice.

"You should have been more careful," Chris whispers.

He throws a lazy salute at Larry's empty bunk and walks out of the cubicle.

A few minutes later he's walking down the gangway to the pier and wondering if this is the last time he'll see his ship, the USS Enterprise.

Sunset is a smear of peach across the sky. The green mountains grow dark. Traces of jet fuel and container cargo coalesce on a faint seaward breeze perfumed with the smell of soil and vegetation. The entire odor prickles at his nose like an industrial-tropical flower.

He wonders how anything can possibly be wrong with his heart after he walks a mile around Pearl Harbor and lets the heavy seabag slide off his back in the medical annex's lobby.

D. Stone is still there, and he's pleasantly surprised when she takes him outside to her van and gives him a ride to the men's medical hold barracks.

"So you do everything around here," he says as they drive past a pier where battleships are tied up.

"I've got duty this weekend, which means processing everyone coming off the ship's for medical care."

"My name is Chris," he tells her, attempting to lighten things up. "What's the D stand for?"

"Deirdre, but you can call me Petty Officer Stone."

"Well, Petty Officer Stone, thanks for your help today."

She drops him outside the enlisted men's medical hold barracks, a dilapidated white wooden house with a crooked front porch surrounded by crabgrass and nestled in a grove of palm trees.

"Report back to the medical annex tomorrow morning at zero eight hundred for indoctrination," she tells him before driving away.

Across the road there's a seawall and beyond that a rocky beach on Pearl Harbor. Above his head, palm-fronds silhouette black against the evening sky.

PART II

Chapter 7: A Wingnut Among Blackshoes

Late in the night Chris wakes up and stretches the long muscles in the backs of his legs.

Outside in the dark, wind rustles the palm fronds.

In the morning he lays there wondering what will happen now that the Enterprise has left him behind. A pang of guilt twitches under his ribs because his ship has gone to sea and he's here on land. Hospitalized in Hawaii, he thinks. How bad can it be?

Even though the room is tiny, with only one bunk, he can't believe how luxurious it feels to have his own space. A single occupancy room is unheard of in the Navy. He looks up at the high ceiling, then out the open window with a screen and a view of tall palm trees and dense flowering rhododendrons behind the barracks.

He slides from under the sheet and goes into the room's private bath.

After a shower, he brushes his teeth. He dumps his seabag into the footlocker at the foot of his bunk and dresses in clean dungarees.

He cocks and crimps his Dixie cup on his head and checks himself in the mirror over the sink.

He walks along the carpeted hall and down the stairs into a foyer that opens onto a lounge full of couches and easy chairs arranged in front of a big screen TV. One of those morning shows with attractive people in skimpy tights doing Tai Chi on a slate patio surrounded by flowering shrubs with the sound turned off. Chris considers turning over a new leaf; quit drinking and smoking, start doing a morning workout. He knows he needs to do something to get rid of the constant ache in his chest but right now he just wants to eat breakfast.

He thinks about Larry Tynan and shakes his head and implores himself to leave Larry's ghost on the boat, but he knows it won't be that easy so he wanders around checking out the barracks.

Right away he realizes the Navy has converted this place from an old mansion. Above the florescent lights hanging on metal rods in the ceiling, there's a dusty wagon-wheel chandelier and fancy crown molding.

He goes outside and sits on a cushioned chair on a stately porch that runs the entire front of the dilapidated building. Wooden columns support the porch roof and white clapboard siding and rows of windows with open green shutters stretch away in both direction. It looks like a shabby New England mansion that should be shaded by lofty oaks instead of palm trees. The view of the harbor from the porch gives the place a retirement home ambience—a rest home for worn out sailors.

*   *   *

Plate heaped with fried eggs, hash browns, bacon, chipped beef on toast and grits, Chris stops at a gigantic fruit bowl and decides he has to take Burkham's advice and start eating healthy. He chooses a banana. He places his tray on a table and heads for the beverage bar. Two trips later he's ready with coffee, orange juice and a big class of milk.

After shaking salt and pepper on his eggs, he splashes on Tabasco, and digs in.

*   *   *

On the asphalt behind the medical annex, Chris stands around waiting with some other guys.

Carlos Devlin is telling how he slipped off a ladder aboard a ship in a storm. "—fell fifteen fucking feet. Smack! That steel deck don't budge, not even a little. Shattered my kneecap into six pieces!" A white plaster cast encases Carlo's right leg from toes to crotch. Carlos drags briskly on a Newport. Curly black hair springs from under his white hat. Although freshly shaved, his square jaw is shadowed black against his mocha-brown skin. "So my doc installed a new Teflon kneecap three months ago and I'm hanging out here in what they call the Navy's bureaucratic ass crack. What's with you two sailors?"

Another guy, Adam, tells about a beautiful woman who hit on him in a bar in Honolulu, then lured him outside where three guys jumped him, stabbed him and stole his wallet. He spent two nights at Tripler, missed his ship and was released from the hospital yesterday.

Chris told about the Pop Rocks and Barium x-ray and the hernia on his stomach.

"What's the matter with you?" Adam asks the fourth member of their group.

Weatherbee smiles a mouthful of brown teeth. He's a tall dude with broad shoulders. He stands on tree-trunk legs and size fifteen boots. His shirt and pants bulge here and there at odd places as if he's really a burlap sack full of pumpkins instead of a man. And his skull has a peanut-pinch to it that makes his hair, forehead and eyes point in one direction and his nose, mouth and chin point in a slightly different direction.

"My condition is pretty complicated." Weatherbee's monotone voice bubbles inside his sinuses. "When I first got here they gave me an endoscopy. That's where they stuck a hose with a camera down my throat and the doctor looked in my stomach." Weatherbee pronounces each word with saliva-greased precision. "Well, the doctor pushed too hard on the hose and he poked a hole in my duodenum, that's the pouch at the bottom of the stomach, and I went into shock and needed an operation for internal bleeding, but then I got a transfusion with the wrong blood type, and ever since I fall asleep for no reason."

"We gotta keep an eye on Weatherbee!" Carlos Devlin snickers. "Any second he could fall asleep even if he's standing up. It's truly a hilarious sight to see. One second he's talking to you and his eyes flutter and he falls asleep like somebody hit his emergency-off button. So be ready to catch him." Carlos Devlin smiles every word, like Weatherbee is a peculiar gadget that he's showing off. "If we don't catch him, Weatherbee will go into a nosedive, snoring all the way to the deck and then smack, he wakes up with a bloody face."

Weatherbee blushes bright red and his mouth opens and his head starts bobbing like he's laughing but he's not making a sound.

It's seriously the weirdest thing Chris has ever seen.

"So, what ship you off?" Carlos looks at Adam.

"Sacramento."

"Supplier, huh?" Carlos smiles enthusiastically with an I-love-the-Navy tone of voice. "You work in underway replenishment?"

"Yeah, I'm on deck handling lines," Adam says. "Operate a forklift and work the booms sending pallets across."

"All right," Carlos looks at Chris and asks, "What about you sailor?"

"I'm off the Enterprise," Chris says.

"You must hate being inside that birdhouse!" Carlos's voice is cold with accusation.

"Birdhouse?" Chris asks.

"Air ... craft ... carrier," Carlos says, oozing contempt.

"It's actually pretty cool, because I'm up on the flight deck all the time—" Chris is about to go into his shtick about launching and recovering jets, but Carlos interrupts.

"Five thousand fucking guys on there, right?"

"Yeah." Chris shrugs.

"Men packed in like bugs crawling all over each other. I knew a bosun who pulled duty on a birdhouse and he said he waited forty-five minutes on the chow line three times a day. I can't imagine waiting forty-five minutes for chow."

Chris has heard a few joking insults told between blackshoes (sailors who work in seaman ratings) and wingnuts (sailors who work in aviation ratings), but he'd always through it was a petty rivalry. He glances around at the group of twenty or so sailors waiting on the blacktop behind the annex, and wonders if all these guys are blackshoes.

"I'd go fucking crazy surrounded by five thousand wingnuts," Carlos says. "Aboard the Cushing we have a hundred seventy-five-man crew. I know everyone and when I go to chow, wait five minutes, that's all. Birdhouse duty is bullshit." Carlos argues his point to Weatherbee, glances at Adam to see if he shares his sentiments. Then he glares at Chris. "Damn air craft carrier's always trying to stay at sea for months at a time, and none of the good sailors below get to see the sun, because the weather decks covered with aero planes."

Carlos is angry now, so Chris decides to back it down and notch, say something nice. "I guess carrier duty is lousy for blackshoes," he says.

"Who you calling a blackshoe?" Carlos demands, his dark glaring at Chris.

Chris feels the peptic ember beginning to glow at the base of his esophagus, beneath the pile of fried eggs and bacon he'd eaten. He toys with the idea of calling Carlos a 'fucking blackshoe' but instead says, "Dude, you called me a wingnut."

"Better watch yourself around here," Carlos growls as he hobbles past, banging Chris's shoulders. "Fuckin' wingnut."

Chris looks after Carlos and considers kicking one of his crutches out from under him right as he's putting his weight on it, but a rare flash of good judgment overrides the impulse. He smirks and shakes his head instead.

A first class petty officer, the man in charge of mustering the medical holding company, emerges from a door in the back of the building, his right arm in a cast and a sling.

"Time for all you sick, lame and lazy sailors to fall in," he shouts.

Weatherbee slinks off behind Carlos.

The group assembles.

"Seaman Abrey!" the broken-armed man with the clipboard calls.

"Here!"

"Bosun Mate Arnold!"

"Here!"

"Boiler Tech Billings!"

"Here!"

"Hull Tech Carlson."

"Here!"

"Bosun Mate Devlin!"

"Here!" Carlos shouts.

Uneasily, Chris realizes that when he left the Enterprise he'd entered the blackshoe Navy. Mild fear runs through him as he imagines all the men surrounding him have the same attitude as Carlos Devlin. The first class calls off gunner's mates and mess cooks, yeomen and diesel mechanics. It dawns on Chris that he was aboard the Enterprise for three years, but he knew none of the blackshoes who worked in the supply division, administration, laundry or reactor plants. Though he shuffled past them three times a day as they slung chow onto his tray, he didn't know the name of even one cook in any of the ship's four galleys. No wonder the blackshoes hate us; all they do is provide services for wingnuts.

Suddenly an elbow pokes Chris in the ribs and somebody whispers, "Answer up."

"Air ... Man ... Marlow!" the guy with the clipboard yells. "Is there an AIR ... MAN here?"

"Yes, sir, right here!" Chris yells.

All the sailor's crane their necks to get a look at this curious creature. No doubt, they'd all learned from their superior officers aboard frigates, destroyers, guided missile cruisers and submarines that wingnuts are not real sailors.

The first class continues calling muster above the mumbling and snickering of those in ranks who look at Chris as if he's a kooky bird.

"Listen up," the first class finally yells. "Anyone with an appointment at Tripler, the shuttle departs every half hour in front of the annex. Anyone new here go to the lobby for indoctrination. Everybody else grab a trash bag and spread out across the grounds to pick up litter. Next muster, thirteen-hundred. Fall out!"

*   *   *

Inside the annex, a few sailors sit in cushioned chairs around a conference room table while a petty officer stands in the front of the room delivering a lecture. Every few seconds he flips a new transparency onto the overhead projector.

"Medical hold personnel shall not," the petty officer reads from the screen, "smoke tobacco or drink alcohol while on medical hold. With the flick of his wrist, a new transparency appears. "Medical hold personnel shall neither go to the enlisted club, nor leave the confines of the Pearl Harbor Naval Station for any reason except to go to a previously scheduled doctor's appointment at Tripler Army Hospital." He looks at Chris as he slaps a new transparency onto the overhead, and says, "You shall not participate in any sporting or athletic activities including swimming, weight lifting, running or contact sports." Then the petty officer hands out sheets of paper and a bunch of pens and asks everyone to sign and date at the bottom.

As Chris reads the paper, it hits him hard that after three years he has left the USS Enterprise—his ship. And now she's gone. Early that morning, his shipmates untied from the pier and steamed onto the Pacific Ocean without him. He reads the paper, which basically restates everything he's just been told. No partying, no sports, no leaving base, etc. The last paragraph explains: "All medical hold personnel are on two week temporary orders. If you do not receive orders back to your command within two weeks, you will be held at Pearl Harbor on temporary duty and reassigned as the needs of the Navy apply."

Chris raises his hand and asks, "Can you explain what happens if I'm not sent back to my ship in two weeks?"

"You'll be in administrative limbo." He smirks.

"What does that mean?" another guy asks.

"That depends," the petty officer explains, "they might kick you out on a medical discharge. On the other hand, if there's nothing seriously wrong with you, they might assign you to mop floors or scrape paint off old ships."

Everyone knows better than to ask any more questions.

"It's a complex decision making process," the petty officer explains, "way above my pay grade." Then he says in a hushed tone, "If you actually do want to go back to your ship, I advise you to get a clean bill of health within two weeks and get the hell out of here."

Chris thinks about the money his Dad had sent, and how he'd spent it on motorcycle payments and a road trip to Vegas instead of depositing it into the Navy college fund. He imagines how disappointed his Dad will be if he comes home on a medical discharge and has no money in his Navy college fund. And that makes him realize that he has to leave Pearl Harbor before his two-week temporary orders expire. He has to be aboard the Enterprise when she goes out to the Gulf of Oman for three months. He has to save every paycheck and deposit them all into the Navy College Fund. If he gets kicked out of the Navy on a medical discharge, his Dad will find out he spent the money and that will suck royally.

He notes that it's Monday morning, so he has this week and next to get better and get back to the ship.

Fuck.

Chapter 8: Nicotine Fit at the Cardiology Clinic

In the waiting room at the cardiology clinic, the urge to smoke a cigarette is overpowering. I have to quit smoking. Fuck, when I get drunk I smoke two packs in one night! Damn, I have to quit drinking too! What if Major Burkham finds something wrong with my heart? I'm starting to believe it, for Christ's sake! Here I am in the damn cardiology clinic! What the hell have I done to myself? And it isn't just smoking and drinking. What the hell is a hiatal hernia? Part of my stomach is pushing up through my diaphragm! How the hell did that happen? He remembers vomiting in the hotel elevator a couple days ago. It's not the first time that happened. Barfing hard can rip your diaphragm, he figures, because he'd barfed hard after binge drinking several times. What if I need an operation? What if I end up disabled, like a freak with a valve sticking out of my belly button? I don't want a disability. I want to live a normal life. But what if I can't, what if I need disability pay because I can't work? What if I have a weak heart and a blown-out stomach? I'll be another lame veteran, probably end up living in a cardboard box with a gross infected belly button valve!

Worrying amped up the nicotine craving.

If I don't quit smoking and drinking, I'll totally fuck up my heart. Chris is thinking about a video they showed in a health class in boot camp. It was about an overweight middle-aged guy who smoked too much and didn't eat right. After he collapsed and got rushed to the hospital, a surgeon sawed through his sternum. And Chris knew that wasn't just Navy propaganda, because he'd read about heart attacks and heart surgery in a book in the ship's library. On top of that he'd read an article in Newsweek about kids under twenty-five who had heart attacks from snorting drugs and popping pills. I've got addiction issues, Chris realizes for the millionth time as he looks around the waiting room where he is obviously the only young person. Several old couples sit together—retirees in for their checkups. He puts his hand to his chest to feel his heartbeat but feels the hard corners of a Marlboro box in his shirt pocket instead. Beneath it, his heart pants like a tired rodent. Addiction. What a terrible thing.

I'm addicted.

I'm an addict.

What am I gonna do?

He thinks about asking Doctor Burkham if she'll send him to an alcohol and drug abuse intervention class but that'll take months and he'll never get back to the Enterprise. Shit!

He stands up because he can't catch his breath, and the only thing he can imagine scarier than death is a doctor descending on his sternum with an electric saw, prying his ribs apart with a chrome chisel and touching a razor-sharp scalpel to the soft pink tissue of his heart.

I want to go back to the ship and work on deck is what I want to do. I'll quit smoking and drinking, I swear I will. I'll stop eating so much greasy food. I'll eat more fruits and vegetables.

"Airman Marlow?"

"Right here."

"Go to examination room number six."

Room six is a dim, windowless box. There's a young woman sitting behind an old wooden desk.

"Morning, ma'am." Chris stands at ease and she motions for him to sit.

She studies the slip from gastroenterology at the top of the pile in his medical record. "You're quite young, Mister Marlow." She speaks in that northeastern educated tone that reminds Chris that he was the one who decided to join the Navy to see the world while everyone else in his high school class went off to college. ·

You're young too, Doctor Penny Brown, he thinks as he reads the nametag pinned to the blouse of her baggy green scrubs. He sees she's slim and small-boned by the way her skin stretches over the bridge of her tanned nose. Her long brown hair is restrained in one of those mesh deals cafeteria workers wear.

He wonders if she's actually a doctor or what.

She flips through the pages in his record, reading, sometimes aloud.

"Patient complains of pain in left chest and left arm especially after eating."

"Patient is hyperventilating due to pressure in chest and back."

"Patient continually complains of pain in left side of chest, radiating into left arm."

Penny Brown's pretty greenish-gray eyes catch his. "What is your command?" she asks.

"The aircraft carrier USS Enterprise, Ma'am." He figures she must be a newbie because "USS Enterprise" is stamped on top of every page in his medical record.

"And the doctors who made these entries?"

"The doctors on the ship," he says.

Closing his record, she says, "Let's start at the beginning."

"Yes, ma'am," he agrees.

"In your own words, what's bothering you?" She looks at him with the concern and intuition of an apprentice Doctor Burkham.

"A couple years ago I was on the flight deck aboard the Enterprise, and we were out on the Arabian Sea near the mouth of the Persian Gulf, and that was the first time I felt a dull ache right here." Chris points to the spot just below his left breast pocket and feels awkward as he notices her noticing his pack of Marlboros. "It hurt a little bit when I carried the chains."

"Chains?"

"Well, the ship is pitching and rolling on the waves so the only way to keep the airplanes from rolling overboard is to chain them down. And that's what I do; carry chains to tie down jets." He knows it's the most exciting and dangerous job in the world, but in this windowless room, telling this college woman about it—well the glamour and excitement of the flight deck sounds like dirty, grunt labor. It also occurs to him, and not for the first time, that it was about a week after Larry got mangled on the propeller of that Hawkeye when all this pain and anxiety started, but he doesn't mention Larry to Doctor Penny Brown. "So, that's my job," he says. "I ignored the pain, half hoped it would go away. But six months later, when we returned to California, I couldn't stand it anymore. I went to sick call and the doc told me to lay on an examination table while he pressed on my ribs. He pressed hard and asked, 'Does that hurt?' and I said, 'No, sir' and he pressed harder. He was crushing my ribs with his big hands. 'Does that hurt, Airman?' he asked again, and I said, 'No, sir,' and then he pressed so hard on the spot where the pain comes from that I thought he was going to break my ribs. And sure enough, a jolt of pain shot across my chest and I screamed. 'There's your problem, Airman' he said, 'You have a pinched nerve.'

Then he scribbled a prescription for Motrin and told me to send in the next man because there was a long line of sailors waiting outside in the passageway to see him."

"And then what happened?" Penny Brown asks, still trying to perfect that concerned look.

"Well, for about eight months, every time I went back to sick call none of the doctors would even want me to take my shirt off. They looked at what the previous doctor prescribed and simply renewed my prescription. Then one time I really complained because the pain was radiating down my left arm and it was hard to breathe, so that doctor ordered an EKG and sent me for x-rays. He said he saw some inflammation on my spine, and from there it started all over again with every doctor I saw prescribing anti-inflammatory drugs."

"Why didn't you go back and see the same doctor?" Penny Brown asks.

"Because Navy doctors are attached to squadrons and ships, and they're always being deployed somewhere."

"How are anti-inflammatories and antacids working?"

"The combination keeps the pain in check but sometimes it flares up."

"How old are you, Chris?"

"Twenty."

"Do you smoke?"

"On and off."

"How long have you been smoking?"

"Two years," he lies. He started smoking at twelve, so he's been smoking more on than off for over eight years.

She leans towards him over the desk and whispers, "Have you been using any street drugs?"

He opens his mouth but words won't come out because he can't bring himself to lie to this woman.

"You have to quit and you have to quit smoking cigarettes too." Then she writes in his record for a few minutes. "Any history of heart disease in your family?"

"No."

"I want you to come in first thing every morning for the rest of the week for an EKG. Then on Friday morning I'll do an echocardiogram on you."

"An echocardio-what?"

"A test, it gives us a look inside your heart."

You're not gonna like me if you see what's inside my heart, lady, Chris thinks and then he wonders if they have a machine that can look inside his head. She says something but he's not fully listening, he's thinking that he's been suspicious of heart disease but had never said it to any of the ship's doctors.

He never mentions the devil, because he does not want the devil to appear.

He thanks Penny Brown and they say good-bye.

*   *   *

As he descends in the elevator, he's soothed by the idea that he's under the care of Major Doctor Burkham, his gastroenterologist, and Doctor Penny Brown, his cardiologist. It makes him feel somehow stabilized, as if his condition cannot get worse while under the care of these specialists. At sea aboard ship, on the other hand, he felt his condition slipping, getting worse all the time. But now he's stabilized and it's reassuring. He thinks back to the times he'd gone to sick call aboard ship. It always felt like a weird medical masquerade. He'd been healthy all his life, so his knowledge of medicine was limited to the elementary school nurse and his mom, God rest her soul, and their thermometers, aspirin, ice packs and Ace bandages. His faith in modern medicine had declined with each visit to sick call aboard ship. Uncertainty about his health gnawed at him. Secretly he suspected the water aboard ship was contaminated with radioactive waste from the reactors, or he'd been exposed to asbestos while sleeping beneath old insulated pipes. Many times he wondered if he was experiencing early signs of heart disease or lung cancer. One time he discovered a bruise on his shin, and another time a clicking inside his knee, and both times it led to anxiety about a pending coronary, blood in his urine or a malignant lump in his armpit.

He hated the way the Navy boasted about its medical facilities afloat. "The USS Enterprise is equipped with a complete operating room and its medical staff has performed such delicate procedures as brain surgery while underway," he'd read somewhere. Right, he thought sarcastically, Doc Tinsdale doing brain surgery on the Bering

Sea, with Corpsman Hathaway assisting. Doc Tinsdale couldn't decide whether to prescribe Mylanta liquid or chewable tablets, he sure as hell wasn't performing brain surgery, not on anyone who lived to tell about it.

He's looking for the neurology clinic and proceeds along a corridor arriving at a room with a sign—ENLISTED LOUNGE—over the open door. There's a coffee mess and snack bar, racks of magazines and the military newspaper Stars and Stripes. On a big TV, a smoking supertanker floats behind the anchorman. Across the bottom of the screen the words: IRAN IRAQ WAR RAGES ON.

Persian Gulf Yacht Club, Chris thinks.

He's spent months out there, several times. He's been in sand storms blown thirty miles out to sea from Saudi Arabia. He clearly remembers standing on the flight deck and watching a brown cloud of sand thousands of feet high blow in across the water.

He'd seen more than a few smoking oil tankers. Iran and Iraq have been at war, sinking each other's tankers, for years.

His good angel tells him to throw the cigarette pack in the garbage, but he ignores it. An ability all smokers developed after puffing away several hundred packs—the ability to snub their own desire to quit. He walks through the lounge and out onto a patio and sits on a folding metal chair and lights up.

As he smokes he thinks, yeah, I'll quit. Doctor Burkham and Doctor Brown told me to. But right then while he's inhaling smoke and the sun is warming his back, quitting doesn't seem that urgent. He'll quit. He knows he can. Tomorrow.

The smoke feels good in his lungs.

*   *   *

The corpsman at the neurology clinic reads the slip and then walks into an office with "Doctor Chu" etched on the glass. A moment later Doctor Chu emerges. He's short and stocky. He's wearing black slacks and a white short-sleeve shirt with a black tie and a pocket protector full of pens. Thick, black plastic glasses frame his eyes. He rakes his fingers through a mop of black hair. He reads the referral slip slowly, deliberately, pronouncing roundly, "Air ... man ... Marlow."

"Good morning, sir," Chris says.

"How can we help you, air ... man?"

"Well sir, sometimes my arm hurts."

"Oh." Doctor Chu looks at the slip. "Burkham? Burkham?" His eyes roll up as if the answer to his question is written on the ceiling. "Ah, yes. Burkham is gastro. It is peculiar for me to have a gastro patient complaining of left arm pain. How is your right arm? Pain or no pain?"

"No pain in my right arm, sir."

"Have you been to cardiology?"

"Yes, they're doing tests on me this week."

Doctor Chu's gaze goes across Chris's neck to his chest. He seems to be looking right inside him. Chris feels like one of those old style anatomy textbooks with the plastic see-through pages, one layer for hair and skin, the next muscles and veins, then bones and below that the organs—heart, lungs, stomach, intestines.

"Well, air man Marlow, I will do a test on the nerves in your arms and your spine to see if there is any abnormality." Doctor Chu steps close and suddenly grabs Chris's left hand in an aggressive take-down move.

Chris is surprised but Doctor Chu begins massaging his arm. The doctor feels his elbow and wiggles his fingertip suddenly between the funny bones. A fingertip probes dangerously deep in the crevice.

Chis is tense. He knows the finger doesn't belong there.

Suddenly a million needles jolt through Chris's arm and he screams, "Ahhhhhhhh!" and tries to pull away but Doctor Chu holds firm.

Doctor Chu is biting the tip of his tongue, chuckling, looking at Chris through his thick glasses.

Sadistic fucker, Chris thinks. He can see a smile in Doctor Chu's eyes!

"No time today for a proper evaluation of your condition," Doctor Chu says, "but my corpsman will schedule you for a thorough examination very soon."

Chapter 9: Chow

After the seventeen hundred muster behind the annex, Chris follows Carlos Devlin along the sidewalk. Chris walks slowly behind the crutching bosun, and when they reach the chow hall Chris walks up and opens the door for him.

"Wingnut!" Carlos says. "Coming to get that good Navy chow?"

"I especially like not waiting forty-five minutes in line to eat." Chris cuts a glance at Carlos to see if he's sincere about, 'good Navy chow.' What kind of thing is that to say?

Chris follows Carlos onto the line. "How long you been on medical hold, Carlos?"

"Three months, and you're only the second wingnut to come through."

"And you were best friends with the last guy, I'm sure."

"Made lunch meat out of him," Carlos says directly in Chris's face and turns curtly away.

"You're taking this wingnut blackshoe thing too far," Chris says.

Carlos smiles deviously and asks, "What do you mean, wingnut?"

"If you got a problem with the way the Navy is set up, hey, that's cool, but there's no need to be hostile with me about it."

"Don't start crying."

They shuffle past the heat lamps as a mess cook clamps a couple Salisbury steaks from a serving pan and drops them on their trays, ladles on onion-and-green-pepper gravy, scoops mashed potatoes into one compartment, peas and carrots into another.

"I ain't crying, man," Chris says. "I just never met anyone who took this nonsense so seriously."

At the end of the serving line, they pick up bowls of fruit cocktail in heavy syrup, and at the dessert cart, they take small plates with large cubes of chocolate cake.

They sit across from each other and Chris asks, "What do you want to drink?"

"Coke with ice."

Chris returns a minute later from the drink bar with two glasses of milk for himself and a Coke for Carlos. Before sitting, he walks to the salad bar and builds a green salad with spinach, lettuce, cucumbers, shredded carrots, three tablespoons of bacon bits and a ladleful of creamy French dressing. He eyes a pan of Jell-O but decides not to scoop himself a bowl when he notices raisins suspended in the red raspberry slab. He wonders if raisins would qualify as a fruit under Burkham's new diet requirements.

Chris sits and reaches for the salt and pepper. "Ok, so why don't you like wingnuts?"

Carlos chews and swallows before speaking. "First of all, wingnuts don't know shit about what's really going on in the Navy."

"Like what?" Chris asks through a mouthful of mashed potatoes.

"Like talking with their mouth full," Carlos says.

Chris rolls his eyes.

"Tying knots, otherwise known as marlinespike seamanship. Can you tie a half hitch?" Carlos asks. "How about a monkey fist?"

"A monkey fist?" Chris asks. "Is that something a blackshoe uses to jack off?"

Carlos shakes his head. "Forget about dropping an anchor or mooring a ship to the pier. These are things real sailors do. As far as I'm concerned, all you wingnuts are a branch of the Air Force." Carlos slides a forkful of mashed potatoes into his mouth with a note of finality.

In order to say something before Carlos cuts in, Chris washes his half-chewed steak down with a gulp of milk and continues. "Aboard a carrier, from the main deck up is airdales, we call ourselves airdales, not wingnuts. And from the main deck down is blackshoes."

"How can anyone stand being on a big floating ghetto like that?"

"It's like a city," Chris says.

Carlos washes down a mouthful of food and says, "Get me a refill, wingnut . . . please."

"Sure, blackshoe." Chris grabs himself another glass of milk, a couple dinner rolls and a few butter pats.

"Do you know what a battle group is?" Carlos asks after Chris sits back down.

Chris is mopping up his gravy with a puffy dinner roll. "Sure."

"Tell me then," Carlos shoots back.

"Well, when the Enterprise heads out from San Francisco on a Western Pacific cruise we bring a few subs, destroyers, cruisers, a supply ship or two and a couple frigates along."

Carlos's eyes harden, and Chris realizes his description of a battle group is a bunch of ships following an aircraft carrier.

Carlos has a forkful of potatoes halfway to his mouth, but he sets it down on his tray and says, "You wingnuts think the other ships are there to watch you put on an airshow. But you're wrong. When a battle group gets underway it includes two supply ships, two fast frigates, two destroyers, a guided missile cruiser, two maybe three or even four submarines and one aircraft carrier."

Chris doesn't say a word.

"All those ships are full of blackshoes, as you call us; half the guys on the carrier are blackshoes too. There's a whole Navy going on, a Navy you know nothing about."

At that moment, a half chewed mouthful of salad and another overloaded forkful half way to his lips, Chris feels a little stupid. Carlos has him believing he isn't really a sailor. He gulps down the salad and asks, "Well, Carlos, why don't you tell me what the Navy's all about then?"

"First and foremost ships are all about boilers and reactors providing propulsion and energy to run the ship. After that it's all about preparation. We drill at general quarters, launch rockets and missiles and fire guns day and night. I'm on the flying squad; we spend a lot of time preparing to fight fires. You ever heard of damage control, now that's what the Navy is all about."

"Watertight integrity?"

"I'm surprised you know that much. Damage control is complicated, but the basics are to keep the ship floating and fighting even if we take a hit."

"With damage control?"

"Damn right." Carlos pushes his fork decisively down through his cube of chocolate cake. "I'll tell you why wingnuts don't know shit about damage control."

"I'm sure you will."

"It goes back to the formation of the battle group. The frigates and destroyers, cruisers and subs are spread out to cover your ass, because if one missile gets through and hits the carrier the good blackshoes down below will keep you afloat but one hole in that flight deck and the carrier war is over."

Having finished his salad and buttered rolls, Chris starts on his chocolate cake. He knows Carlos is correct. If even a bullet hits a flight deck fueling station it could set off an explosion that could kill dozens and blow holes in the ship.

"Carlos, you ever heard of gunboat diplomacy?" Chris asks.

"Sounds like political bullshit."

"Political bullshit or not, that's what the Navy's all about," Chris says, remembering how Larry explained it. "It's like this; when the US, meaning the president and his buddies, want to influence another country, they park a carrier off their coast and fly jets up and down the beach. It lets them know we can zap them whenever we want."

"So what you're saying is wingnuts are all about a bunch college boys breaking the sound barrier for deadbeat politicians." Carlos pushes his fork sideways through his cake again.

Chris refills his milk and Carlos's Coke. He'd already eaten his cake so he scoops a bowl of red Jell-O, plops on a dollop of whipped cream and returns to the table. He's stuffed but eats the Jell-O anyway; raisins and all. Talking about war makes him anxious, and when he's anxious he gorges on chow.

"You know something, Marlow?"

"What?" Chris sets his spoon down in the empty bowl.

"For someone who's got an ulcer or whatever, you eat an awful lot."

Every compartment in Chris's tray is wiped clean. Not a pea nor a carrot or even the fruit cocktail's heavy syrup remains. There isn't a crumb on his cake plate. If he hadn't used both dinner rolls to mop up the gravy, he would've wiped the last streaks of French dressing from his salad bowl.

"The doctor doesn't know what's wrong with me. I hope it's not an ulcer." Chris attempts to dismiss Carlos's comment, but he knows he's eaten way too much again. The familiar cramp tightens beneath his sternum.

They leave the chow hall and walk past the piers on Merry Point and continue walking out along the Harbor Road. Off in the west, across Pearl's East Loch, a mountainous ridge of clouds glows orange along its high peaks.

Carlos crutches and Chris walks slowly beside him. Carlos lights a

Newport. Chris lights a Marlboro. They stop to sit on a bench while they smoke.

"Another thing about wingnuts," Carlos says. "They all hate the Navy. F.T.N. they say. I seen a wingnut with F.T.N. tattooed on his arm." Carlos pulls a quick drag. "Imagine that. F.T.N. permanently printed on your arm, what a dope!"

F.T.N stands for Fuck the Navy.

"Do you hate the Navy, Marlow?"

"No," Chris says. "How about you?" He draws a shallow drag off his Marlboro; afraid that smoking will aggravate the burning sensation in his chest.

"I love the Navy." Carlos smiles.

"Really?" Chris asks. He'd never heard anyone say those words before and he wonders if Carlos's sentiment is popular among blackshoes.

"Marlow, you silly wingnut." Carlos chuckles.

Even though it's an effort to breath, Chris still feels compelled to smoke.

"Here you are on beautiful Oahu, jewel of the Hawaiian Islands, you ate all that good Navy chow, and you're getting paid for it. You got nice uniforms and medical care. All for what? You don't even know what's wrong with your little belly. The Navy takes better care of you than you take care of yourself."

Chris crushes the half-smoked Marlboro under his heel. He draws a deep breath and tries to ignore the now acidic fire burning in his food-stuffed gullet. He takes a cellophane packet of Mylanta from his pocket, tears it open and pops the two tablets.

Carlos points at the ships moored at the Merry Point piers. "That's a mine sweeper, and that's a new Ticonderoga class destroyer."

Chris swallows the mouthful of foam hoping it will smother the fire within.

"Look at that conning tower, Marlow!" Carlos points across the water, "That's a sub setting out to sea." Carlos follows the black conning tower with longing eyes. He raps his cast with his knuckles and says, "I can't wait to get back out to sea."

Horizontal fins protrude from the sides of the conning tower and a red bulb blinks on a short aerial.

The Mylanta is working. The pain lessens and Chris feels a little calmer. Perhaps, he thinks, it's not the Mylanta at all; it's the thought of returning to sea. He breathes easier. He tries to project his thoughts out across the dusky harbor. On Ford Island, he sees a satellite communications drum atop a derrick of steel girders, and white concrete buildings. The bone-white Arizona Memorial seems to hover between the dark water and the orange and gray tinted clouds. "You ever been out there?" Chris asks.

"Where?"

"The Arizona," Chris says.

"I go out to the memorial and pay my respects every time I visit Pearl," Carlos says proudly.

Chris feels a new discomfort in his chest, not indigestion, but guilt. Guilt, because he's been to Pearl Harbor more than a half dozen times, but he's never visited to the Arizona Memorial.

Chapter 10: AWOL

Sailors afflicted with broken bones, hernias, thyroid dysfunction and blueberries, stiff necks, exotic rashes and torn ligaments muster on the pavement behind the medical annex every morning at zero eight hundred. Christopher Marlow is at a loss because he can't describe his condition with a dramatic tale of woe as many of the other sailors can. He has neither fallen overboard in rough seas nor lost his mind after three months submerged in a nuclear submarine.

A gray bearded old salt claims to be suffering from a rampant case of carbuncular rectal warts and proudly recounts his unmuzzled exploits in the whorehouses of Pusan, South Korea.

If Chris were a raconteur, he would exaggerate his hiatal hernia into a life threatening heart murmur or a drink-induced peptic ulcer, but when he does explain his ailment, the blackshoes regard him with incredulous looks; silent accusations that he just wanted to get off his ship.

After roll call and trivial announcements, the formation disperses. Several men go inside the annex for janitorial duty while others prowl the parking lot, plastic bags in hand, picking up cigarette butts, flip tops and candy wrappers. A few stragglers roll up their sleeves, light cigarettes and lean on the brick building in the shade telling sea stories until lunchtime.

Chris boards the shuttle to Tripler Army Hospital.

Sitting in the back of the van, he looks out the window and realizes that every military base he's been to was neatly enclosed behind barbwire-topped fences, but Pearl Harbor is different. It's a sprawling complex of shipyards, airfields, buildings and weapon depots, interspersed with family housing, golf courses, a Navy Exchange shopping mall and beaches. The Nimitz Highway spills six exit ramps into a melee of parks, supermarkets, gas stations and fast food joints that inundate the military area with free enterprise. Likewise, taxicabs and busses entered Pearl's gates as freely as military personnel drive and walk off. People in uniforms and civilian clothes all seem to be affiliated with the military. Sitting in the back of the van—the medical hold short bus—Chris looks out the window and can't quite tell where the base ends and the civilian world begins.

*   *   *

Inside an examination room at the Tripler Army Hospital Cardiology Clinic, Chris lays on a narrow, thin-cushioned table while a humorless Army sergeant attaches sensors to his chest, wrists and ankles. For several minutes, the EKG machine transforms his heartbeat and pulse into a series of jagged red lines on a rolling strip of graph paper. The sergeant removes the sensors from his chest and Chris says, "See you tomorrow."

By 9:15 in the morning he's on the public transit bus heading back to Pearl Harbor. He's wondering what they'll make him do when he arrives back at the Medical Annex when the bus stops at the Navy Exchange shopping mall. He notices there's a grocery store, a department store and an assortment of shops, so he decides to hop off the bus and have a look.

After browsing around, he purchases a blue nylon backpack, Bain de Soleil suntan lotion, a three-dollar pair of dark tinted sunglasses, a pair of blue rubber sandals and knee-length swim trunks printed with a motley array of Sphinxes, Aztec Sun Gods and smiling Buddhas.

After the lady at the checkout rings up his purchases, Chris gives her a twenty and a five. She sets two quarters on the Formica counter, but he slides them back to her and snatches a copy of The Stars and Stripes newspaper from a rack next to the cash register.

As the day's first heat wrinkles rise from the parking lot, Chris exits the store and walks toward the bus stop. At the same moment he's considering how much nicer it is to have a bag of beach gear slung over his shoulder than sixty-five pounds of steel chains, two Marine Military Police step in front of him.

"Hold it right there, sailor!"

Chris freezes. He's intimidated by their crisp uniforms, complete with holstered pistols, radios, mace, blackjacks.

"Identification," one of them demands.

Before he can pull out his wallet, two Navy Master at Arms roll up on bicycles to join the investigation.

"Sailor, you are unauthorized in this area during normal working hours," one of the Master at Arms informs him.

"I didn't know," Chris replies, eyeing the guy's sporty mountain bike and his belt loaded with cop-gear. "This is my first day here. I'm on medical hold at Pearl."

"Why not let us handle this," one of the Master at Arms says to the marines.

The marines look at each other and one of them says, "Sure."

Chris is unaccustomed to the street-walking technicalities that are a regular part of military behavior ashore. He's a fleet sailor, and at sea there's a high regard for rank and tradition, but nobody sweats the small stuff, like shined shoes, haircuts, shaving or neat salutes.

"We could write you up," the Master at Arms says. "You'd go before the executive officer. He's a marine and does not like sailors one bit. He'd doc your pay fifty dollars and make you stand a seabag inspection. But on account of the fact that you're here for medical reasons we're going to let you off with a warning."

"I appreciate it," Chris says.

"Now listen up! On weekdays, between zero eight hundred and seventeen hundred you must be in dress uniform if you are on the premises of the Navy Exchange. You will not wear torn, frayed or faded uniforms. You will polish your shoes! Shave every day and have your hair trimmed every week. Do you understand?"

"Aye, aye!" Chris throws his shoulders back and restrains a smirk.

He boards the next bus and rides it for half a mile. Stopped at a congested intersection with a McDonalds, 7-11, Texaco and a used car lot crowding the four corners, Chris looks out the window for any sign of military police. As new passengers pay their fares, he slips off the bus. He looks around to see if the Master at Arms have followed him but the coast is clear, so he runs for the Texaco men's room. Inside the toilet stall, his heart races as he strips off his dungaree uniform and stuffs it in his new backpack. His hands shake nervously as he tears the tags off his new swim trunks. He's worried that the Master at Arms are staking out the bathroom and calling for backup on their radios.

Transformed into a civilian beach bum, he puts on his new sunglasses, opens the door and steps into the glorious Hawaiian sunshine. No sign of the MAA.

Inside the Texaco, Chris zaps two beef and bean burritos in a microwave oven, then leaves the Texaco and walks across the street to the bus stop where he sits eating and waiting for the bus. After a while, he decides to smoke a cigarette, and then he can't tell if it's the anxiety he feels over running away from the Navy or the burritos or the cigarette that's got his stomach belching fire into his esophagus. It doesn't matter, he decides, as he washes down his last Amobarbital with a swig of orange Hi-C.

A bus route map on the Plexiglas wall indicates the A bus will take him to Honolulu and Waikiki Beach which lights up his brain with visions of bars and beaches packed with bikini-clad girls. He knows he can have a frosty mug of beer with lunch and sun himself on the beach all afternoon. He easily imagines going to a night club at sundown. The bus route map also shows that the C bus goes over the island's central mountain range and drops down onto the North Shore, where there are world-famous surfing beaches like Banzai Pipeline.

His thoughts teeter between cocktail lounges full of tourists, maybe stumbling shitfaced through another night at the Waikiki discos, or chilling at a beach on the North Shore, maybe renting a boogie board for the afternoon.

He decides to leave it to fate and board the first bus that shows up.

So it goes, he thinks as he sits on the bench and lights another smoke—waiting for the Amobarb' to do its thing.

*   *   *

The C bus weaves through Pearl City, north to Wahiawa at the center of the island and down through sprawling pineapple plantations to Oahu's North Shore. At a fork in the road, they follow a sign for King Kamehameha Highway and Chris sees beaches in the distance.

He picks a stop to get off the bus at random, simply because there's a beach and not much else. Trapped air hisses from the big vehicle's brakes, and then it drives away. He lifts the new sunglasses off his eyes and looks past green bushes, through palm trees and ironwood boughs, across the sand at the in-rolling breakers.

He follows a trail down to the beach and strikes out along the sand, a wayfarer on the island's northern fringe. Waves erase his footprints as he traverses the empty beach, always getting closer to a distant vanishing point ahead. He meanders through haymow drifts of seaweed red and brown and does a little spelunking in kelp-strewn strands of black, volcanic rock. He finds a cave and climbs into the cool darkness. He hunkers down in a blowhole and sits listening to storm-surges crashing on the rocky outcrop. White spume sprays skyward and salty drops, like monsoon rain, splash on his bare back. He listens to mermaids burbling water music, as the crashing waves carve new caverns beneath him in the rocks.

Walking along, the Amobarbital numbs the sun burning his shoulders. When beads of sweat break on his brow, he coats himself with Bain de Soleil. For a while he sits on a desolate stretch of sand and smokes a cigarette, listening to the wind whisper in his ears. Things begin to appear in the blue sky, like winged horses swooping along faster than airplanes and then fireworks that turn into algebraic equations. He shakes his head, smiles and laughs and enjoys the show. After a while he just sits there knowing somehow that time and space are infinite and this means somewhere out there exists an exact duplicate of himself, sitting on the same exact beach, hallucinating. What really freaks him out is he knows his other self, at this exact moment, is thinking about him.

"Wow," he whispers.

After walking for a great while he comes upon a lifeguard stand, people sunning themselves on blankets. A thatched-roof shack called The Belly Buster up near the road rents umbrellas, surfboards. There's a snack bar selling sandwiches, fruit and soft drinks.

Chris lies on the sand and settles in for the afternoon.

Waves roll up and churn against the shore. Golden rays imbue the beach, its sparse vegetation and pliant occupants with a brilliant light. Drowsily buffered on the outskirts of sleep he swirls in chimerical dreams spurred by roaring breakers, impassioned surfers hooting and the static-peppered broadcast of a sand-filled FM radio cranking out the latest new-wave hits. Each time he reaches the precipice and is rolling over the edge into a foreboding sleep, a breeze sends fusillades of sand against his skin, a dog barks or an excited Frisbee catcher yelps for joy. Each sensation lingers, flickering across the blackness of his closed eyes before disappearing into his swarming subconscious.

Sometime later, arising from his comatose state, Chris pulls the Stars and Stripes newspaper from his pack and lethargically begins reading the headlines.

McDonnell Douglas Rolls 100th FA-18 Hornet Jet off Long Beach Assembly Line

Reagan Okays 20% Pay Hike for Armed Forces Personnel

Congress Appropriates $25 Billion for Star Wars Defense Initiative

Secretary Projects Future Navy: 600 Ships

None of it means anything until he wonders, why do we need so many ships to patrol the Atlantic, Pacific, Indian Ocean and the Mediterranean? What are we gonna do, park a half dozen battleships off the coast of every nation with a beach? The number 600 makes no sense to him at all.

Secretary Projects Future Navy: 600 Ships

As we rapidly approach the 21st century, our Navy is tasked with a vital and difficult mission: Defending freedom and keeping shipping lanes open in an increasingly hostile world.

Northern Korea, Libya, Iran and Iraq, several African Nations and Japan are currently preparing to or have already declared increases on their coastal boundaries. These nations are claiming that up to 200 miles from their shores, out into the open sea, are no longer international waters. These adjusted boundaries are in contradiction to U.N. policies and League of Nations' accords. The United States has claimed only 20 miles from her shores for over 100 years and she does not plan to deviate from her policy. Another hostility faced by our Navy in our efforts to control the sea is our duty to police warring nations. For thirty years, we have stood watch over Vietnam, the Persian Gulf, Libya, Egypt, Israel and both sides of the Central American Coastline. And for more than forty years, we have stood watch over the Philippine Islands, South Korea, Japan, the Suez Canal, Guam, Cuba, the

Panama Canal, the North Atlantic and the Mediterranean. We must also support the Coast Guard in their mission, patrolling our coastlines at home. Today's Navy faces a challenge greater than any armed force has ever faced in the history of the human race. Our mission calls for courage, glory and honor. In order to accept this challenge, to grasp our destiny, our Navy requires more high tech equipment, crews of highly trained men and an enormous budget.

The Pentagon staff has been working on a plan that will go to congress this month. It considers the future, encompasses our goals and demonstrates a need for a Navy of 600 ships. Our fleets will increase by 147 ships; including six super-carriers, nineteen nuclear submarines and eleven guided missile cruisers. We will design, build, fit out and commission all these vessels during the next five years. This is the most broad-ranging, forward-looking plan the United States Navy has ever conceived. It is a plan that will ensure our control of the sea in the 21st century. As this plan goes to Congress for approval, I implore all sailors to heave ho! Our Navy is performing crucial tasks every minute of every day. I insist that every man, from the fleet admirals down to the deckhands, renew your pride and dedication to our cause, and let it reflect in your uniforms and your professional attitude. We are setting a course for the 21st century, where our 600-ship United States Navy will rule the waves.

Pride stirs in Chris's breast. "Rule the waves," he mumbles, still feeling whacky from the Amobarbital. "Damn," he whispers, looking at the number 600. Six-hundred ships! He has a sense of belonging as a member of the most powerful team on the globe. He stares out over the incoming waves, toward the horizon. He takes a deep breath of salty air and imagines the Enterprise's long steel keel cutting through the waves, jets rocketing off her bow. His dilated pupils visualize submarines gliding through deep-sea canyons far below the ocean's choppy surface. The secretary is right, he realizes. It makes sense. Chris now feels that he understands—America can only control a hostile world by controlling the sea. It's so obvious!

Right then, everyone on a nearby blanket suddenly leaps to their feet, shouting and pointing out at the waves.

Chris sees a surfer a few hundred feet away, riding atop a huge swelling crest. He's a square-shouldered, black-haired bronze god glissading along on an enormous aqua-blue wall of seawater. The stance of an Egyptian deity carved in hieroglyphics keeps him atop his plank. He's streamlining along the steep watery slope, gradually nearing the beach, where the wave ahead crashes. He slides down the watery wall's face and carves a quick S-turn by cocking his hips in several fluid twists. The wave's crest thrusts upward, forming a fluttering knife-edge over the surfer's head before bending forward and throwing back a hiss of saltwater spray.

Impressed, Chris watches the surfer crouch low on his board as the cylinder of water closes over him, and Chris fears for the surfer consumed inside the crashing wave. But as it curls over and begins to collapse, the wave sends up a tremendous splash and the surfer shoots out of the crashing watery mayhem and glides toward shallow water where rocks protrude through the surface. Suddenly, the surfer transfers his weight to the board's tail and turns around and rides back up the wave's crashing face and launches off its frothy crest. Like pitchforks and rakes in the hands of an angry mob, the top of the wave churns beneath him, clutching at the fins on the surfer's board. Sunshine shimmers off his tanned, wet flanks, and he shakes his head, sending a spray of jewel-like droplets flying from his black hair. The surfer traverses the bowl of blue cloudless sky, knees bent, palms flat out to his sides as if supported on invisible parallel bars. Still against the blue Hawaiian sky, the surfer's hieroglyphic stance contrasts sharply with the angry shore-pounding surf beneath him.

*   *   *

One after another, surfers ride the furious walls of water toward the beach. Chris wants to splash around in the shallow area but he feels unworthy. To enter the water, he fears, will be like jumping on stage during a live performance.

He's hungry.

The Amobarb's afterglow barely lights his brain.

He walks up to The Belly Buster and orders a veggie sandwich, sprouts, tomato, avocado and cheese on whole wheat, and a guava nectar. When he pays and thanks the girl working the counter, he notices an index card tacked to a post, "Learn to surf!" it tells him. "Ask

74

for Jack Holland at The Belly Buster, $15 an hour, long or short board, wet suit included. Private lesson, no reservation needed."

I can't afford it, he tells himself. I'll break my neck on the rocks. I can't ride 30-foot waves. He glances over his shoulder and realizes that even way up here near the road, under the palm trees, he can hear the surf rumbling as load as a freight train.

He sits at the picnic table and eats his sandwich while he imagines falling off the top of a thirty-foot wall of water, slamming headfirst onto a coral boulder, and then having a two-story houseful of saltwater collapse on him. "No way," he tells himself, "surfers here are pros." He glances at the index card tacked to the post. It's old. The ink is runny. It was probably tacked there during low season.

Then he realizes that he's visited this damn island over a half dozen times, and all he's ever done is swill cocktails at nightclubs and pass out in hotel rooms on Waikiki. He sips the last of his guava nectar and stands up to ask about surfing lessons. It's only water, he figures. The worst thing that'll happen is I'll get wet.

"Hi," Chris says to the girl working the snack bar. Alien feelings shoot through him as he thinks for a second that he's just a normal guy on vacation. "I saw the sign for surfing lessons, is Jack here?"

"I'll find him," she says.

Chris knows everything is going to work out fine. He sits at the picnic table and waits.

"Jack's out surfing," the woman yells. "He'll be in any minute."

Chris gives her a thumbs-up, then smears lotion on his shoulders and relaxes. He closes his eyes and soaks up the rays. Before long, someone casts a shadow across his face and when he opens his eyes there's Jack Holland, the dude he saw surfing a few minutes earlier on that massive wave.

"Did you ask about lessons, bro'?"

"I did."

"Cool. I'm Jack." He flashes a friendly smile and speaks with that So-Cal dude accent.

They shake hands.

Jack sits at the table. He's wearing dark trunks. Black, curly hair past his ears.

"I saw you surfing," Chris says.

"The waves are cracking great today," Jack says as he drums his fingers on the table. His hair drips and he bites his lower lip.

Chris glances at the gold ring on Jack's finger.

"Just got married four months ago,' Jack says.

"Congratulations."

"She's a great lady." Jack breathes deep and drums his fingers some more. He flashes a smile at Chris as if they're sharing an inside joke.

Chris wonders if he's missed something.

"I met her right here at the Pipeline," Jack says, holding up his left hand, staring at his wedding band.

"That's great," Chris says.

"You'll have to cut me some slack, Chris," Jack says and exhales hard. "It's been months since we've seen waves like this, bro, and I've been out in it all morning. I'm trying to get a grip, let things slow down a little."

"It's all good," Chris says, hearing the rumble of the big waves out beyond the beach. He wonders what really goes on out there, what it takes to ride those monsters.

Jack shakes his head and water drops fly in all directions. "Done any surfing?" he asks.

"No," Chris confesses, feeling like a total nugget.

"No worries. It's easy to get up on a stick and ride."

Chris glances at the giant waves crashing into furious foam. They rumble like bombs exploding on the sand.

"Aloha!" Jack says laughing. "You're not riding those, big chief. Experts only on the Pipeline in these conditions! You and me gonna drive around the point to Yokohama Bay, where we can roll on the mellow swells."

"Ah, okay," Chris says.

"Let's go." Jack stands.

Chris swings his backpack on and wiggles his toes into his sandals.

They cross the street and walk uphill on a dirt road. Colorful stucco bungalows are tucked back in the trees. Perched atop the hill, a pink house with a wraparound deck looks out at the ocean.

In a garage under the deck, mountain bikes hang on hooks screwed into the beams. Greenpeace and Earth First! stickers on the wall. A block of wax sits on a neon-pink surfboard lying across a pair of sawhorses. Scuba masks and snorkels hang on nails and several surfboards hang in a rack on the wall. Jack grabs a long surfboard, hands it to Chris, looks him up and down and rummages through a trunk full of wet suits. He hands one to Chris and on the way out grabs another long board.

They lash the boards atop of a red Volkswagen Beetle, hop in and take off.

Jack drives back the way Chris had walked, passes the bus stop and cruises along the blacktop hugging the island's coast.

A few miles later, they turn onto a dirt road that winds down a mountainside toward the beach. In a clearing, men sleep in the shade under tarps strung on tent poles beside the road. One man leans on a tree strumming a ukulele. Jack waves and the man waves back as they continued downhill. Along the way, Chris sees several more tailgate picnics, groups of Hawaiian's hanging around smoking barbecues and snoozing in the shade under tarp tents. The tall grass and trees part and they park in a gravel lot close to the sea. Chris pulls out money to pay.

"We'll deal with the finances later, bro."

Chris is surprised to discover that he will learn to surf on a long board. He'd figured it would be easier on a short board but Jack says no.

Jack carries his board under one arm and his wet suit in his free hand. Chris does the same as they wade into the water.

Jack doesn't offer any pointers on how to stay on top, but he does say, "Just do what I do, and I'll tell you everything you need to know when we get out there."

Jack straddles his board, dunks his wet suit and says, "You don't have to get it wet before you put it on, that's just the way I like to do it."

"How far out are we going?"

"Pretty far."

They lie on their boards and paddle out over the swells. Each sizzles as it lifts them. Atop the waves, Chris glimpses the vast expanse of water all the way to the horizon and when he slides down between the waves he notices patches of white foam and clumps of seaweed on the surface.

After a long while paddling, Jack sits up on his board.

Chris paddles beside him and looks over his shoulder and sees the beach is a white strip threatening to slip off over the horizon behind them. "If I explain everything it'll just fill your head with stuff, so I'm gonna have you get on top and ride and take a few splashes, okay?"

*   *   *

Chris remembered Scarborough Beach on the Indian Ocean in Perth, Australia.

He and Larry Tynan figured they'd swim out and paddle around, but it turned out to be a bad idea. As soon as they dove in and swam past the first line of breakers, the current pulled them way out from land. And while they swam for their lives trying to get back to shore, two lifeguards stood atop a wooden lifeguard stand blowing whistles and waving their arms. Chris remembered how scared he was, wondering why the lifeguards weren't coming out to rescue them, and how his fear turned to panic when the lifeguards climbed down from their stand and stood on the beach blowing their whistles and waving their arms for everyone to get out of the water. All the while the current pulled Chris and Larry further and further from land. Chris noticed the lifeguards didn't have a boat. He and Larry gave up trying to swim. Instead, they tread water, yelling back and forth to each other while choking on gulps of saltwater. Finally, they began a swimming frenzy that lasted over half an hour and landed them on the beach about a mile from where they originally entered. Chris clearly remembered the relief he felt, thoroughly exhausted as he rode the crest of the last huge wave that slammed him into a mix of watery sand and ground-up shells. With his last ounce of strength, he leaped to his feet and ran for the beach where he collapsed. After a few minutes of panting on all fours like shipwrecked sailors washed ashore, Chris and Larry saw one of the lifeguards jogging toward them; his nose coated with white sunblock, wearing orange Speedos and a straw sombrero.

"Ya bloody fools!" the lifeguard said in a youthful cockney accent, "What ya thank ya doin' paddlin' out s'far? Wanta be bait for the great white, do ya?"

"Great white?" Larry gasped.

"Yea, the bloody beasts are cruising all the coast this time a year."

"Great white sharks?" Chris asked.

"Yes! My mate an' I saw a school o' six abou' an hour ago, and under such conditions we do not go in a wat'a after anyone."

"Great white sharks?" Larry asked again in total disbelief.

"Ga' day, mates," the lifeguard said and jogged away down the beach.

*   *   *

First thing," Jack says to Chris, "relax, bro', and feel the rhythm. I can see you're feeling it already. Remember, the worst thing is you get wet. Now, when you're standing on top bend your knees, sit back, lean forward. If I say anymore it'll mess with your head."

"Okay."

"You stay here, I'll paddle out and ride back past you and you check out my stance when I go by."

Chris waits and watches Jack paddle out and watches him surf back past him.

"Right foot a little out front," Jack shouts, "left foot under your bottom, knees bent, arms out for balance, stay loose." With no fancy moves, Jack rides past, then sits on his board, then lies on it and paddles back.

"You make it look easy," Chris says.

"Go ahead. Paddle out there and ride back past me."

Several swells roll beneath him as he gets into position, then he picks his wave and paddles fast as it surges under him. Leaping to his feet, the breeze whips at him. He grips the sticky board with his feet as a million tons of water rolls beneath him. Tapping the power scares him a little, so he squats down and spread his arms for balance. Jack bobs on the wave just ahead. A little laugh quivers in Chris's chest, because surfing is easy.

Then he starts sliding off the back, so he leans forward and lowers his butt, which sends him sliding down the face. He flies over the board's nose and belly flops into the water right in front of Jack.

Salt burns his taste buds and adrenaline flows in his veins. The board bonks him on the head. Undeterred he climbs on and paddles over to Jack.

A few more tries, and they're surfing side by side.

"Find your limits," Jack yells.

Chris is giddy, high on Mother Nature, because now he understands that she curls up thousands of these beautiful waves every day off this fuzzy green coast, right here under the warm sun. He glances over the tip of the board into the deep trough ahead and feels the wave sizzling around his ankles.

It fills him with good fear.

After every wipeout, Chris climbs back on, paddles out, picks his wave and leaps to his feet.

Now he's atop a large one. The crest throws freshets of foaming salt water as high as his hips. When he slips off the back, he leans forward and when he feels momentum taking him over the front he leans back and relaxes.

"Looking good, big chief!" Jack shouts after they ride what seems like a hundred yards.

Chris's mind sparks with the physics of wave dynamics.

"You're doing it!" Jack shouts.

Chris turns to look at Jack and the surfboard shoots down into the trough, going sideways but he bends his knees, reaches down and grabs the edge. "Wow," he whispers as it straightens and rises to the shoulder of the wave.

"Nice," Jack shouts.

Ahead, Chris hears breakers roaring. His wave quickens and the crest foams up around his ankles. The front wall steepens before him. Chris considers diving off the back, but his stability on bent knees reassures him. Besides, he reasons, it's only water.

With a loud churning, the wave ahead curls over and breaks.

Out of nowhere, he visualizes Major Burkham's face and remembers he's on medical hold.

That's when his wave bucks like an elephant rising on its hind legs. The blare from the beast's trunk fills his ears. The water in the trough below sucks up the face of the wave.

"Banzai!" he shouts and leans forward. He accelerates, turning sideways, traversing the wall of water. The lip rises behind him and splashes over like an elephant spraying water from its trunk.

"I'm getting tubed," he whispers as the wave crumbles on top of him, tearing him off the board and spinning him inside an industrial washing machine. One of his knees comes up and hits him in the eye. The other leg wrenches backward. His foot touches the back of his head. Tons of churning seawater grinds him into the sandy bottom.

He's glad it's not a coral reef. His head pops up and he gasps for air but another thousand gallons of frothy seawater slaps him in the face. He tightens every muscle as the undertow scrapes him against the sand while pulling him back out. Another wave tosses him over the falls again. He lands on his knees, jumps to his feet and runs three steps before tripping over his surfboard. He half swims, half crawls to the beach, where he lays on his back and laughs at the sky.

On the ride back, Chris pays Jack for the lesson and says, "I'm going to be here for a few more days and definitely want to take another lesson."

"That's cool," Jack tells him. "These next few weeks there are competitions and luaus going on, so come and hang loose, big chief."

Chapter 11: Temptations and Revelations

The next morning after his EKG, he's standing at the bus stop across the street from the Texaco, looking at the route map and asking himself if he wants to go back to the North Shore or down to Waikiki. He considers doing another surfing lesson with Jack, and the motivation to take his surfing skills to the next level stirs within. But the Waikiki beach scene exudes its appeal on him too. I can surf there, he reasons. A day of tanning on Waikiki is easy to imagine. In the back of his brain, under a lying, piece-of-shit trap door, he knows he can stay out late and party with the tourists if he goes to Waikiki.

He thinks about how nice it would be to meet a girl. Down there they're all on vacation, far from home—far from their reputations. He'd met girls there before but had to admit the ratio wasn't good. Dozens of times he ended up bar hopping into a late-night blackout when what he really wanted was to land between a set of hotel sheets with a cute girl. But it can happen; he could meet someone today—the sirens sing their sweet song, pulling him toward—toward what? He wonders. Will I end up shattered on the rocks with a wicked hangover, scrambling tomorrow morning to get back to base? Or will I meet her—the girl I've been searching for all these years. He remembers the sorority girl with the great breasts and the chastity belt. Even though he doesn't have her address, doesn't even know her name, he imagines writing letters to her from the ship and her reading them in her college dorm room. She'll probably send me a breakup letter like that chick sent to Larry. Fuck! Chris hopes she doesn't screw him over like that. He doesn't want to walk into an airplane propeller because his head is fucked up over some girl.

He concentrates on the bus route map and the timetable under Plexiglas. Someone stuck a wad of gum on the map right on Diamond Head Crater, and someone else stuck a cigarette butt right in the wad of gum.

He looks away, tells himself to get his shit together.

82

It can happen, he reassures himself, I can meet a girl on Waikiki.

Another twisted bit of logic unravels in his head when he thinks about showing up for his EKG the next morning, still soused if he does go bar hopping tonight. Might actually be a good idea—induce a wicked hangover with intense chest pain and all the anxiety that goes along with it and then have an EKG. If there's something wrong with his heart, as he fears in his darkest moments, getting an EKG while experiencing a wicked hangover is certainly one way to find out.

The bus for Waikiki pulls up to the curb and he climbs aboard.

He listens to the engine in the back, growling like a trapped mechanical beast, and he knows he's twisted his better judgment—what remains of it after his years in the Navy, and now he dreads the possibility of ending up in a bar on Waikiki Beach with a cigarette in one hand and a drink in the other.

He challenges himself to take the situation as a test, to see if he can spend a day on Waikiki and avoid the dens of industrial tourism—the bars and nightclubs. Somehow he knows it will be like avoiding fire while walking through hell.

*   *   *

The Waikiki waves are lazy walls of water that roll for a long way over a shallow bottom and then break on a shoal before reaching the beach.

A surfing instructor at the Surf Rider Hotel refers to the wave as "perfect four foot point break" and he teaches Chris how to stand forward on the very front of the long board and do a nose-ride. He teaches Chris to stay right in the sweet spot, which he calls the shoulder—the spot on the wave just to the side of the breaking crest where the wave curls over. After an hour-long lesson and an hour of splashing around out there by himself, Chris rides several waves for a hundred yards without wiping out.

By noon, he'd been riding for over two hours. He walks out of the water with the surfboard under his arm and salt water sluicing off his skin. A deep sense of contentment fills him when he looks at the towering white hotels and the fuzzy green mountains. Sunbathers with different shades of tan glisten in vibrant colored swim suits. He returns the surfboard to the shack where he rented it and then finds a spot to spread his towel.

He rubs on Bain de Sole and for the better part of the afternoon lays in the sun. The scent of bodies coated in coconut oil roasting and the faint thunder of waves crumbling in the distance tantalizes him as he slumbers on the sand.

Later, he orders a grilled chicken sandwich and a 7up in the cabana bar at the Surf Rider Hotel. Somebody drops a few quarters in the jukebox and a bunch of college kids start dancing. Sure enough, a half-hour later Chris has a pint of Foster Lager in one hand and a Marlboro in the other. Everything's fine, he tells himself. Alcohol and nicotine fill him with a relaxing buzz, but he can't get himself to forget that his problems come directly from the curl of blue smoke on the cigarette in his left hand and the frosty pint in his right.

"It's okay," the evil angel whispers in one ear. "There's nothing seriously wrong with you."

"Everything is not fine," the good angel says in his other ear.

On a thousand evenings in the past he'd have been wholly absorbed by the scene, the music and the hip kids partying. He'd have asks a girl to dance and gotten lost in the night—but something has happened, something went wrong inside him somewhere along the way.

Is it his stomach, his heart, his mind—all of the above, he wonders. He takes a drag and can feel the smoke in his lungs, and imagines the nicotine molecules attaching to his blood cells. He feels the sensation spreading through his limbs, along his veins and nerves, into his brain. And the suds from the cold beer spike his taste buds, and soak into his belly.

It doesn't feel right.

He looks at the cigarette between his fingers. The tan speckled filter-tip, the white paper cylinder with faint ringed lines, and the word Marlboro printed there. Blue-gray smoke rises from the smoldering tip. Over the years, he'd barely thought about the habit, but when he did it always passed for a social thing. "Let's go have a smoke," he'd said to hundreds of friends and acquaintances, without giving it another thought. But now, he can't get by on that. So what if this is the ultimate vacation destination with droves of beautiful people relaxing. He hears the evil angle telling him, "Don't get so uptight. It's not that big a deal." But he knows this won't do any more. He isn't like these people. He looks at the smooth faced kids. They're on break from college where they go to class and listen to professors lecture about history and business management. They can come here to Hawaii and cut loose, drink a little, smoke a few cigarettes and return to their safe lives back home without a care. But he can't do this. He lives on a battleship, works hard labor, smokes and drinks in dive bars across Asia. This life is rough and he has to take care of himself.

He looks at the cigarette and the mug of beer and realizes he's doing exactly what he'd told himself he wouldn't do!

He snuffs the cigarette in an ashtray on the bar. He puts down the mug and walks out.

He takes a bus into downtown Honolulu and roams the streets. His habits are so well weaved into him, every time he sees a woman's face or a neon beer sign he wants to slide up onto a barstool, light a smoke and order a pint and a shot. He knows the girls hanging out in bars in the afternoon are looking for cash.

He wonders if he has enough in his wallet.

Self-disgust hacks at these thoughts as if they're serpents sliding down out of the jungle in his mind.

He wanders through shopping malls and the capital buildings, parks and parking lots. He wonders if this is all there is to life as the angel's in his head argue; the bad angel trying to convince him to go sit on a barstool and smoke and drink and chat up girls, and the good angel telling him not to do it.

Is this what being an adult is about?

Is this why I joined the Navy?

He stands on the sidewalk outside a bookstore and thinks about browsing the aisles for something to read. He can go back to the base and lie in bed and get lost in tales of adventure.

He pauses before the stone steps of a cathedral and gazes up at the spires and stained glass windows. He knows it will help to go inside, kneel down and pray to God for help. He needs divine intervention to beat his bad habits, but he walks away along the cracked sidewalk instead.

The display in the window of a sporting goods store makes him stop, attracted to the backpacks, surf boards, scuba equipment and bicycles. "I'm such an asshole!" he whispers. "Look at all this stuff made for having fun, but all I do is smoke and drink booze and prowl for sluts. What the fuck is wrong with me? Why am I such a degenerate?"

He goes into the store and wanders around.

In an aisle full of aquatics equipment he chooses a pair of swimming goggles. At the checkout he snags a surfer magazine.

Chapter 12: Earth First!

The next day, after his EKG, Chris changes his clothes in the Texaco men's room.

At the bus stop, he waits for the North Shore bus.

*   *   *

Big waves roll in toward the beach but they're smaller than the waves two days ago. A lineup of surfers bob on their boards and peel away and paddle atop the rising crests, then one or two of them leap to their feet. These waves don't race in with the storm speed of the waves two days ago. They don't rise up as high, but they do curl over and form a tube. And the tube, from the beach where Chris stands, looks like a churning white steamroller spreading out across the wave's face as it crashes.

At the Belly Buster Chris asks for Jack, but the girl hasn't seen him. She tells Chris to cross the road and go up to the pink house and ask for him there.

The red Volkswagen Beetle is gone, and Chris considers coming back after lying on the beach for an hour, but he decides to knock at the door instead.

He walks up the wooden stairs and onto the deck. Rattan thrones face each other across a wicker table where a pink glass vase full of dried flowers sits. A long, cushioned table is off to one side. Chris wonders what it is and then sees a contoured oval pillow on a steamer trunk beside bottles of lotion and he knows it's a massage table.

*   *   *

He's been to a few seedy establishments billing themselves as massage parlors, but the Fleet Club in Singapore was an authentic Oriental massage parlor. Looking for alcohol and sex, he and Larry had entered the Fleet Club and were initially disappointed. There were no chicks lounging around in high heels and skimpy lingerie. There were muscular and slightly overweight men in tank tops, cloth pants, rope-soled shoes and tank tops. Chis wanted to leave, but Larry convinced him to loosen up with the thirty-five Singapore dollars and pay for the club's full therapeutic treatment. For the next two hours, the Malaysian men ushered the towel-wrapped sailors from steam room to cold showers and then to Jacuzzi tubs and back to the massage tables. They cracked every joint in their bodies, from their necks to their fingers and toes. They rubbed them and stretched their arms and legs.

Afterwards, when they walked onto the street, their legs felt rubbery like stretched pieces of salt-water taffy.

*   *   *

Chris knocks on the door and a tall woman in a flowing, colorful wrap answers. She's a big boned girl, attractive and vibrant. Her skin glows with an olive tan over muscles that are clearly the result of weight training.

"Hello." She smiles.

"Hi, I'm Chris. Is Jack here? I'd like to take a surfing lesson."

"You're welcome to wait. He'll be here in just a few," she says.

"It's okay?" Chris asks.

"Sure."

He sits in one of the rattan thrones and looks out over the palm trees to the water beyond, where surfers float in a lineup on the incoming swells. A minute later, she comes out and gives him a glass of iced tea. He glances at her diamond solitaire and gold wedding band.

"Thank you," he says.

"I'm Marsha."

"I'm Chris," he says again, feeling awkward without Jack there. "I took a surfing lesson from Jack the other day and wanted to go again. This is excellent iced tea by the way."

"Thanks. I made it with raspberry and let it sit in the sun all afternoon yesterday."

Chris takes another sip. "Who does massage?"

"Me. I'm getting back into it after being away from it for a while. I have a job interview for a masseuse position at a health club in

88

Honolulu tomorrow. I really should be reviewing a few things."

"Don't let me keep you," Chris says. "I'll go wait on the beach."

"I've been away from massage for almost a year and rusty so I've been working on Jack and some of our neighbors. Just now I was reading over my notes from massage school, but I need a body to work on."

Chris is sure Marsha is politely telling him to get lost. He wonders what Jack will think if he arrives home and finds Chris having a glass of iced tea with his wife. He drains his glass and sets it on the table.

"Could I ask you a favor?"

"Sure," Chris says.

"Let me practice some massage techniques on you."

He thinks about asking if Jack would mind, but realizes that'll sound sleazy. "Sure," he says, feeling a bit awkward.

"Take your shirt and sandals off and lay on here," she says, smacking her palm on the cushioned table. She attaches the contoured oval pillow. Chris lies down.

"I can tell you're into weight training." Marsha throws a sheet over him and folds it down off his back. She squeezes lotion into her hand. A light mint fragrance teases his nose as she goes to work on his neck and shoulders. She presses hard on the muscles, untying knots of tension. She pauses to consult a textbook open on the steamer trunk.

"I can't believe how tense you are!"

Her fingers dig into his shoulders and his concentration slips away. She squeezes more lotion into her hands and goes back to work on the other shoulder. She pulls the sheet over his torso and folds it off his left leg. "A good massage along with your workouts will reduce the aches and pains of recovery."

Chis perks awake from his euphoric state and says, "Pain?"

"From lifting weights, the pain in your muscles from constantly trying to rebuild after being torn down."

"I'm on a ship all the time, where it's impossible to get a massage."

"Are you in the Navy?"

"Yeah, but now I'm seeing a doctor at Tripler for a stomach problem.

She pops his toes one at a time.

"Oh! That feels good."

"How long has your stomach been bothering you?"

"A few years."

"How have you been dealing with it?"

"Navy doctors have been giving me pain killers and antacids, but I finally got fed up with that and insisted they send me to see a specialist."

Marsha strokes Chris's right hamstring. "Your problem could be stress related?"

"My job is stressful. I work on the flight deck of an aircraft carrier."

"Wow."

"The work is hard but the travel is nice." Chris hears Jack's Volkswagen coming up the road. "But you're right, I've been stressed out." The car stops and the door slams and Jack runs up the stairs.

"Hi babe," he says. Marsha stops working on Chris's leg and they kiss. Jack asks, "Who's this?"

"Your Navy friend."

Chris wants to explain. He feels caught in a compromising position. The only contact he's had with women since joining the Navy is sex, and now with Marsha, a new bride, and her husband having just burst in upon them engaged in a relaxing physical activity, makes him feel caught in the act. But Jack didn't exhibit a grain of suspicion.

Jack only smiles and says, "Hey, Big Chief! How are you, buddy?"

"I feel great after a relaxing massage."

"I can't believe how tense this guy is."

"The military does that, I guess," Jack says as he enters the house. He returns with a glass and the pitcher of iced tea. He sits in one of the rattan thrones, fills all the glasses and says, "So, what's the Navy all about?"

Chris rests on his elbows and Marsha returns to massaging his leg. "It's like a big corporation," Chris says.

"War Incorporated." Jack chuckles. "How about you, what do you do for the corporation?"

Chris tells them about his job on the flight deck and his visits to ports in Asia and Africa. "I'm here to have my stomach checked at the Army hospital."

Marsha covers Chris with the sheet and sits beside her husband. "How's that?" she asks.

"I feel great." Seeing them side by side now, presents a portrait of everything Chris isn't—a handsome guy with a beautiful girl.

"You don't seem like the gung ho military type," Jack says.

"I'm not."

"Ever think about what the Navy puts in the ocean?" Jack asks.

Chris recalls the article he read in Stars and Stripes. Six hundred ships. "What do you mean?"

"Nothing personal, but do you ever think about how much stuff you guys throw off your ships into the water?"

Chris thinks about it. "In one day," he says, "the Enterprise throws a few tons of trash overboard." He's seen mountains of full plastic bags, crates, steel drums, bucket of food-slop and broken aircraft parts thrown off the ship. And the Enterprise is only one ship.

Jack drains his glass, stands up and says, "Come on, Chris, I want to show you something."

As he slides off the massage table, Chris feels so relaxed that his knees almost fold beneath him. "Thanks, Marsha."

"No problem," she says.

"Good luck on your job interview."

"Thanks."

Chris follows Jack down the steps, off the deck and around the house. They walk along a path. Hip-high ferns grow beneath tall palm trees.

Suddenly Jack stops and turns to Chris with a friendly smile. "I don't want you to get the wrong idea," he says. "I'm sure you've got some kind of patriotic contract with the Navy, so don't take this personal, okay?"

"What are you talking about?" Chris asks.

"Let me just say the Navy is a litter bug." He turns and continues down the path.

They walked along, then cross a road, and Chris follows, wondering what he's about to discover. The beautiful blue ocean spreads out to the horizon on their right and a green mountain on their left. At a bridge spanning a deep, narrow gorge they climb down a rocky cliff by clinging to vines and roots. At the bottom, they stand in a secluded cove where a creek runs from a crack in the rocks and flows into the ocean. Gigantic boulders are strewn on the sand. Waves crash on a jagged outcropping. They walk along the beach until they come to a mound of junk that spills from a crevice in the base of the cliff.

"This junk's been collected over the past few years," Jack says.

Chris sees rusty steel drums, plastic packing crates, wooden pallets, yards of bubble wrap and chunks of Styrofoam.

Chris picks up a clear plastic cylinder.

"Lots of those," Jack says.

Inside are the remains of a sonar beacon. Military stock numbers and the words Lockheed Aerospace are embossed in the plastic end cap. "An airplane flies along," Chris says, "and drops about forty of these in a line a couple miles long."

"What for?"

"They ping the bottom with sonar and send signals back to the guys in the plane overhead who are looking for Russian subs."

"Techno-trash," Jack says.

Chris picked up a rusted five-gallon can that he recognizes as aircraft cleaning compound. Greenish sludge oozes out and he jumps back and drops it, watching the sludge pool in an indentation in the sand. "That's aircraft cleaner."

"How do you mix it?" Jack asks.

"What do you mean?"

"Do you use it straight or mix it?"

"We have to mix it, straight it'll strip the paint off the fuselage." Chris wonders what happens to fish that swim through a slick of aircraft cleaning compound. He and other plane captains had fun on washday. When a can of cleaning compound was empty, they filled it with water, screwed the cap on tight and threw it from the flight deck, cheering when it hit the water and made a big splash.

"The Navy has a bad attitude about throwing shit over the side," Jack says. "It's like something over the side means it magically disappears. But the ocean can't swallow any more trash. Does anyone in the Navy ever tell the sailors that there are huge garbage slicks on all of the major oceans?"

"No," Chris says, wondering why as a sailor in the world's biggest Navy, he knows nothing about the oceans. He's never learned about currents, environmental hazards, weather systems, longitude and latitude or sea life. He feels stupid realizing that he knows nothing about the ocean while Jack, a surfer dude, knows so much.

"I'm not blaming you." Jack sits on a rock and looks toward the sea. "This isn't even the bad shit," he says.

"What's the bad shit?"

"Rad-waste, medical waste, sewage, dolphins killed in tuna nets,

Japanese killing whales and sharks, Russian factory ships farming the sea out."

"What's Rad-waste?" Chris asks.

"Radioactive waste. The US military dumps tons of it. You said you're off an aircraft carrier. It's nuclear powered, right?"

Chris hesitates, wondering what kind of sabotage Jack has in mind but he glances at the garbage with naval stock numbers on it, and it's clear who the saboteur is. "Yeah, the Enterprise has eight reactors. I read somewhere that it's the largest conglomeration of nuclear reactors in the world."

"Did you know that there's a trap door in the hull under every reactor on a Navy ship?" Jack asks.

"Yeah," Chris says. "If a meltdown starts they can open the door and dump the reactor into the ocean."

"Do you think the Navy would report that if it every happened?" Jack asks.

Chris knows the Navy would only go public with a story like that if the press found out about it.

"Ever heard of Farrallon Island?" Jack asks. "It's fifty miles west of San Francisco."

"No."

"The military stashed ninety-thousand drums of rad-waste near Farrallon Island back in the forties and for the past twenty years it's been leaking into the ocean. In the sixties the Navy lost two nuke subs. They sank to the bottom of the Atlantic, and they've lost a whole bunch of nuke bombs over the side. And now with all the talk of arms reduction they're gonna start dismantling and burning nuclear weapons on a little island south of here. I bet they never told you any of this stuff." Jack smirks. "But it's not just the US; the Japanese, the British, the Russians—they're all up to no good."

"Sounds bad," Chris says.

"I am totally patriotic," Jack says, "which means that these problems are only going to be solved when lots of people raise hell about them."

"Are you raising hell?"

"We send pictures of dead fish and garbage slicks to all the politicians, but direct action works a lot better."

Chris wonders what direct action is.

"Every once in a while we dump a truckload of this shit at the capitol building in Honolulu or outside the main gate at Pearl Harbor."

"That's cool," Chris says, thinking he'd like to join in on some direct action. "Do you get busted?"

"Oh sure, we've spent a few nights in jail; had our pictures in the paper, sometimes the judge suspends the fine."

"Think that'll change the world?"

"World's gonna change, I'm just trying to nudge it in the right direction." Jack slides off the rock and says, "Let's get out of here."

They scramble up the rocks, cross the road and walk along the path through the ferns.

They enter the surf shack under the deck, and Jack says, "You want to take a ride around to Yokohama Bay?"

"You think I can surf here?" Jack says. "These waves ain't so big."

"You want to surf the Banzai Pipeline, Big Chief?"

"Yeah," Chris tries to sound confident.

"Well alright." Jack hands Chris a short white board with three small fins on its tail.

They emerge from under the deck and Jack shouts upstairs to his wife, "Marsha, let's go surfing!" A minute later, she comes down the steps and grabs a surfboard from the shack.

"I'll be glad to give you some pointers," Jack tells Chris as they walk down the dirt road toward the beach.

"I appreciate it."

"But seriously I think you're gonna get pounded today."

"Pounded?" Chris asks.

Chapter 13: The Giants

Indoor swimming pools, tennis and racquetball courts, an expansive roomful of free weights and Nautilus equipment, a sauna, steam room, several gigantic hot tubs. Free loaner surfboards and bicycles, snorkeling gear, scuba diving charter trips, sailing and golf lessons. Tacked to a bulletin board, brackets track club sport tournaments including softball, water polo, basketball, flag football and volleyball. Chris's head swims with thoughts of adventure and athletic diversion.

Angelo was right, he realizes, this is the best rec' center in the Navy!

He enters the weight room and walks slowly across the blue, rubberized carpet, through rows of shiny chrome weight machines and racks of dumbbells, he can't comprehend the dimensions of the room. Women in vibrant colored tights and guys in shorts and tank tops pedal exercise bikes and jog on treadmills.

Accustomed to lifting with Angelo in the weight room aboard the Enterprise, a shadowy steel box squeezed between the anchor chain lockers in the ship's bow, Chris doesn't know what to do with himself.

He remembers, during flight operations, the space aboard ship filled with the deafening roar as aircraft launched from the catapults on the deck above. It sounded like subway trains colliding in a dark tunnel. Barbells clanking and metal weights jangling as the massive ship rode on rough seas. Except to growl or grunt a rush of adrenaline into their veins, the men lifting weights aboard ship rarely spoke. On calm waters, he benched 175-pounds, but on rough seas, he strayed between 125 and 200. When the ship rose on a steep swell, no matter how hard he pressed, the weight stuck to his chest, but as the ship rolled over the top of a swell and began sliding down into the trough, the weight rose. There were times when the ship took a swell broadside and barbells became lopsided, weights slid off. Men sometimes limped to sickbay with smashed toes. The captain eventually ordered all hands to wear steel-toe boots in the ship's weight room.

Rolling around on the springy, spacious floor-mats in the Pearl

Harbor weight room, Chris stretches and does crunches to warm up. He glances around, checking out the people exercising, and right away realizes these aren't ordinary sailors getting a little exercise. There are several guys, weight-lifting giants, with thighs like beef shanks, bulging chests and massive arms, abdomens as flat and hard as a dinner plate. These are Hawaiian body builders, men Chris has seen strutting along Waikiki Beach, slicked in a film of Coppertone. And women too who are buff with bodies as trim and hard as a Barbie doll. He figures some of these people are Navy SEALS or Marine Recon—highly trained killing machines. He realizes again that his job as a jet mechanic isn't typical for most people in the military. Some of these folks look like they run ten miles before breakfast. They aren't like him; they haven't taken a barhopping tour of the world. Some of these people have been training in the jungle, learning to kill people.

Feeling good in this well-lit, chrome-spangled gym, he thinks, Damn, I gotta straighten up.

After loading a fifty pound weight on each end of a barbell, he lays on his back on the bench. He reaches up and grabs the bar, spaces his hands evenly apart and presses upward until his arms are fully extended. Smoothly, he lowers the barbell to his chest, inhales and pauses, then pressing the weight back up until his arms are fully extended again.

After a few reps his biceps are buffed up and his pecs are square. But to make a set really count, to achieve the burn that tears the muscle, he knows he has to exert himself until his chest and arms strain so bad they cease to press. He knows he needs a spotter to help him lift during the final difficult reps.

Between sets, Chris contemplates the giants. It seems the purpose for developing such massive muscles is simply to flex at the beach and earn the right to massage tanning lotion into the svelte, brown backs of sunbathing beauties; a worthy goal in his opinion but not one he's likely to ever achieve.

As he sits on the end of the bench he remembers what Angelo always said, "If you want to build muscle mass, you gotta maintain good form and push every set to failure." So Chris steps over to one of the Giants and asks the guy to spot his next set.

Then Chris lies on the bench and presses the loaded barbell through eight reps. As he lowers it, his arms shake and his back bows up off the bench. From the ribs up, his skin blushes a tint of blue and blood red and every muscle, including his jaw, eyelids and ears, clench. His muscles are locked up and he can't lift any more.

The giant stands at the head of the bench and places an index finger under the bar to assist him with a tiny effort, all while saying "Push it, come on, you can do it."

Chris shivers and presses with all his might and raises the barbell in slow, shaky increments. And when his arms are finally straight and his elbows locked, he sighs. He moves to place the barbell on the rack, but with one finger the giant prevents him and whispers, "One more, come on, make it hurt."

Chris inhales and slowly lowers the weight and feels a vigorous determination to embrace self-improvement as a new way of life. He pushes as hard as he can. It feels like his eyes are going to pop out of his head. The muscles across his chest and arms lock up tight and he simply cannot lift the weight at which point the giant presses a finger under the bar and it slowly rises.

Next, Chris decides to swim a few laps.

He puts on the new goggles he'd purchased at the sporting goods store in Honolulu and dives into the pool. He swims so fast to the other end he has to stop and catch his breath. Pushing off from the side, into his second lap, he swims slowly, and after a few strokes falls into a lazy, comfortable pace. He swims ten laps and feels no shortness of breath. With each stroke, he stretches his arms ahead and cups his hands as he paddles through the water. He kicks his legs powerfully. He stops lifting his head out of the water to breathe, instead he turns his neck to the side once every four strokes and only far enough for his mouth to break the surface so he can inhale. He exhales into the water so every breath lasts exactly four strokes.

He swims with thoughts unfettered by worries of addiction. The zero balance in his Navy College Fund does not disturb the tranquil emptiness of his mind. As he kicks, strokes and breathes he isn't afraid of the Iranians. The anxious claustrophobia that he knows will come during ninety days trapped aboard ship on the Persian Gulf doesn't trouble him. The steady rhythm of water surging past makes him forget about Larry and how he died and what happened after he was killed in the accident on the flight deck.

He turns his head and inhales once every four strokes. And he isn't nervous about the results of the medical tests on his nerves and his heart.

He kicks, strokes and breathes like a machine programmed with confidence. He swims countless laps, switching between freestyle and backstroke. Chlorinated water sluices around him. When he hooks his arm over the pool's concrete edge after more than thirty laps, he's breathing deeply and his heart pounds strong in his chest.

He watches two girls in bikinis walk by and suddenly wants to dressed up and splash on cologne. Have a few drinks and dance at the nightclub on base. But the discipline developed during a few days of working out whiplashes on these temptations. Pride swells in his chest after only smoking a few cigarettes over the past couple days. He's been eating light meals and only drank a couple beers since that night at the Wave.

After a short soak in the Jacuzzi, Chris takes a long shower, gradually turning it from hot to freezing cold. He stays still as the icy spray pours on his scalp, running cold over his shoulders. His muscles contract and his skin clams up as the cold shock turns to numbness.

He's frozen to his bones and it feels good.

He leaves the recreation center and walks along the dark Harbor Road, past several mighty battleships tied to the pier. In the quiet evening he listens to the ships humming and gurgling as he walks back to the barracks to go to sleep.

Chapter 14: Shellbacks and Pollywogs

In the TV lounge, Weatherbee snoozes with his head slung over the arm of a cushioned chair.

Chris can see that he's going to wake with a painful kink in his neck and says "Hey, Weatherbee! Wake up, man!" Chris shakes the green-tinted guy by the shoulder. But Weatherbee snores louder, a gob of phlegm gurgling in his throat.

Grimacing, Chris steps back.

He climbs the stairs and walks down the hall toward his room.

"Yo, wingnut!" someone shouts as he passes an open door.

Carlos Devlin is sitting in a desk chair, his white plaster cast propped on the footboard of an unmade bunk. He's shirtless, revealing several tattoos on his arms and chest. He holds a moisture-glazed can of Budweiser. A pyramid of ten empty cans stands on the desk behind him.

Adam sits on a metal folding chair, holding a can of beer too. His Dixie cup hat is pushed forward on his brow.

"Hey guys," Chris says as he leans in the doorway, wary about entering. He's spent many nights in barracks-drinking-bouts, and doesn't want to wake up tomorrow with a hangover—not with his big cardio evaluation first thing in the morning.

Carlos reaches into the tin garbage pail, pulls a beer from beneath the crushed ice and tosses it to Chris.

"Have a beer, wingnut!" Carlo is drunk.

Chris doesn't open it. He doesn't want to drink it.

"You know, Marlow, you're alright—for a wingnut."

"How long you been in, Carlos?" Chris asks.

"Two years, what about you?"

"Almost four," Chris says. "I was on my third WestPac when I got off the ship here."

"Third in three years?" Carlos doesn't believe it.

"It's true," Adam says. "I've been on the Sacramento steaming alongside the Enterprise the whole time."

"Three Western Pacific cruises in three years," Carlos says in disbelief.

"The Enterprise and the Sacramento should only have made two WestPac cruises in that time," Adam explains. "But we got sent out after a short turnaround that one year. What was that all about, anyway?" Adam asks Chris.

"We were supposed to have a full year in San Francisco," Chris says. "But there was a plane crash on the USS Midway, so they were held up in the yards for repairs and couldn't go to the Persian Gulf, and the Enterprise was the only carrier they could send."

Chris glanced at Adam and knew he was a Shellback if he'd been steaming aboard the Sacramento alongside the Enterprise for the past three years. Then he considered Carlos, with all his trash talking and wondered if he was still a lowly wog. "You been across the line, Carlos?" Chris asks.

"Twice now," Carlos says. "What about you, wingnut?"

"I'm no wog!"

Carlos glances at Adam.

"I'm no wog," Adam says. "Where'd you cross the line?"

"About a week after boot camp," Carlos starts telling his story, "I boarded the Cushing in San Diego and the next week we left for a training cruise down around South America. The Captain didn't want to initiate any wogs until the way back so the cruise got off to an easy start. We went through the Panama Canal, and then we cut hundred-mile-long figure eights off the Yucatan for a couple weeks. Every day we went to battle stations, did fire drills and launched a few Tomahawks. After that we went south, and had a week off in Buenos Aires. Went around Cape Horn, and came up for another week off in Chile."

"Sounds like a pleasure cruise to me." Chris recalls the half dozen times the Enterprise had made month-long training cruises without ever pulling into port.

"The Cushing ain't a carrier trying to set the record for the most days at sea, Marlow. The blackshoe Navy knows how to enjoy time off in port." Carlos takes a long pull on his beer and lights a Newport. "Now, where was I?"

"Liberty in Chile," Adam reminds him, smirking.

"Yeah, like I was saying," Carlos continues. "So we start steaming back north to San Diego, and all the wogs start getting worried. The Shellbacks reminded us that we had narrowly escaped the wrath of King Neptune on the way down. They told us the captain had made a deal with the Royal Order of the Deep to thrash us double bad on the way back."

"How many people aboard the Cushing?" Adam asks.

"Out of one hundred and seventy-five there were eighty or so Shellbacks," Carlos says. "Well anyway, my Chief Bosun, a man the size of a steel buoy, was a fearsome character, a giant with a big nose, little bitty eyes and a head like a horse. One morning, at zero five hundred all the Shellbacks, dressed like pirates, come to wake up us pollywogs. They forced us to wear our clothes inside out and backwards, with skivvies on the outside. Some guys got shampoo put in their hair but weren't allowed to shower, and I got shave cream put on my face but couldn't shave. Every Shellback had a two foot length of fire hose and they whipped our asses hard and herded us on hands and knees to the galley for a breakfast of green mashed potatoes, prune juice and sour milk."

"On the Sacramento we had to drink raw eggs and eat raw potatoes covered in pepper," Adam says.

"The captain came over the P.A. and announced that during the night, Davy Jones and his pirate crew had snuck aboard and taken over the ship. Then King Neptune's voice comes over the P.A. and says he's taken the helm, he's hoisting' the jolly roger and all the pollywogs were going to be punished for wandering onto the equator."

"You were scared like a little bitch I bet," Adam said.

"Hell yeah, especially after my Chief bosun got a hold of me. He said, 'Devlin, my little pollywog, did I hear you complaining about a toothache?' And he put a leash around my neck and took me to the quarterdeck where one of the cooks was dressed up like a mad scientists. First, he gave me a heaping spoonful of garlic powder and ordered me to hold it in my mouth. Seemed like an hour I was breathing through my nose holding that shit in my mouth. Then the cook has this contraption made out of an enema syringe and a hose and he sprays a foul concoction in my mouth and orders me to gargle and swallow, but I spit-up on Chief Bosun's shoes so he paddles my ass until it stung so bad I couldn't feel it anymore."

They all laugh.

"My worst memory from wog day," Adam says, "was the garbage tunnel 'cause they saved all the leftovers for two weeks and then on wog day they unrolled a big canvas tube on the deck and shoveled in all the rotten vegetables and chicken bones and rotten potatoes and they made us wogs crawl through that nasty shit!"

"I went through a garbage chute on the Enterprise," Chris says. "I held my breath and crawled as fast as I could."

"I tried," Adam laughs, "but when I got half way, somebody stepped on the chute and I couldn't back up because more wogs crawled in behind me. And the stench in there was awful. The rotten food must have been six inches deep. I almost passed out, scrunched up and practically suffocating with Shellbacks beating on my back through the canvas and yelling at me to move it."

"What'd you do?" Carlos asks.

"I was so nauseous," Chris says. "I threw up."

Carlos and Chris break out laughing.

"You barfed!" Carlos says.

"All the pushing behind me finally bowled over the Shellback that was standing on the chute and I got pushed through the slime right out onto the deck. I was like Jonah getting spit out by that damn whale."

"I went through my initiation on the way down to Mombasa," Chris says, "it was horrible, but I enjoyed it on the second cruise when I went through wog day as a Shellback."

"The second time is a lot more fun," Adam says.

"Going through as a Shellback, paddling wog ass is much more fun indeed," Carlos says.

Smiles bean on their faces.

"What other ports does a carrier go to?" Carlos asks, "I hear you all don't get very good liberty."

"This is the sixth time I've been to Pearl Harbor, and I've been to Subic Bay, Sasebo in Japan, Hong Kong, Thailand, Singapore, Mombasa and Perth, Australia." Chris peeled the flip top off his beer can and took a swig.

"I guess with over five thousand guys on board you can only pull in at the big cities."

Chris knows Carlos is correct.

"On the Cushing we only have a hundred and seventy-five sailors, so we pull into little bays, port towns, fishing villages. On my last cruise we had liberty in the tiny country of Brunei on the island of Borneo. The people were so friendly." Carlos took a long swig of beer.

"Once my ship visited Perth, Australia," Adam sits up straight. "We had a good time walking around the city and going to nightclubs, but a month later we pulled in at Bunbury, a small town down the coast from Perth and in Bunbury families came to the pier, picked guys up and took them to their homes. The family I went with made a barbecue. They called it a barbie and they cooked up the biggest prawns and lobster tails I've ever seen, and the man of the house, Mister Grogan, he kept asking us to tell him about the Navy."

"Australians are awesome," Chris says. "They were with us in World War II, Korea and Vietnam. They're tough as hell."

"That's just the beginning," Adam continues. "Then about nine o'clock that night we pile into Mister Grogan's station wagon and head to the pub, and as soon as I belly up to the bar this gorgeous woman, tall, big boned, reddish-blond hair, named Alison comes right up and tells me there's hardly any black men in Australia and she's curious about taking a black man to bed." Adam's smile beams from ear to ear. "We talked for hours and finally Mister Grogan waved goodbye, and he winked like he knew the deal, and Alison kidnapped me to her family's beach house. We drank strawberry wine and stayed in bed for two days except for a walk on the beach."

"Damn!" Carlos says enviously.

Chris fondly remembers a girl he met in Perth, Australia and her accent that he liked so much.

"Take it from me on a supply ship," Adam says. "I've been to more ports than both of you put together and it's a fact, the small ports are better than the big cities."

"A small town would be total chaos if a carrier showed up and five thousand guys descended on the bars," Chris says. "The poorest guy off a carrier has five-hundred dollars burning a hole in his pocket and he's horny as a mule."

"Wingnuts are the plague of the Navy," Carlos says.

"I'm sure you've seen inside few bars," Chris says.

"Yeah, but all wingnuts do is prowl around till they find a strip club and then get drunk and start fights."

"Not everybody off a carrier is a drunk," Chris says, and realizes he's not talking about himself.

"Carriers are full of drunks who spread the clap all over the world."

"You're as big a drunk as any wingnut," Chris says, glancing at the pyramid of empty beer cans.

"Is it true about the clap lines on a carrier?" Carlos asks.

"Yeah," Chris says. "There's a line of six hundred men, including officers and chiefs at sick call after we leave Subic Bay and all they do is give VD tests and Penicillin shots." Chris takes a long pull off his beer and sets the empty atop the pyramid of cans. "They got this one strain of the clap in the Philippines that is so strong, the only way to get rid of it is a needle right in one of your nuts."

Carlos offers Chris another beer but Chris says, "I got medical tests tomorrow. I gotta go easy."

"What's two beers?" Carlos tempts him.

"This is the first time I've ever stopped after one. Usually I don't stop till I pass out."

"That's what happens when you're off a carrier." Carlos drops the beer back into the crushed ice.

"I've gotten drunk in bars on four continents," Chris says.

"You can't blame the Navy for that," Adam says. "It's up to you what you do in port."

"That's what Chief Bosun told me after my first liberty in Ecuador," Carlos says. "I came back to the ship with a wicked hangover and was talking shit about drinking as if everyone spent three days in the bars like I did. The Chief took me on the side and told me that not all sailors are drunks, and if I didn't want to be a drunk I'd take up golf and photography and I'd go on guided tours and eat at fine restaurants. Ever since then, when the Cushing hits a port I find a classy restaurant and drop a hundred bucks on dinner."

"I do the same thing but then I end up in the bars," Chris says. He wishes someone had taken him off to the side three years ago and told him that all sailors aren't drunks. "I gotta hit the sack you guys."

"Alright Marlow, good night."

In his room, lying beneath a white sheet, Chris looks out the open window at black palm-fronds silhouetted against the starry sky.

"When the Enterprise hits port," he whispers, "I feel like I'm part of a gold rush along with everyone running to the bars."

Chapter 15: On TV

In the morning, after a light breakfast and muster behind the annex, Chris rides the shuttle to Tripler Army Hospital.

At the cardiology clinic, he lays on a bed next to a cart with a twenty-six inch Sony Trinitron, a computer keyboard, VCR and an assortment of electronic boxes covered in buttons and dials.

"Hello, Airman Marlow." Doctor Penny Brown enters the room wearing baggy green scrubs. Her brown hair falling in shining curls over her shoulders.

"Good morning, Doctor," Chris says.

She sits on a cushioned stool on wheels and starts typing on the keyboard. A pepper-speckled target appears on the screen. Static blasts from a speaker. She lowers the volume and continues typing and flicking switches. Beeps and purrs from components on the cart. She removes a bundle of blue wires from a drawer along with a phallic object that swells with a bright blue rubber knob at one end.

"With these," she holds up the wires, "I send sound waves into your chest."

"What about that?" He points at the phallic object, a bit worried.

"This picks up the sound waves and transmits them to the monitor." She slips a tape into the VCR.

"Are you going to record my heart on video?"

"Yes and a team of specialists will watch it and diagnose you."

She squeezes little dabs of goop onto his chest and sticks metal tabs to them. Next she plugs the wires into a box next to the TV.

"Roll onto your left side," she tells him, "so your heart drops out from behind your sternum."

Chris rolls towards her, disturbed at the thought that his heart actually moves around inside his chest.

He wonders if there's an empty space in there for it to swing like a pendulum on a knot of arteries. Or do his lungs move aside as it slides over? Thinking about it gives him the willies.

The TV screen glows a dull yellow now as she places the blue rubber knob against his chest. The beat of his heart sounds softly from the TV's speaker. Suddenly a reddish-gray shape, hooked like a kink in a garden hose, surfaces through the yellow glow. It swells and contracts in time with each beat of his heart.

Chris stares at his throbbing aorta on the screen and can't believe the constant violent spasms taking place inside his chest. He thinks of the times when he touched his own chest to feel his heartbeat and it seemed like a light steady thumping and then just barely, but here on the screen this thing is expanding and contracting like a machine. It shocks him to realize that he has no control over the forces that actually keep him alive. An autopilot, like another person he doesn't even know, living inside his own skin, in charge of running his most vital systems. What he'd thought of as his life, the little he'd actually thought about it up until now—his personality, his wants and desires—he realizes they're just vague whims compared to his heart, this knotted muscle pumping blood through hoses and tubes to his brains and organs and limbs.

That's my life, he thinks, and it just happens on its own.

She types on the keyboard with one hand and nudges the rubber knob across his skin with the other.

A red oval, a foot across, appears on the screen. It flashes black and red. Three flaps closing simultaneously, turning the oval black and instantly the flaps shrink away, turning the oval red again.

"Your tricuspid valve," she says.

"What are you checking for?"

"All four valves should open and close in sequence and seal tightly. If the valves don't seat firmly, blood could be forced in the wrong direction."

"What happens then?"

"That condition is known as a heart murmur."

"Is that common in guys like me?"

"In your age group," she thinks for a moment, "one in a thousand."

Suddenly the yellow glow clouds the valve and static crackles from the speaker.

Heart murmur, Chris thinks.

"You can't talk so much," she says. "I'm picking up vibrations from your larynx."

She moves the knob slightly on his chest. A different valve appears. This one opens and closes the same way but only has two flaps. "Your bicuspid valve," she says. "There are two more valves." She types. "Here's the pulmonary. It controls the flow of blood to your lungs and its partner, the aortic valve, controls the blood flow out of the heart."

On the screen, red against yellow, countless millions of blood cells are sluicing through his valves.

"Your heart appears to be healthy, timing is precise, and your valves close firmly." She switches to his aortic valve. It looks like the pulmonary valve; a gate closing and opening rapidly.

"How big is that?" Chris whispers.

"Little bigger than a dime," she says.

And there on the TV, nearly a foot across, the valve appears to regulate the flow of gallons of blood surging from his heart.

She presses a button and an opaque ruler appears on the screen. "Now I'm measuring the dimensions of your valves and chambers. We can learn quite a bit from measurements."

She maneuvers the ruler on the screen. Typing again, the valves appear one at a time. "This is the entire heart muscle." She holds the knob firmly against his ribs. The jiggling organ fills the screen.

He realizes that these pulsing chambers and mechanical valves are the root of his constant hunger and fear.

Doctor Brown disconnects the wires and gives him some paper towels to wipe the goop from his chest.

He asks, "How long until I hear the results?"

"We'll send a report to Doctor Burkham. Are you in a hurry?"

"My temporary orders only last another week."

"I'll expedite it," she says.

Chris hops off the bed. He buttons his shirt and says, "Thank you, Doctor Brown."

She says, "Good-bye, Airman Marlow."

*   *   *

The urge to smoke has been creeping up on him all morning and now it pounces because he feels relief, especially since she said his heart valves were the right size and they sealed properly. Walking along the wide corridor, he starts thinking, "What's the big deal? Just smoke one lousy cigarette." And then he implores himself not to, "Doctor Burkham told me to quit!" He walks along. "It'll be okay," he tells himself. "Besides, this ache has nothing to do with smoking," he reassures himself. "It's from a hiatal hernia, not a heart condition."

He takes the elevator down and heads for the lounge, all the while repeating in his head, "It'll be okay. Don't worry about it. It'll be okay. Don't worry about it." He strolls through the lounge and goes outside on the patio on the roof of the emergency room. He approaches a tall Marine sergeant standing in the sunshine smoking.

"Can I bum a smoke?" he asks.

Without saying a word, the marine reaches into the big pocket on the front of his camouflage blouse and pulls out a cigarette from a pack he has in there.

"Got a light?" Chris feels like such a grub.

The marine points the tip of his cigarette at Chris's face and says, "You want me to smoke it for you too?"

"Sorry," Chris mumbles as he pressing the tip of his cigarette against the marines' cigarette and puffs.

With great disappointment he tastes menthol, like cheap candy.

Fuckin' menthol!

"Thanks," he says, but the marine ignores him.

Chris smokes the KOOL slowly, every shallow drag of phony mint flavor mocking him for succumbing to his nicotine addiction.

*   *   *

When he arrives at Doctor Chu's office in the neurology clinic, the corpsman leads him to an examination room where the blinds are open, and sunlight fills the room.

Rows of blinking green and blue lights line the face of a large electrical test bench that takes up most of one wall. Several dials, the shape and size of old-style car speedometers. There are drawers, no doubt filled with electrical gadgetry that Doctor Chu will plug into the bank of receptacles.

Black numbers run from -30 to +150 on one of the gauges, and he figures they measure electrical current and that's scary. "I hope he doesn't shock me again," Chris whispers.

"Good morning, Air Man Marlow," Doctor Chu says as he enters the room. He's wearing a white lab coat and carries a legal-size clipboard. His mass of black hair is stacked atop his head, and his black plastic-framed glasses magnify his eyes.

"Good morning, Doctor," Chris says.

"Please take off your shirt," Doctor Chu says. "And sit in this chair by the electromyography machine."

Chris pulls off his shirt and sits.

Doctor Chu runs his soft slim fingers along Chris's left arm, probing the muscles and connective tissues like a masseuse.

Chris remembers the shock Doctor Chu unleashed from his funny bone during their first meeting. He struggles against the impulse to yank his arm away.

Then Doctor Chu opens a drawer and pulls out a tangle of rubber straps and wires that look to Chris like a torture device.

Doctor Chu puts a chrome-studded, black rubber bracelet around Chris's wrist and another around his upper arm in his armpit. Next he attaches a chrome-studded rubber strap to the bracelet and winds it tightly around Chris's arm all the way up to the strap in his armpit.

Chris feels it cutting off his circulation.

Then Doctor Chu plugs several black wires into receptacles on the front of his machine and runs them to a black box covered with switches and dials. More wires are attached with alligator clips to the studs on the rubber strap.

It all makes Chris think about bondage pictures he saw in a dirty magazine in Japan.

Doctor Chu double-checks all the connections. "Air man, you must relax," he says, "and do not tighten any muscles in your arm."

"Yes, Sir."

"I'm checking the continuity of your nerves."

Doctor Chu throws a switch, and the machine hums softly.

Chris wonders if they should be wearing safety goggles.

Needles jump on the big dials. Little green and red bulbs blink on the face of the machine. A faint hum surges to a low growl.

Doctor Chu throws a switch and turns a knob, and then he observes the needles on the dials. He does this over and over, and each time he jots numbers on a form on his clipboard.

"Now I will check your reflex," Doctor Chu says. "Stay relaxed!" He reaches over and throws a red switch on the face of the machine.

"KA-POW!"

A blue spark jolts along the metal studs on the rubber strap wrapped around Chris's arm and he jumps back in shock.

Many of the wires unplug from the electro whatever-it's-called.

Doctor Chu quickly plugs everything back in, and Chris thinks he sees a smirk on the man's face.

"Reflexes look good, huh?" Chris asks.

"It's too much voltage." Doctor Chu restrains a snicker.

A tinge of burnt hair lingers.

Doctor Chu flicks the red switch again and the muscles in Chris's arm tighten up a little.

"Very good," Doctor Chu says as he opens a drawer and takes out a metal probe that looks like a curling iron. He plugs it in and touches it to Chris's wrist, holding it there. Then he presses a button and holds it down.

Chris's hand curls into a fist. He tries to unclench it, but it's locked shut.

When the doctor releases the button, Chris's hand relaxes.

When the doctor presses the button again, Chris's hand curls into a fist again.

Doctor Chu does this over and over and each time Chris's fist clenches. Dials bounce on the gauges and the doctor scribbles something on his clipboard.

Chris tries to relax his hand but can't because Doctor Chu's machine is controlling him.

Next the doctor presses the curling iron against Chris's shoulder and when he pushes one of the buttons, Chris's arm bends at the elbow, his biceps tightening into a knot. Several times the doctor cycles Chris's arm through these routine movements, stopping now and then to jot notes on his clipboard.

Gradually the odor of warm rubber replaces the smell of singed hair, all while numbness spreads from Chris's fingertips to his armpit.

Finally, Doctor Chu removes the apparatus wrapped around Chris's arm and says, "Lay on the table so I can examine you."

The tension from the shock treatment dissipates as Doctor Chu delicately traces the contours of Chris's scapulae and collarbones. His fingertips burrow in the crevices along Chris's vertebrae.

The doctor seems to be counting his ribs. Then, with a cloth tape he measures many angles on Chris's back and shoulders, making notes on the dimensions of Chris's skull, the circumference of his neck, the length of his arms, the width of his hipbones.

He turns on a light-box mounted to the wall and it illuminates the backbone x-ray taken on Chris's first day in port. The doctor stands beside the table for a long time comparing the x-ray to Chris's back. He runs his fingertips along Chris's spine, stopping here and there. He cautiously works his fingertips between two vertebras and performs a sedating acupressure.

This goes on for a while and Chris lays there without saying a word. It feels good to have someone touching him, even if it is Doctor Chu.

Chris almost dozes off.

"Airman Marlow," the doctor startles him, "I will give Major Burkham a full report on my evaluation, but I wish to tell you that you have very good bone structure and strong muscles."

"Thank you, Sir," Chris says.

'You may put your shirt on and go about your business."

Chapter 16: Payday Mentality

A clerk with thick lenses in his glasses and a black mustache sits behind a folding table in the medical annex's air-conditioning machinery room. It's Friday and it's payday and the clerk is paying everybody on medical hold out of two strongboxes full of cash.

A freckle-faced Marine in camouflage fatigues stands beside the table with a loaded pistol on his belt.

Chris hands over his identification and starts to worry because the clerk looks at it for too long. Chris is concerned that transferring his records from the Enterprise to Pearl has botched something up, and he dreads having to go to the dispersing office to file an earnings correction request.

Three times the clerk checks Chris's identification and three times his fingertips click the keys on his adding machine, total it and tear off the paper tape that ticks out. And three times, he crumples the tape, tosses it in a wastepaper can and shakes his head in disbelief. When he finally looks up with what Chris is sure will be bad news, the clerk says, "Six hundred and forty-four dollars."

He'd expected only half that but doesn't say anything. He'll gladly take all the cash now, even though he suspects they'll discover the overpayment and garnish it back.

The clerk counts out a stack of fifties and twenties.

Thoughts of a seafood dinner, crowded nightclubs, pints of cold beer and a luxury hotel room swirl in Chris's mind. With a stuffed wallet, he exits the machinery room, and as he walks past the chow hall and out the Harbor Road, he struggles to reign in thoughts of partying all night on Waikiki. He decides to burn off his extra energy at the gym.

In his room upstairs in the barracks, he unbuttons his shirt, tosses his hat on the footlocker and reclines with the pillow folded behind his head while gazing out the window. A tropical flower fragrance rides in through the screen. He likes gazing at the shadows cast by the palm trees on the grass. The thick pile of bills in his wallet makes him think about a fine meal at one of the nice restaurants on Waikiki. He knows that another plate of food at the chow hall won't satisfy him and already his mind is wandering to the nightclubs near the beach.

"I'm on medical hold," he reminds himself. "Something is seriously wrong with my stomach and I might have a fucking heart condition." Just go to Waikiki, his mind immediately counters, goes for the counterpoint. Eat a nice dinner and stay in a hotel. Relax. You don't have a heart condition. Then why is Burkham having me evaluated at cardiology—and in the same instant he imagines himself at the Wave, knocking back a few shots and dancing with a pretty girl.

He jumps up from the bed, goes into the bathroom and splashes cold water on his face. He looks at himself in the mirror. "I feel fine. There's no pain at all in my chest. Calm fucking down."

He grabs his hat, buttons up his shirt and bolts from the room.

The simple act of walking, the mild aerobic, repetitive swinging of the arms and striding along the sidewalk plays like a soothing tonic to his harried mind. Just as he'd mastered his anxiety earlier while walking out the Harbor Road to the barracks, he masters it again on his walk to the gym. The clear-headedness that comes with a leisurely stroll makes him decide to eat at the chow hall after working out.

In his mind he's mapping out a plan. He thinks, while everyone else celebrates Friday and payday, I'll watch TV at the barracks and go to sleep early. On Saturday, I'll sleep in. On Sunday, I'll take the bus to the North Shore and attempt surfing the big waves again.

He enters the gym content with his weekend plan and right away he sees that the place is deserted. Not even the giants are there loading fifty-pound steel disks onto barbells. Chris decides to mix up his usual regimen and work on muscle groups that he usually avoids. With forty pounds on a barbell, he cranks through several sets of wrist curls and alternates them with sets on the leg machine. It's a hard workout, and he watches himself in the mirrors. As he does curls, the sight of his bulging biceps puffs up his self-esteem. He removes his shirt and flexes his pecs. After 150 sit-ups he admires his hard abdomen.

In the pool, he paces himself through the first ten laps doing a leisurely freestyle stroke. A meditative trance settles in as he follows the black stripe on the bottom of the pool. He switches to backstroke and counts light fixtures in the ceiling until he can tell exactly when he will reach the end of the pool. For a long while, only Chris and the lifeguard occupy the pool area. He watches light fixtures slip by overhead as he kicks his legs and windmills his arms with steady momentum. The thought of spending a weekend laid back on the beach encroaches on his mind. Yokohama Bay? There are no hotels. Where will I stay? North Shore? The big waves will pound me again. Waikiki? No! He exhales sharply through grit teeth, yet his mind flashes on the droves of tourists and college girls on vacation. I'm lonely, he realizes for the millionth time. He knows he's searching for companionship on the neon-lit streets and in the crowded clubs. Partying all night does have a certain appeal and right then his forearm cracks on the pool's concrete lip.

Slowly sinking to the bottom he clutches his aching arm and growls, bubbles gurgling through his clenched teeth.

He switches to sidestroke and another swimmer passes him going in the opposite direction. She has dark hair and a lime-green one-piece. With one eye above and one below the surface, Chris watches her torso slip by in a fury of splashing limbs. She'll never keep up that pace, he thinks with a macho air.

Two laps later, she passes him and three laps after that she passes him again.

Chris picks up his pace and lap after lap they pass at the center of the pool. She seems to have no trouble maintaining the sprint, but Chris feels a shortness of breath coming on.

Who is this chick, he wonders.

Unable to swim any further, he hangs his arms over the edge of the pool and daydreams about the love life he wants but knows as a fleet sailor, he's not going to have. For three years, he's never been in one place for more than a few months, usually no more than a few days. His relationships with women consist of infrequent one-nighters and cathouse romps. It's not his preference, but he's a sailor. Relationships are impossible. Sex is a perverted routine reenacted in every port. At sea there's Rosie Palm and her five sisters.

He lifts himself onto the side of the pool and sits there watching her as she cruises like a missile toward him, her arms and legs churn up the water.

It's been a long time since he's had sex; two maybe three months. He remembers a guy passing out cards on a busy intersection in Honolulu a few years ago. He took one and read the message: Island

Girls of Oahu Catering to the desires of discriminating gentlemen at all the fine hotels. The memory came back, and he fantasized with it. It was almost two years ago. He'd shoved the card in his pocket and later that night he called and they sent a girl. She was a tall bleached-blond with a perm and she wasn't the least bit shy. She handled him like a nervous amateur. His mouth was so dry, when he tried to talk his tongue clicked. During her little routine, he felt like a lusty dog. Afterwards he was ashamed, because he'd paid a hundred dollars for an hour but it was over in ten minutes. They hadn't even pulled the slipcover off the bed.

Now she's swimming back toward his end of the pool, and the shamed memory makes Chris realize how much nicer it would be to spark a relationship with a real girl. But what could she possibly see in me, he wonders, a wingnut on medical hold? Medical problems, the phrase flashes in his mind like the emergency lights atop an ambulance. Island Girls, he knows, will take the complications out of it. He climbs out of the pool and goes over to the hot tub.

*   *   *

Swimming laps brings a wonderful trance. Sliding through the water, she forgets the records department and her phone watch at midnight. She swims and feels better. Sometimes she swims and the forgetful trance does not come, but today is payday. That makes her feel good, having to stand watch later is the downside, but, she reasons, I won't spend any money this weekend. The swim lanes at the pool are never crowded on Fridays. Only one guy, a guy who can swim like an eel, she notices. She picks up her pace a little, gives him a race.

She thinks of herself as a water bug since arriving at Pearl.

Back home in St. Louis she learned to swim at the neighborhood pool when she was five, and she'd only been in water over her head a few times prior to joining the Navy.

Now she's in the water all the time.

Who is this guy, she wonders and a lap later she notices he stopped. I won, she giggles. Now he's catching his breath on the edge of the pool. She turns at the end of the lap and glances at him. She jogs her memory, tries to recall where she's seen him. Working in the records department, she's seen everyone on base. He looks familiar. Where have I seen him? In the middle of her next turn she realizes that he's checking her out. And short hair, maybe he's a marine, with that crew cut, but it's not short enough for a marine, not quite a crew cut, but it's short. His abs look hard. He must do a lot of sit-ups.

*   *   *

Slowly he sinks into the hot, effervescent water and positions himself so two jets pulsate on his lower back. He closes his eyes and tries to reason with himself, but it's useless. He thinks about the hotel-room carpet under his bare feet and a king-size bed in a room at one of Waikiki's big hotels. Outside the sliding glass doors, there's a balcony with a view of Diamond Head. Ten floors below, palm trees, the beach and the lazy energy of a world on vacation. He wants a shark steak and a fog cutter. "Skip the fog cutter," he whispers. No fog cutters, no smoking and no nightclubs. I'll watch a movie in the room, sleep until noon tomorrow and then rent a surfboard, maybe take another lesson. A mellow weekend. Spend a hundred bucks at the most.

Then his resistance crumbles as he imagines slipping three crisp fifty dollar bills into his wallet—for an Island Girl.

He slides over to make the jets blast another part of his back.

Someone slides into the tub across from him. It's the girl in the lime-green one-piece. To his surprise it's Petty Officer Stone.

"Hi," Chris says.

She smiles.

After they'd met the previous weekend, he forgot about her, figuring she had dozens of guys hitting on her every day.

"You set a quick pace," he says.

"So do you," she replies. "You look familiar."

"The medical annex."

"You work there?" she asks.

"I'm on medical hold." He tells himself nothing is going to develop with her.

"What's wrong? If you don't mind me asking."

"I have a hernia."

"Swimming doesn't aggravate it?"

"No," he says. "It's not a real hernia, it's a hiatal hernia."

She nods and leans back.

"How do you like Pearl?

"Island life suits me fine."

"I feel more relaxed every day," he says. "I took surfing lessons a few days ago."

Then she remembers who this guy is. She met him on the pier with the marine in the wheel chair. Their eyes met in the rear view mirror and she almost hit a pedestrian.

"Surfing?" she asks.

"Yeah," he says, and realizes she could rat him out for sneaking off base while on medical hold.

She knows he's not supposed to be going to the beach, never mind surfing! "You're off the Enterprise, right?"

"They left me here last weekend."

"I think it's unfair they won't let women serve on combat vessels."

"Women should be able to do all the jobs in the Navy," Chris says, but secretly he thinks if there were babes like you on the flight deck guy's would be dropping bombs on their toes and walking into spinning propellers. "What do you do when you're not at the records department?"

"I live for the records department." She says.

Chris laughs.

"I like scuba diving," she says.

"Sounds adventurous."

"There are so many great dive sites around Oahu."

"I think I saw something about a dive club here on base."

"I went with them a few times," she says, "but I like going on dive charters with the locals."

"It must be nice to break away," he says. "When the ship pulls into port all the guys want to go get drunk. I'm totally sick of it."

"I partied so much when I first got here," she says, "but not anymore."

Chris wants to say, me too, but knows he has a ways to go to get over his struggle with alcohol and drugs. For a second, he despises her because she can separate from the Navy every day at five o'clock. She'd never know the sensory deprivation that comes during weeks at sea.

She checks the time on her bulky dive watch and stands up to leave, steamy water sluicing off her torso.

"I'm going to eat dinner before muster," she says.

"Didn't you have duty last weekend," he says.

"I did, but this weekend I'm filling in for a friend." She climbs from the tub. "The dining hall closes in half an hour."

He wants to invite himself along to eat with her, but he chokes. "I'll see you around," he says.

"Bye."

Angry at himself, he sits in the bubbling hot water as loneliness and frustration settle in. He wants to meet someone, even just dance and talk awhile.

Island Girls flashes in his mind.

He sees Larry Tynan's face and feels overwhelmed by dread.

The number three thousand pops into his head. That's how many dollars he has to deposit in the Navy college fund.

I've gotta straighten up and get off medical hold. I've gotta get back to the Enterprise. I've gotta put three-thousand dollars into the Navy college fund!

He takes a deep breath and knows he doesn't need to analyze it any further.

The Jacuzzi stops and the water around him is suddenly tranquil.

                            *   *   *

He puts on a pair of khaki shorts and a T-shirt, throws a few necessities in his backpack and stops in the TV lounge on his way out of the barracks.

"Weatherbee, what's up?" he says.

"Marlow, how's it going at the hospital?" Weatherbee's lips and teeth are orange from stuffing handfuls of Cheeze Doodles into his mouth.

"Pretty good," Chris says. "Had an echocardiograph today."

"Seen your heart on TV, huh?"

"Yeah, it was cool."

"I had one a few weeks ago," Weatherbee says.

"How'd it go?"

Weatherbee takes a long swig of Mountain Dew. "Did that gal doing the test put a tape in the machine?" he asks.

"Yeah, so the doctors can diagnose me," Chris says.

"Let me tell you, Marlow," Weatherbee says, "this medical hold is a bureaucratic crack. You can fall in here for months, maybe even a year and nobody will figure out what's wrong with you. I've been to cardiology, gastro-ology, radio-ology, neuro-ology, and every other 'ology' up at that dang hospital. I had explanatory surgery and none of them doctors knows what's wrong with me. Every time they try something they put me in worse shape."

Chris remembers what Weatherbee said about getting a transfusion with the wrong blood type. "Maybe there's nothing wrong with you, Weatherbee."

He tosses Cheeze Doodles into his mouth and takes a long pull on his Mountain Dew. "There's definitely something wrong with me," he says.

Chris doesn't doubt it. Weatherbee is the goofiest looking guy he's ever met.

"I've lost faith in medical science," Weatherbee says.

"Me too," Chris says.

"And know what, Marlow?"

"What?"

"That VCR tape that gal put in the heart machine, the echo' whatever you call it?"

"Yeah."

Weatherbee takes a conclusive gulp of mountain Dew and says, "I think the tape was playing what was on that TV screen and not recording it."

"No way!" Chris wonders if that really was his own heart he'd seen on the TV or a recording of someone else's heart. He figures Penny Brown wouldn't commit a fraud like that, but the suspicion lingers.

"Well, any old way," Weatherbee says. "All these doctors are full of—"

Instantly Weatherbee's peanut-shaped head falls back on the big recliner's headrest, and the Cheeze-Doodle-orange lips go slack. Weatherbee's mouth falls open and Chris can see a mash of chewed-up orange mush splattered across Weatherbee's teeth and tongue.

A thin snore wheezes from Weatherbee's throat.

Hilarious, Chris thinks as he walks across the porch. He swings his backpack over his shoulder, walks across the base to the main gate and sits on a wooden bench to wait for the bus to Waikiki.

Chapter 17: Tricks

For sixty dollars, servicemen receive excellent weekend accommodations at the Fort DeRussy Hotel. Every room has a color TV, two queen-size beds, thick cushy carpets, air conditioning and spectacular views of Waikiki, Diamond Head and the Koolau Mountains.

With a belly full of mahi-mahi, fruit bread and string beans Chris strips naked and opens the balcony's sliding glass door. He gathers all the pillows on one bed, slips between the crisp, white sheets and grabs the remote.

An anchorwoman wearing a blue blazer and a white blouse with a tiny blue bow tie appears on the screen. Her blonde hair looks great against her deep tan. She reports an active volcano on the big island and a plane crash in Japan.

The two fog cutters Chris drank at dinner bestow a maudlin glow on his face. He smiles as the anchorwoman signs over to a foreign correspondent, and Chris's smile vanishes when a frighteningly familiar scene appears on the TV.

Ashen gray clouds in a pewter sky. The steady spinning of a helicopter's rotary wings whisk the camera's eye above the ocean.

"Today, Iranian fighter jets crippled an Exxon supertanker in the Persian Gulf," a British correspondent's voice as a tanker, listing on its side, appears on screen. From a crack in the hull, thick black crude gushes into the sea. A black slick spreads across the water. Orange flames flicker on the ship's deck, and a tower of night-black smoke erupts skyward. Two Navy helicopters circle the crippled hulk.

Chris licks suddenly-dry lips as he watches the blazing ship.

He wants to go to the bar and have a few more drinks.

"This is the seventh vessel bombarded by Iranian aircraft in ten days. Six Panamanian crewmembers died in the explosion and two more died fighting the fire. Iranian military officials ordered American battleships out of the Gulf but a statement issued by the US State

Department shortly after today's incident indicates that Navy battleships will remain on station until a cease fire agreement is reached by Iran and Iraq."

The correspondent recounts the old issue of Middle Eastern religious fanatic warfare fueled by a multibillion-dollar oil industry.

Chris grabs the remote and clicks it off.

He gets out of bed and dumps his backpack. He splashes on cologne, pulls on his pants and shirt and heads for the door.

"I'll be sober for three months when I get to the Persian Gulf," he whispers to the empty hallway. Just a couple beers, he promises himself. In the elevator, he shakes his head trying to forget that the Iranian jets mentioned on the news were American made Grumman F-14 Tomcats. Grumman and other defense contractors, Chris knows, swindle the US government with thousand-dollar screws and five-thousand dollar screwdrivers. But only in his bleakest thoughts does he consider that Navy admirals and elected officials are supplying the enemy with replacement parts, rockets and missiles. He suddenly thinks about Larry Tynan and the dead Panamanian seaman he'd just heard about on the news. They'd gone to their graves in a war run by power-hungry politicians, greedy corporate executives, and over-zealous military commanders.

Chris knows he's a tiny cog in the war machine.

His heart aches.

His throat is dry.

He walks across the lobby and out into the night, trying to lose himself in the crowds of happy tourists.

*   *   *

When the sable vest of night comes on, the masks of day are put away and those of night are painted on. The Empress of nocturnal spells and queens of sunless boulevards voguishly don their wanton wear. Muscular boys in surfing shorts, tanned and shoeless, carouse among men in thin ties and shiny shoes. These masquerading clients crowd the silver-luster scene, on the street before the Wave they are prepared to misbehave.

*   *   *

121

He waits half an hour in the crowd.

Pushing, practically shoving finally puts him within a step of the chaotic entrance.

Inside he gulls against gyrating bodies.

Strobe lights flashing.

Blasting pop music assaults his ears.

And finally—he makes it to the bar.

Below the mirrored shelves ranged round with decanters, flasks and long neck carafes, handsome bartenders hustle about, gladly selling delirium and death.

Chris purchases two bottles of Becks, thereby avoiding another wait at the bar again too soon. Down his throat goes the first, where it soaks into his belly. The music's fluid rhythm imparts its appeal. Bopping, colorful sport shirts and miniskirts all around compel him to flex his knees and tap a foot.

A girl turns him away when he asks her to dance. But another with wavy brown hair, a belly shirt and a miniskirt dances a few songs with him. Then she disappears when the musicians take a break.

He lurks about in the crowd, feeling a little foolish and missing his friends. The scene is different, not the same, without them. He drinks two more beers, standing silent and alone against a black wall. He feels the social apparatus synchronizing him into snippets of overheard conversation. Electronic beats pulse through the space and meld with each swig of beer. He whiffs smoke from nearby cigarettes but resists. An undetected, all-consuming urgency compels him to stay in the club for the duration of the night. His presence in the scene, he decides, is more than important; it's necessary.

He finds a place at the bar and orders a shot of Wild Turkey.

The nightlife exudes a magnetic effect on him. Leaving the club and going back to his hotel room, getting a good's night sleep crosses his mind but immediately he dismisses it because that would be boring.

He pushes through the crowd, catching more whiffs of cigarettes. It's tempting to smoke, but instead of bumming one from a stranger, he goes upstairs to the air-conditioned lounge.

A raucous group mobs the bar, and spontaneously Chris joins in. They cheer each other as the man of bottles pours elixir directly into each patron's mouth. Chris brandishes his billfold, peels off a ten and bends backward over the bar.

His molars are submerged in Tangy Kamikaze.

Standing up after the dose of social lubricant, a rush of jubilant faces fills his eyes. A woman gives him a high five and keeps coming. They embrace and he inhales tufts of her perfumed hair. The crowd's attention shifts to her, and he catches only a glimpse of her face before the momentum forces her backwards over the bar.

Her turn for Kamikaze.

She bounces back into the maddening crowd, they press again, filling each other's personal space. The crowd approves with a cheer as a flourish of paper money showers the bar. An incoming tide of anxious drinkers forces them aside.

They hold each other, and she asks, "What was that?"

"Kamikaze, I think," he says.

"Are you with these people?" she asks.

She wears a sleeveless blue top, a string of pearls, a blue skirt and white heels. Color accents her eyes and a thick bunch of brown hair cascades onto her shoulders.

"We're all friends, I guess," Chris replies, thinking she looks a bit older and that excites him.

"I'm here with my cousins. One is probably asleep in a corner and the other is out to dance with every girl in the place. Are you on vacation?"

"I'm in the Navy," Chris replies.

"The Navy!" Her eyes open wide as she leans back against a railing over the dance floor and takes a long look at him.

"You on vacation?" Chris asks.

"My whole family is here to celebrate our grandparents' fiftieth anniversary."

"Are your grandparents here tonight?"

She smiles.

A peal of feedback from an electric guitar downstairs.

Someone shouts, "The band is back!"

"Let's dance," she says.

"Sure," he says. "By the way, I'm Chris."

"And I'm—" Another peel of feedback sets every ear to ringing.

She grabs his hand and leads the way.

A barrel-chested black man blows his saxophone through a medley of R&B hit while Chris and his friend shimmy with the crowd.

Half an hour later, sweat-soaked from scalp to soles, they join the stampede to the bar. Amidst the confusion, she introduces him to her cousins. Their names garbled in a cyclone of new wave music roaring from a stack of amplifiers. There's a girl cousin from Missouri and a dude named Mark or Mike.

Music annihilates their attempt at conversation.

The cousin from Missouri frowns under hair molded like an Army combat helmet. She stares straight ahead and nurses a slushy drink. Mark or Mike, as it were, loads his lower lip with a plug of Copenhagen, spits on the floor between his feet then he stands up and crashes through the crowd. Chris watches three girls in a row turn him away before he clears a space on the floor and does something like the twist alone.

Chris fights his way to the bar, purchases another round of drinks and returns to the table. Mark or Mike lights a cigarette and says, "Let's get the hell out of here! None of these bitches want to dance."

"Where to?"

"How about the punk club?"

"The Cage?" Chris has been there. It's hard-core.

"Yeah," Mark or Mike says.

Chris's friend puts her hand on his thigh and leans over close. He feels her lips on his ear. "Hey, sailor," she whispers, "will you take us clubbing?"

They slam their drinks and leave.

Outside, Mark or Mike taps a cigarette from his Marlboro soft pack and lights it with a Bic.

Chris wants one. "I just quit," he says.

"I quit fifteen minutes ago," Mark or Mike says, "but I decided to start again." He holds the pack toward Chris with several filter tips extended.

The last shred of sanity in his brain implores him not to take one. He figures his female friend is not a smoker, and if she sees him smoking, that might ruin any chance he has of making out with her.

A taxi pulls up and they hop in.

Mark or Mike smokes in the front seat.

The cab glides along Ala Wai Boulevard. Chris opens the window. A breeze washes his face. Don't smoke, he tells himself. He and his new friend are holding hands. It feels good. Years of working the flight deck has toughened his hands, but hers are soft.

Amazing.

He tightens his grip, just enough to assure himself she's real. He wracks his brain to figure out some way he can learn her name. He thinks about cornering Mark or Mike when they get to the Cage and asking him.

He imagines her ditching her cousins and coming back to his room—and they sleep together, not even have sex. That would be cool.

"We've got to go back to our hotel," she says. "Driver, please pull over at Seaside Avenue?"

"What's up?" Chris asks, embarrassed at his panicky tone.

"She's sick."

Helmet-hair looks pale, eyelids droopy. Drool overflowing her lip. Chris looks close and sees it's barf—she barfed in the cab.

"Nice meeting you, Chip." His friend lays a kiss full on his lips before climbing out of the cab and slamming the door.

Mark or Mike reaches back with the pack of cigarettes and Chris ends up smoking two before they arrive at the Cage.

Unlike the Wave, this joint's clientele is from Honolulu's crooked backstreets, not the hotels lining Waikiki. Chris is the only patron whose clothes deviate from basic black. Spiked Mohawks stab the streetlamp's yellow glow like the spiny backs of extinct dinosaurs. Many of the juveniles appear androgynous and tattooed from wrist to chin. Their ears and noses stuck through with studs and hoops. On the street, goons and sinners lean on concrete like a lineup of crime suspects.

A herd of leather boots, black jackets and dark mascara crowd the stairs leading up to the Cage.

Chris has drunk himself blind in some of the roughest bars in Tijuana, Hong Kong, Perth and dozens of other ports across the Pacific and Indian Ocean, but nothing compares to the Cage. Barbed wire and jail cell doors and yards of chain link fence are bolted to the walls and ceiling. Shards of glass litter the floor and a downpour of pulsating strobes flicker through the darkness over a sea of bobbing heads.

Chris gives Mark or Mike a five for beers and approaches a punk girl. She wears ripped fishnets, black miniskirt and a leather bra. She gives no reply when Chris asks her to dance, but she does turn an anemic look of disgust toward her mates before grabbing Chris's hand and pulling him to the dance floor.

A look of disgust must be favorable in punk, Chris thinks as he shakes his ass and takes a better look at this dance partner. Music like chainsaws and colliding automobiles blares from speakers obscured above in darkness. A vocalist rants in a cranky British accent, the words not discernible above the destructive sound of the instruments. A thick coat of shellac covers broken disco records, bottle caps and double-edged razor blades imbedded in the floor.

Chris is so drunk he dances for a while before realizing that the punk girl has vanished in the crowd.

He slinks from the floor to look for his beer. When he finds Mark or Mike, they sit at a table in the back. They smoke and drink while Chris talks about the Navy. "It's fucking incredible man, but dangerous. You should join for sure."

"Ever seen somebody die?" the kid asks.

Chris's swaying head snaps to a halt and through bloodshot eyes he gazes at his companion's smooth face. Raising the cigarette to his lips, Chris takes a big drag and fills his lungs. While holding in the smoke, he chugs his beer, drains the bottle and closes his eyes. He knows, even in his lost and stumbling drunkenness, he'll never wash away the memory of Larry Tynan—his dead best friend.

"Yeah, I seen this one fucking guy get ground up in an airplane engine," Chris says.

"No way!" The kid smirks.

"Yeah, and afterwards we had to—" Chris stops and swears that after tonight, after this last alcoholic bender, he'll quit drinking and smoking and clean himself up.

He leaves Mark or Mike at the table and never sees him again.

He pushes through to the bar and orders four fingers of Wild Turkey, a Becks and a pack of Winston.

*   *   *

As if etherized upon a table, he sees the crowd swaying around him. Pollutants course through his veins, erasing logic and reason. Limbs regressing to oafish, rubbery things; all memory lapses to inky black. Later he sees weird, distended faces looming in his eyes, and then a shiny orange taxi is blowing its horn at him. An angry Samoan man with arms covered in tribal tattoos waves a thick middle finger in his face and shouts, "Fuckin' haole boy, I'll kill you!"

Chris darts away, along a side street, laughing.

Painless.

Sometime later, a scene slowly comes into focus and he finds himself in a dimly-lit dive bar with one hand clenched on a mug of beer and a cigarette smoking between his fingers.

A rough-looking woman has her hand on his thigh. "Hello, sailor," she whispers.

His alcohol-soaked eyeballs translate her face, smeared as it is with lipstick, rouge and mascara, into a dreamy portrait. His sopping mind transmits manly sounds but only slurs come from the stinking orifice below his nose.

She strokes his thigh and flutters her eyelids, playing him like a magic trick.

Aberrant logic convinces him that he has this little sex kitten purring.

Secretions from glands inside his skull mix with the alcohol in his blood to further contaminate his perception. A peep show in his mind rehearses climactic scenes from triple-X movies. Oh, he's certain sex will occur in a most fleshpot way.

She suggests they go to her place so he swigs the dregs of his beer, snuffs his cigarette and follows her into the night. Lust and lunacy ravish his brain. He doesn't think it's strange when she steers him, arm in arm, into an alley between two buildings. Beyond the streetlamp's dingy glow, swallowed in darkness, he unpacks some words, "Can you make me a cup of coffee at your place?"

"With cream and sugar?" she asks.

"I need something sweet," he says, thinking he's being witty.

"I've got something sweet for you," she says as she trips him into a trashcan.

*   *   *

He's on his hands and knees in food scraps, crawling on busted-open garbage bags.

Everything is blurry.

He closes one eye, searches for his wallet—finds it looted on the concrete.

A policeman appears above him in the streetlight's glow.

"What's your problem?" the cop asks.

Chris shakes his head and croaks, "No problem, officer." He tries to stand up.

"You've got all kinds of problems!" The cop shoves him into the alley, comes after him, shoves him again.

Chris stumbles backward over a dented garbage can.

The cop whacks him across the side of the head with a nightstick.

He collapses on a pile of garbage.

*   *   *

He stumbles back to the room at about five and passes out, decrepit and penniless. It's cool outside so he leaves the balcony door and the drapes open and the air conditioner off. By mid-morning the temperature in the room shoots up to a stifling ninety-one. Dazzling sun shines through the open balcony door, baking Chris's bare legs. The glass magnifies the sun, nearly blistering his exposed back. Still drunk and passed out at noon he rolls over but doesn't open his eyes or gain consciousness. The temperature rises steadily to a searing ninety-nine degrees.

He's dreaming about a Thanksgiving turkey cooking inside an oven, when suddenly he sits up startled. One eye opens, then the other.

He sees his shit scattered on the bed.

Cologne, T-shirt, suntan lotion, swim trunks, socks, coins, matches. They mean nothing.

Bits of thoughts fall like dandruff flaking from a scratched scalp.

Ink stamps on the backs of both hands tell the story.

He slides out of bed and walks toward the bathroom, turns and walks toward the balcony, turns again, feels dizzy. He leans on the desk. He shuts his eyes against the furnace-like heat. A twinge of pain shoots through his skull. He touches the tender lump above his ear.

He has no recollection of being beaten by the cop in the alley, but his heart slides into an abyss of guilt anyway.

Breathing is difficult because the dead air in the room feels like clear smoke.

Drink all night and wake up thirsty—it makes no sense at all.

He's desiccated to the center of his bones.

Hanging his head under the shower's cold spray, Chris tries to absorb some moisture. He opens his mouth and gulps water from the showerhead. From neck to hips, his torso feels like a bag stuffed with old wool sweaters but dammit the water won't soak in.

In the mirror, his gaunt face sags like soiled linen. The bright lights burn his bloodshot eyes and scream in his ears. With a toothbrush he attempts to scrub his teeth and his conscience clean but it doesn't work.

He slams the balcony door, cranks the AC and sits on the bed.

"I gotta stop." He rubs his eyes with shaky fingers. "—been this way too long."

*   *   *

His memory flashes on a green plastic garbage pail. A whorehouse in the Philippines. He'd been writhing on a futon and hanging his head off the edge to vomit in that green plastic pail. Filipino girls whisper and giggle in the hallway. Empty bottles of rum and Coke on the night table. A day earlier, when he passed out, they laid a cold towel on his forehead. When he came to, they fed him warm sticky rice.

Another night he'd passed out in a park in San Diego and woke up face-planted in the grass. A police officer was tapping a nightstick on the bottom of one of his tennis shoes. "You better get up and walk away," the cop said. Tequila in Tijuana had done it to him that time. At least he'd made it back across the border. He roamed the streets for an hour before figuring out where in Diego he was. That afternoon at sick call on the ship, a corpsman gave him the vial of Amobarbital.

What the fuck was that corpsman thinking, Chris wonders, wishing he had an Amobarb' right now.

And those times, like many others, he nursed a wicked hangover and swore he'd stop and clean himself up but he never could stop binge drinking, because every good alcoholic knows the best time to get completely wrecked is after you'd been sober for a few days.

Empty promises.

Useless fucking words.

Drinking liquor is just too easy.

Lying to myself should be hard, but I'm good at it now.

"I'm gonna stop drinking," he whispers, wondering if he's lying to himself right now.

*   *   *

"This time I mean it!"

But even as he speaks, an urge in his lungs triggers a habit in his brain and he looks at the nightstand, at the crumpled pack of Winston beside the clock radio. Even now, when it hurts to breath, he wants to smoke a cigarette. Placing his hand over his heart, he feels it throbbing, working too hard.

"What the fuck is wrong with me?"

He can't inhale deep enough because there's a load of rocks piled on his chest. He sucks air, puts a hand on his sternum feels his ribs rising and falling. His feet and hands are numb. Pain shoots through his heart. Heart attack, he thinks as he stands up in a panic.

With one sock on, he looks around for the other.

Deranged by fear like sparks popping inside his head, he goes out onto the balcony.

His brain throws out half-clipped thoughts like flakes of snow that melt and vaporize in the hot air.

"I was healthy when I joined the fucking Navy." He thinks about all the liquor he's poured down his throat, all the empty bottles he's left around the world, all the smoke he's sucked from a hundred cartons of cigarettes—the stomach-churning hangovers and the drugs—it all comes back on him like a polluted geyser erupting in his mind.

Even if the doctors can't tell, he knows his stomach and nerves—maybe even his brain—are damaged.

He foresees a miserable life ahead, strung out with painful hangovers, stretching for years into the future.

He steps up onto a patio chair.

Self-disgust and lousy memories.

Hopelessness.

Salvation on a concrete slab twelve floors below.

A few miserable seconds away.

He places one foot on the railing and steps up with the other.

Now he has both feet standing on the balcony railing.

He stretches his arms over his head and presses his fingertips on the bottom of the balcony of the room upstairs.

He looks out over the palm trees, past the hotels toward the green and black cliffs of Diamond Head.

His eyes settle on the blue sea stretching to the horizon.

He thinks about Larry and his knees wobble.

He sways.

His foot slips.

A tear leaks from one eye and runs down his cheek. It drops from his face and evaporates in the air long before hitting the sidewalk far below.

He closes his eyes, trembles and falls.

His fingers claw at the sky.

*   *   *

His butt hits the railing hard and he flips backward.

His head bangs into the glass patio door.

His elbow bangs on the concrete balcony.

"You asshole!" he growls with bittersweet rage.

*   *   *

"Do you need an ambulance?" the woman's hospitable voice through the phone.

"No, I can walk if it isn't too far."

She gives him directions. "Are you sure you don't want a taxi?"

"I need to walk."

"I hope you feel better," she says and hangs up.

After walking through the city streets, he stands in front of the receptionist at the emergency room in the Honolulu Medical Center.

"I'm stationed at Pearl Harbor," he says, "but I need to see a doctor."

"You should go to Tripler Army Hospital."

"I feel really lousy."

She slides a form at him.

He fills in a few boxes, then says, "My chest hurts and it's hard to breath."

"How long ago did it start?"

He wants to say, several years ago, but instead says, "About an hour."

She places her finger gently on his wrist, checks his pulse.

"I feel kind of shaky."

"Come with me." She waves him around to the end of the counter.

There's a handsome doctor with short dark hair. Confident and self-assured, he says, "Tell me what's going on?" He puts a hand on Chris's shoulder and gently grabs Chris's wrist to check his pulse.

It bangs against the doctor's fingertip.

"My chest hurts and it's hard to breath."

"Any history of a heart condition?"

"No."

"Come back here with me." He leads Chris through swinging doors into the ER.

Narrow beds on wheels, green oxygen tanks, IV racks and equipment in glass cabinets. Whispers and beeping machines behind closed curtains.

A man groans in pain.

A mother consoles a sobbing child.

"Take off your shirt and hop up on that bed," the doctor tells him.

A nurse unlaces his sneakers. The doctor puts his stethoscope on Chris's chest.

Another nurse attaches EKG sensors.

"We want to give you oxygen but need to draw blood from your arteries first," the doctor says.

Now there are four nurses, each with a thin glass needle in hand. They stand one at each wrist and one at each ankle.

"We'll draw blood directly from the arteries in your extremities. It might hurt a little," the doctor says, "but I need to see how much oxygen is in your blood."

The two nurses standing at the foot of the bed each grab an ankle, and the two at his sides each grab a wrist. They feel around for his arteries and then poke him with their glass pins.

It hurts and Chris yanks one arm away. A vermillion bead of blood forms on his wrist. The nurse grabs his arm and pokes him with the glass needle again.

Blood fills the thin tubes in rapid spurts.

He feels crucified.

They drop his ankles and wrists to the bed, attach cotton balls under

Band-Aids. They slip out through the curtains.

The doctor puts his hand under Chris's chin. "Open wide," he says. Chris complies and the doctor presses a tiny pill under his tongue. Then he fastens a green rubber oxygen mask over Chris's mouth and nose with an elastic strap.

Radiating from under his tongue, the pill sends a surge of power and vitality into his neck and through his chest.

It feels so good! He wants a vial of this miracle drug.

His heart begins pounding in sharp, steady beats.

The pain and tension that had seized him is gone.

The mask forces fresh oxygen into his lungs.

He feels so good, it's unbelievable. He wants it to last forever, but then he glances at the green cylinder and he thinks about the old man who rode out of the elevator on the big, white bed with the tubes and wires keeping him alive.

"Oh, shit!" Chris whispers, his voice muffled by the mask. "I'm that guy now!"

Effortlessly, Oxygen enters and exits his lungs.

Under his tongue, the little pill dissolves.

I'm that guy, Chris thinks fretfully as he dozes off.

He's zonked out when the doctor pushes back through the curtains. "Chris," he says, "How do you feel?"

Chris pulls the oxygen mask aside, "So much better."

"That's good. Your blood oxygen level is normal. Your lungs are clear. I think your difficulty breathing is related to acid indigestion," the doctor says. "Have you eaten anything spicy?"

"No," Chris shrugs.

"Well, you need to watch what you eat—" he looks knowingly in Chris' eyes "—and be careful about what you drink because you may have a stomach acid imbalance or an ulcer that can cause severe chest pain."

"What was that pill you put under my tongue?"

"Nitroglycerine."

Chris wonders if it's the same thing as the explosive.

They put him in a wheelchair and park him in an empty hallway behind the emergency room.

The doctor comes out and hands him a pint-sized beaker filled to the top with a white frothy concoction. "This is my special heartburn milkshake," he says. "I want you to drink all of it and sit here for a while."

Chris takes a long swallow and instantly feels a cool numbing sensation coating his insides.

"What's in this?" he asks.

"Three parts liquid Mylanta and one part Benadryl," the doctor winks. "I call it a hangover eraser."

That's a recipe I have to remember, Chris thinks as he chugs the soothing white liquid.

*   *   *

Afraid to eat but hungry, Chris walks the nightlife strip of Waikiki. Passing bars with neon lights glowing in the windows, liquor stores and restaurants where smiling people sit around tables enjoying lavish dinners. He sees a woman in a miniskirt, catches a glimpse of her smooth thighs. A handsome guy in a muscle shirt struts through the big doors of a palatial hotel lobby. A line of tourists wait at an all-you-can-eat twenty-four-hour buffet. He wanders, like a spy among the happy vacationers and wracks his brain, trying to figure out how he can curb his vices.

Addiction. The word bangs around inside his head.

"I'm just lonely is all," he whispers into the night.

PART III

Chapter 18: Xerox

Weatherbee is still sleeping in the lounge when Chris returns to the medical hold barracks on Sunday afternoon.

The view from a helicopter hovering above an erupting volcano fills the TV screen. Magma and brimstone spray skyward.

"Volcano Goddess Pele is getting restless on the big island again today," the reporter says over the chopper's thwocking blades.

A river of molten lava ignites a palm tree.

Chris pops two Mylanta tablets into his mouth and chews.

On the screen, lava flows across a beach and into lazy blue waves where it breaks into a furious boil. Steam rises around the helicopter and is whipped by the spinning blades. Through the dense vapor, orange lava flickers beneath the waves.

Chris gulps the frothy concoction as he walks upstairs to his room.

*   *   *

Monday morning the sun rises on a breezeless eighty-nine degree day. Chris stands in formation next to Carlos Devlin, on the blacktop behind the Medical Annex. His shirt collar rubs against his neck like cardboard, and his feet, inside black leather boots, bake like loaves of bread in a brick oven.

When the first class who calls roll stops to speak with a woman who came out of the annex, Carlos leans over and whispers to Chris, "Where you been, dancing?"

"I got a room at a hotel on the beach."

"Medical hold sailors ain't supposed to leave the base except to go to the hospital!" Carlos says. "When they figure out the game you're playing, you're going to be in a world of shit, Marlow."

"Hey," Chris says. "I got no appointments till next Monday, that's when my test results come back, so I'm stuck here all week."

"Time to pick up cigarette butts with the rest of us."

"I'm dreading it."

"Air Man Marlow," the first class shouts over his clipboard. "Front and center!"

He can prove he had appointments every morning during the previous week, but if they looked into it, they'll discover he's went AWOL every afternoon. His tan shines like a shade of guilt especially among all the pasty blackshoes.

Chris wonders what is going on when he sees D. Stone standing beside the first class. A white tropical skirt accentuates her shapely hips and tapers snuggly at her narrow waist. Her brown hair, parted in the middle, winged back from under her uniform cap. Her smooth face is tan and lightly made up. She has a dangerous smirk on her lips, and she's staring directly at Chris.

"Where were you last week?" the first class growls.

Chris's first thought is that D. Stone ratted him out after he told her about taking surfing lessons. He knows he's on shaky ground. He's learned during several years in the Navy that being absent without leave, referred to as AWOL, can carry a stiff penalty, like restriction to the barracks, loss of pay and demotion in rank. Moreover, he knows that lying to a senior officer is a serious offense that carries a grave penalty. So he locks into the rigorous military bearing he developed during hours of marching and standing at attention during boot camp years ago, and he says to the first class, "I've been at Tripler Army Hospital, cardiology and neurology clinics."

"Every day?"

"Yes," he says, walking a fine line along the edge of the truth. "I had daily appointments, a complete medical work-up on my heart, nerves and stomach."

The first class decides Marlow has his shit together well enough. "Go with Petty Officer Stone," he says. "She's got a job for you."

The blackshoes are all whispering and mumbling as Chris holds the door for Petty Officer Stone. He glances across the ranks, searching for Carlos Devlin and when he sees him glaring, Chris winks.

Inside the air-conditioned annex hallway smells crisp and clean, the floors waxed to a brilliant shine. Doctors and nurses scurry about in uniforms and scrubs.

Chris thinks about sitting with her on Friday in the hot tub at the recreation center. He's trying to remember her name. Doris, Debbie, Donna. He's hopeless with names. His memory serves up vivid images of her pretty face, practically flirting with him. She's into scuba diving and lives off base and she left him with the impression that she isn't haughty about it. Oh, what the fuck is her name, the electrons in his head scramble through the alphabet. D-A, Daphne, Da—, no. D-B, D-C, D-D, he smirks. D-E. Debbie. He's worried that getting so drunk on Friday night has permanently scrambled his gray matter. Dear! Yeah, Dear, Dear . . . Deirdre. How could I forget such a sweet name? Deirdre Stone!

Chris follows her along the corridor, his heart racing at the thought that they'd met on Friday afternoon and now on Monday morning she boldly plucks him from the ranks and puts him to work inside the annex. They enter the records department. Big windows with reinforced wire mesh offer a view of the lobby.

Chris follows her back behind the reception counter, between shelves crammed with medical records, all tidily arranged in rows like library books, color-coded green, red, blue, etc. As they continue walking further back in the narrow aisle, they pass between shelves stacked with old brown folders stuffed with papers from floor to ceiling. The musty feel makes him think it's some kind of archive. A light overhead buzzes loudly. Another blinks and several are burnt out creating a shadowy area where some of the files smell a bit moldy as if they'd been water damaged. There are pages sticking out at odd angles from some of the files. A section of shelves looks like it collapsed to the floor and a hasty corpsman had shoved the records back in place leaving them in jumbled disarray.

They pass by the records of Vietnam riverboat crews, beyond the files of the men who bombarded the coast of Korea from battleships on the Sea of Japan and into shelves weighed down by the records of men who sank dead to the bottom of the Pacific during World War II. Perhaps back here are the records of the men still inside the hull of the USS Arizona. In the way back, there are no lights at all and it's dark among the records of the dead.

Dust tickles his nose.

Petty Officer Stone's heels click ahead of him as she leads the way through the darkness.

"Back here," she says, stopping suddenly, "we have a copy machine."

Chris walks into her and his crotch area presses right against her bottom. Her hair fills his face. A sweet powdery fragrance rises from her neck.

She giggles.

"A copier," he steps back. "Excuse me," his voice thick.

She opens a door and flicks on the lights. Half a dozen florescent tubes blink inside a windowless room. A copier bolted to the floor. Cardboard boxes of medical records stacked nearly to the ceiling along one wall. An old wooden desk and a chair crammed to one side.

Chris notices the Xerox logo on the top corner of a white panel on the side of the machine. "We met at the rec' center, right?" he asks. "And your name's Deirdre."

"Since you're on medical hold," she says, "being a jet mechanic and all, you can figure out how to operate this thing." She hooks a thumb at the copier. "My last copy guy got orders back to the fleet before training his replacement, and now we've got a backlog."

"You know what I'd be doing outside?"

"Picking up litter," she says.

He can't tell if she's flirting or what. He feels anxious about being in this tiny room with her. One hand goes to a box of records. He flips the lid absentmindedly. The weight of having to be witty suddenly crushing him. He never could say those subtle things to set the mood with a woman, to put her at ease. But, he reminds himself, she came outside and plucked him out of ranks and brought him back here and now she's letting one second turn into two and three. The reason she isn't explaining where the extra paper is or telling me the job related details, he figures, is because she wants me to chat her up. But the weight of her expectations continues crushing him, and he has no idea why. He suspects it has something to do with how pretty he finds her face and how that makes his glands secrete too much hormones into his veins—making his thoughts run in a continuous nervous loop.

Awkwardness fills the space between them, but out of nowhere, and to his surprise, words are coming from his mouth. "I might only be here another week."

"Is that all?" A grain of disappointment in her tone.

He's senses that they've entered into a secret conversation, where they can talk about him working the copier and fan a spark of friendliness.

"Next Monday I get all my test results and, well, I don't think I'll need an operation or anything."

"Nothing major wrong with you then," she says with none of the disappointment he detected a moment ago.

"My doctor will probably send me back to my ship." What an idiot, he thinks as her smirk dissolves and her focus shifts from his face to the concrete blocks in the wall behind him.

"You get the machine going and I'll have you train someone who'll be here longer." She plucks an old file out of a box, "Practice on this."

He takes the file and she walks out.

"I'm such a jerk!" He runs his hands along one of the white plastic panels on the side of the machine and tugs it open. A web-work of black plastic gears and levers are riveted together. On one end of the machine, a plastic bins hold a few sheets of blank paper. He walks to the far end and sees a tray that catches the copies.

Chris closes the side of the machine and opens the cover over the copy glass. He flips a switch on the control panel. Mechanical clicking sounds and a low hum from inside. A row of green digital zeros blink on the control panel. He presses a button engraved with the letters B-O-S-S. A flash of white light bursts from the glass and a sheet of paper, grungy-gray on one side, ejects from the far end of the machine.

He opens the record Deirdre gave him, lifts the metal tabs holding the pages and pulls them out. He shoves them into the chute and hits the B-O-S-S button. One at a time the machine sucks in each page. Duplicates eject into the tray on the end; originals into a tray on the lid.

Deirdre enters with her arms stacked full of thick folders. "Very good, Airman Marlow, I knew you'd figure it out. Here's a few records to copy before lunch." She dumps the files on the desk.

"What're the copies for?" he asks.

"People getting discharged or next of kin."

Her dark hair, he notices, and her eyebrows and lashes make the whites of her eyes seem bold, magnetic even.

"I don't know what good these copies do," she says, "nobody can read a doctor's handwriting anyway."

The Xerox emits a harsh buzz and the steady click, flash and hum ceases. On the control panel, Chris reads the illuminated words, "Add paper."

He follows her through the dark aisles between shelves stacked with medical records to another windowless room.

They rummage through metal cabinets and move boxes around searching for paper.

Chris asks, "Did you go scuba diving over the weekend?"

"No. I had duty. How about you, do anything fun?"

Can't tell her about my trip to the emergency room, he thinks. "I kicked back at Waikiki." He remembers what they'd told him at indoc' about no leaving the base and no sports, and he thinks maybe he shouldn't tell her. "I always wanted to try scuba diving," he says.

"It's awesome," she says, but the gear is heavy. You said you have a hernia, right?

"It's no problem. I lift weights all the time." My hernia only acts up, he thinks, when I drink ten beers, knock back several shots of whiskey and smoke forty cigarettes.

Deirdre sits on the desk, puts her feet on a chair. "I know the dive master who runs the scuba class," she says.

"How much does it cost?" Chris pulls boxes of blank medical records off the shelf to see what's behind them.

"About one fifty for the class and the book, plus equipment, and that's a great price. I took an advanced wreck diving class that cost two fifty and then I bought another two hundred worth of equipment."

"Shipwrecks?" He tosses a box onto a shelf and looks at her, impressed.

"Sunken airplanes too."

"Wow." He slides boxes around, looking for copy paper.

"We did classroom and pool instruction and then we made nine dives on two different wrecks, two at night."

"Shipwreck diving at night?" This chick is crazy.

*   *   *

Deirdre is crazy, according to her mom.

When Deirdre calls home her mom says, "Deirdre! Scuba diving?

140

You're crazy! You'll be dead before the attorney your father hired prosecutes that damn recruiter that tricked you into joining the Navy."

"Mom, nobody tricked me, I volunteered," Deirdre says. "I was bored in Saint Louis."

Deirdre has been calling home weekly for almost two years but her mother still doesn't fully accept that her baby-girl is in the US Navy. Her mom still curses "the recruiter that tricked you out of college." But truth is Deirdre hated her classes at the Saint Louis Secretarial Institute. She'd actually dropped out and gotten a job as a clerk in a supermarket bakery before going to see a Navy recruiter.

Deirdre's father, Baxter, collected a disability for a ruptured disk after twenty-two years hoisting beer kegs at Anheuser Busch. When Deirdre last saw Baxter he was in the neighborhood's corner bar hoisting seventy-five cent glasses of Bud. She didn't argue with her mom. She knew her dad hadn't hired a lawyer to get her out of the Navy. He wouldn't waste the money he could spend on beer.

When she first arrived on Oahu, Deirdre lived like a sailor on shore leave. Enticed by the glitzy nightclubs at the hotels on Waikiki, she spent her weekends on the beach and her nights dancing. On base, men constantly approached her. Whether she was shopping at the Navy Exchange, licking a cone outside Baskin Robbins, eating in the dining hall, walking along the street or handing a medical record over the reception counter, there were men, men, and more men looking her in the eyes and asking her out on dates. Many were handsome. Some had neatly trimmed beards and mustaches, other smoothly shaven. They came in all shapes and sizes—tall and short, skinny and chubby. Some of them were buff—amazingly buff studs. They all wore nice uniforms, some in khakis and others in whites or dungarees.

When she first arrived at Pearl Harbor, she found it impossible to pass up an invitation to dinner. She wanted to make friends and there were so many great restaurants outside the base. She didn't know anyone, so when a guy asked her to go on a hike or a picnic or a bike ride or out for drinks and dancing, she accepted and went along.

Quickly she learned that sailors are a transient, horny, two-timing, easy-spending bunch. After three months at Pearl Harbor, Deirdre had two full time boyfriends and three casual acquaintances. She was becoming a sailor. Back home she never ran around with boys, but on Oahu she found it difficult to say no several times a day to handsome, seemingly well-mannered men. Eventually she could not go to the gym, the Navy Exchange or the dining hall for fear of the awkward situations when she encountered two or more of her male-friends at the same time.

She'd only had sex with three men during those six months, but one day she read a medical bulletin about world-travelling US Navy sailors spreading sexually transmitted diseases.

She immediately ended all relationships.

To divert her attention from guys, nightclubs and the stereotypical sailor-ashore lifestyle, Deirdre enrolled in scuba lessons at the recreation center. Once certified, she escaped the Navy most Sunday mornings on a dive charter out of Honolulu. With local divers and tourists, she explored the underwater sites around Oahu. She browsed the surf shops and subscribed to Scuba Times Magazine. She read books about diving, joined the Cousteau Society and woke up in the morning from underwater dreams. After every dive, she wrote in her log, describing the fish, corals, shades of blue and impressions of the various equipment she rented. She took Red Cross classes and earned First Aid and CPR certificates. She put a wet suit on layaway. Making friends with locals and diving with travelers from Europe, the US and Canada, Asia and Australia instilled a sense of wonder and worldliness. Beneath the ocean's surface, miles off the coast of Maui, Oahu or the Big Island, she felt independence and daring coursing through her body; the feelings that made her join the Navy in the first place.

In order to make the records department, the Navy Exchange, the recreation center and the on-base Baskin Robbins safe to work and hang around, Deirdre bought a cubic zirconia solitaire and practiced rejecting men in the mirror on the back of her locker door.

"Sorry," she'd say, after a man asked her out, and then casually she'd touch her cheek with her left hand, flashing her "diamond" engagement ring, "but my fiancée wouldn't like that at all."

She could tell when a man was about to pop the question and she would touch her hair and flash the ring. If he didn't notice, or, like most sailors, saw the ring but popped the question anyway, she assumed a shocked expression and gasped, "I'm engaged to be married."

That kept men away until Steve Laroo sat across from her in the dining hall one sunny day at lunch. Steve was tall, muscular and tan, with curly, dirty-blond hair. She put her hands under the table, yanked that tacky stone off her finger and discovered that he was from Moro

Bay, California and he was single—one of those shy but strong surf-and-turf California boys. He'd just completed boot camp and would be at Pearl for six months. Steve was attending the Navy Diver Training Program on Ford Island. Deirdre liked that he did not ask her out or flirt with her at all during that first meeting in the dining hall.

She was proud of the way she sized him up and realized she could handle herself. Not like Tracy from Dallas, Deirdre's first roommate, who got knocked up with twins two-months after arriving at Pearl Harbor from boot camp. Tracy didn't know who the father was. So she told each of the nine men she'd had sex with over the past two months that she was pregnant, and luckily one of them manned up and admitted the twins were his. They had a hurry-up wedding and were living happily in Navy housing. Within fifteen minutes after meeting Steve Laroo, Deirdre wanted to be friends with him. Two days later when she met him again, she asked him out.

Infatuation transitioned quickly to lust and fluctuated fantastically between the two for six months.

Steve, a certified diver before joining the Navy, dove on Sundays with Deirdre. The Deep Sea Diver Training program he attended was the most comprehensive and intensive program in the world. He could rarely leave the base and was only free for Deirdre on Sundays.

The only thing exceeding the speed at which Steve's six-month training program flew past was the speed at which they fell for each other. They knew that outside one slim chance, Steve would soon leave Pearl for permanent duty at a distant base. Their only hope of staying together was that Steve would graduate first in his class and thereby earn the privilege of picking his choice of the twenty sets of orders his class would receive. Among those orders, a Navy detailer had informed the class, there would be one set for permanent duty at Pearl Harbor. Scared by the knowledge that time was running out for them, rather than study every moment and prepare for his weekly exams, Steve spent time with Deirdre every chance he got.

Thirteenth out of twenty in his class, the Navy sent Steve to Guantanamo Bay, Cuba where hostile Cuban guards occasionally shoot at Americans who cross the base's perimeter fence. Steve and Deirdre swore they'd love each other forever, and they actually did write each other letters for two months after he left.

Broken hearted, Deirdre put in a request for extra pay so she could

live off base. She bought a car and alienated herself from Navy people.
She put her cubic zirconia ring back on, avoided the dining hall and the
Navy Exchange. She only came on base to work, stand watches and
swim laps.

But when she met Chris at the recreation center, she could not get
him out of her mind. She came into the records department Monday
morning, looked over the list of men on medical hold and found,
"Airman Christopher Marlow, temporary orders, USS Enterprise." She
bit her lip and schemed for a moment before walking into her boss's
office. Lieutenant Ward was on the phone, smoking a True menthol.
When Deirdre suggested they get someone off the medical hold crew to
take care of their duplicating backlog, Ward said, "Great idea, Stone.
Got anybody in mind?"

"There's a jet mechanic on the muster sheet, ma'am."

"Go get 'em, Stone."

Deirdre promptly went outside and rescued Chris from his job of
litter-picker-upper.

With him, she figured, she'd have a friendly relationship. If
anything got started, he'd likely be leaving soon anyway.

He probably isn't mister right, she thought, but he looks like mister
right now, with his tan, his muscles, his neatly trimmed hair and a
dangerous smile.

*   *   *

"Shipwrecks are awesome," she says. "We went down a hundred
and ninety feet to an old cargo tanker off Maui."

"A hundred and ninety feet!" Chris is sliding boxes around.

"Sport diving you follow a table and you can only descend one
hundred and thirty feet. But my instructor took us to one ninety because
we'd already logged several deep dives." She looks at the way Chris's
back tapers from his shoulders to his waist as he tosses a fifty-pound
box of medical tape onto a shelf above his head, and she decides to get
the form for his scuba physical signed off. Even if he is seeing a
cardiologist, there's nothing wrong with his heart.

"I found it," Chris says as he sets a box of copy paper on the desk
and wipes his brow with the back of his hand. He wants to smoke a
cigarette, but instantly snubs the foolish idea. It's his second day not

smoking.

Seeing his straight teeth close up, she figures he must floss every day. And so tan. The guys off the ships are usually white as milk. The flight deck, she remembers, that's where he said he works. He must get a lot of sun up there. I bet it's hot.

"If I was going to be here longer I'd take a scuba class," he says. "I'm a good swimmer."

And he's kind of dumb too, she thinks happily. He doesn't even realize he's on medical hold? He's supposed to be on light duty, but he went to a hotel on Waikiki for the weekend.

She decides again, she likes him.

"Are you going to the recreation center to swim laps tonight?" she asks.

"Sure," he says. "I'm working out hard this week."

"I'll introduce you to Afram, the dive instructor."

"I um, well," he stutters, and feels some weird pressure from her to take a scuba class.

"A friendly introduction," she assures him and opens the door.

Chris hoists the box onto his shoulder and follows Deirdre back to the copy room. He thinks about the breakfast he'd eaten; a piece of toast, a glass of pineapple juice, a cup of tea, and a banana. I'll eat a salad for lunch with a glass of water, he thinks. Scuba, what am I getting myself into? Am I really going to take a scuba class? That's crazy!

Chapter 19: Chiefs

Chris removes a stack of paper from Chief Ordnanceman Jeffrey Johnson's red cardboard folder, stacks it in the Xerox's chrome feed-chute and presses the B-O-S-S.

He glances at the blank walls, sighs, put his elbows on the desk. He reads, "Larsen, Allen, A., USN" on the tab of a dog-eared, green folder protruding from one of the piles in front of him. With a spark of curiosity, he pulls it out and opens it. The top pages are the most recent entries, but Chris decides to follow Larsen, Allen A.'s medical history in chronological order, so he bends the metal tabs up and lifts the stack of paper. He places it face down on the wooden desk and flips over the back page, the very first entry.

* * *

Allen Larsen was eighteen in July, 1951. He entered the Navy at Chicago, Illinois. Chris imagines gusty winds whipping through canyons created by old, ornate skyscrapers. He imagines trolley cars and a smiling young man in a cotton T-shirt, canvas pants and leather boots. Allen Larsen wore his hair slicked back in a D.A. style, Chris decided. He carried a comb in his back pocket and a pack of Lucky Strike rolled in his shirt sleeve on summer nights. Larsen received a series of inoculations at Great Lakes Naval Training Center in Wisconsin and got his first orders to the fleet; San Diego Shipyard, USS Ajax.

San Diego, 1951: The tan facade of the Spanish Mission in Balboa Park glowing almost pink in the Southern California sunshine. The Silver Strand, sprinkled with lazy palm trees swaying on Pacific breezes, stretches from the Hotel Del Coronado south to Baja. Chris imagines Larsen, stripped to the waist, sweating profusely, shoveling coal into the Ajax's cast iron boilers.

Chris flips over a yellowed routine-physical exam, the paper thin as onion skin. A long lost corpsman had pressed the rubber stamp of the Sasebo Japan, Medical Clinic on the top right corner of the form and neatly printed Oct 14, 1956 in black ink, revealing that Larsen hadn't needed an aspirin or even a Band-Aid during his first five years in the Navy.

Then in 1957 Larsen got orders to Whidbey Island, State of Washington. Apparently, he reenlisted for shore duty after five years at sea. Nothing but routine physical exams and inoculations while working in the dry docks. In 1960, Larsen hurt his hand; "treated laceration on left thumb with [not legible], x-ray shows no broken bones. Sick in quarters for seventy-two hours. Pt. will return for wound redress and follow-up."

1965: USS Iowa. Now there's an old battlewagon with great big guns.

Scribbled in a box at the bottom of a form: GM1 Larsen. Chris knew that stood for Gunner's Mate First Class. He counted 51 to 65 on his fingertips and whispered, "He'd been in fourteen years and finally made first class."

"Pt. reports abdominal pain. Dispensed [not legible] and aspirin, return if discomfort persists."

Chris remembered a training video they showed in boot camp; the Iowa's sixteen-inch guns, three per turret, emitting cracks of thunder, bursts of fire and smoke when they shot projectiles as long as his arm and as big around as a dodge ball. He wondered if Larsen and his gun crew bombarded Vietnam in 1965. Clearing the way for democracy—

Chris wondered if the tremendous bang from those cannons gave Larsen a case of indigestion. On the next ten pages, Chris saw that Larsen had gone to sick call fifteen times in three months. The same diagnosis reworded and scribbled in several different handwritings; Tagamet, Motrin, aspirin, Mylanta. "Pt. will return if discomfort persists."

Chris knew that run-around because doctors on the Enterprise had put him through it.

Larsen landed in the Los Angeles Naval Hospital in January 1966. Captain Scopes, a doctor with excellent penmanship, took Gunner Larsen off all medication and ordered a series of tests. Captain Scopes' lucid pen summarized the lengths of EKG tape and lab slips taped to pages in Larsen's record. "Tests indicate excessive levels of sugar in

Pt.'s blood and urine. He complains of persistent thirst and excessive discharge of urine. Thirty-mc insulin per day has restored Pt.'s sugar levels to normal limits. Pt. referred to LANH Diabetes Clinic at this time."

"Diabetic," Chris whispered, "those bonehead doctors were treating him for indigestion. Fuck, I hope I'm not diabetic."

From 1966 to 1969, Larsen worked at the ship repair facility in Long Beach, where they gave him monthly prescriptions at the medical annex.

Chris wonders if Larsen was married or had kids. He wonders about L.A. in the late sixties. Race riots. Jim Morrison. New ten-lane freeways full of big American-made sedans. Allen Larsen drives to his Chevy Impala through a crowd of hippies protesting the war when he arrives at the shipyard every day for work. Larsen probably supervised a crew of metalsmiths who welded armor-plate steel and repaired ship's guns for a living. He must have been a tough old salt.

Chris wonders why he's copying Allen Larsen's record when Larsen would have been in the Navy for twenty years and eligible for retirement back in 1971.

The Xerox stops. Chris unloads Jeffrey Johnson and the duplicate. He puts Dickey Wilson, Boiler Technician First Class, in the chrome chute and presses the B-O-S-S.

Gunner Allen Larsen must have been a lifer and gone for the thirty-year enlistment. Chris wonders what type of medical calamity lay ahead.

He glances at a routine physical and a few prescription slips, and then he turns over a thick white sheet of paper that isn't a standard medical form. Pins and needles tingle up his spine, and send a shock bristling across his shoulders before they ground out in the back of his neck where several hairs stand on end. Dated March 14, 1972, someone used red and blue pencils to color in a black-line sketch of Larsen's heart. The caption reads, "Double coronary bypass on Gunner's Mate Chief Allen Larsen." The sketch shows two tubes spliced into Larsen's aorta and routed to his heart muscle. A note explains that they used veins from Larsen's legs.

Pinpricks cross Chris's chest and he winces. He tries to fend off the images but it's too late, he asked for it. He'd reanimated Larsen's medical history in his imagination, and now he sees them shaving

Larsen's chest. Silver hemostats hold the skin stretched back from an incision that runs from his Adam's apple to his breastbone. Under white surgical lamps, a masked man in a lab coat and a hairnet pushes a grinding circular saw through Larson's thick sternum. A shiny tool, like a jet mechanic's pliers, spread Larson's ribs apart and a hand, sealed inside a rubber glove, reaches in and fondles the clogged, pulsating knot that is Allen Larsen's heart. A surgeon touches a shiny scalpel to the aorta and Chris shuts his eyes. He shakes his head, trying to make the horrifying visual go away.

Even after heart surgery, some people can't quit smoking and drinking. In 1974 at a clinic in Greece, Larsen complained of chest pain. In the middle of an illegible entry, a frustrated flight surgeon neatly printed, "Senior Chief Larsen has been ordered to quit smoking immediately. He is showing signs of emphysema." Monthly entries seemed to indicate Larsen was treating himself well. According to a Navy doctor in Greece, Senior Chief Larsen lost weight, quit smoking and drinking liquor, gave up sweets, salt and red meat. He must have quit eating in the chow hall. Before leaving Greece in 1975, Larsen earned a promotion to master chief petty officer; the highest rank attainable by an enlisted person in the US Navy.

Because the medical record provided only a peephole into Larsen's biography, Chris sat back and wondered why Larsen, a diabetic with a double bypass and early signs of emphysema, continued to reenlist.

Chris wondered why the Navy didn't put Larson out on a medical discharge.

*   *   *

Chris thought about Chief Miller; the Teflon Tyrant back in his squadron aboard the USS Enterprise.

Back when Chris first came aboard the Enterprise, Chief Miller commanded the squadron's maintenance control desk. Chris recalled the half-quart coffee cup Chief Miller had permanently attached to his left hand and a Parliament 100 clamped under his gray-black mustache. The chief's face looked like the skin off a piece of Kentucky Fried Chicken. He cursed every other word, talked on the phone with several people—putting one on hold to ask a question, then putting them on hold to give the answer to another—all while simultaneously communicating over a three-channel walkie-talkie with jet mechanics, flight deck directors, plane captains and hangar deck control. The chief also briefed pilots on the status of their aircraft and imposed tyrannical order over all other personnel in the maintenance control office.

Occasionally Chris took a rack of fuel sample bottles to maintenance control for Chief Miller to inspect. Chris waited patiently, watching Chief Miller do ten things a minute. He kept track of all the jets, pilots, and mechanics with a sharp pencil and a yellow legal pad. He could smoke a Parliament 100 in thirteen drags, and seemed to top off his black-inside coffee mug every few minutes.

He'd tell everyone on the phones, the walkie-talkie and everyone badgering him in the maintenance office to, "Fuckin' handle it and get back to me!" then he'd take a break to deal with Christopher Marlow.

"What's happening on the roof, Airman?"

"We've been hot seating tankers all morning, chief."

"No shit, who's the cocksucker left the canopy up on three zero seven?" Chief Miller didn't wait for an answer. They both knew Trombini had aircraft 307 and word was he ran off on a smoke break and left his cockpit canopy open when the ship steamed under a downpour. "The electricians are growing tits 'cause half the black boxes shorted when they applied fuckin' power." The chief took a deep drag, "Is this kid Trombini a shit bird or what?" Chief Miller twisted his Kentucky Fried face into an inquisitive scowl. A cloud of cigarette smoke flowing from his lips.

"Trombini is from Detroit."

"What the fuck kind of answer is that?" the chief snapped. An amused smile stretched his extra-crispy skin as the Parliament rolled from one side of his mouth the other.

"Trombini thinks the Navy should give Chrysler a contract to build jet engines," Chris said. "He asked if I thought a Cummins eight cylinder diesel with a turbo blower could get an A-7 Corsair off the flight deck."

Chief snatched the cigarette from his lips and howled, "Eight cylinder with a blower—" he laughed. "That's rich!"

"Yeah, it is," Chris said smiling.

Chief Miller actually had to dry a tear from the corner of one eye when he recovered from the fit of laughter and coughing that wracked his respiratory system. Then he became extremely sober as he held a fuel sample bottle up to the light. Chris could hear him wheezing but the chief never plucked the cigarette from his lips without pulling a drag from it, and he never snuffed one unless he immediately lit another. "These samples are just fine, Airman," he'd say and wink a smart carry-on.

Then the chief sat at his desk and slugged a mouthful of hot, black coffee and started taking maintenance briefs and barking orders into telephones and walkie-talkies—doing what he loved—playing jet mechanic hard ball in the squadron maintenance control office.

One night Chief Miller unexpectedly flew off the ship. Rumors claimed he suffered a stroke or a heart attack, maybe both. Chris had hear what laid Chief Miller low was a combination asthma attack and bleeding ulcer induced by smoking two packs of cigarettes and drinking two gallons of coffee per day. Chris fancied that the old chief was still kicking, definitely still smoking and probably sneaking out to a country western bar on Saturday nights. Either that or he was dead, because he sure as hell wasn't passing his golden years playing bingo and shuffle board, eating pitted prunes and applesauce.

*   *   *

Chris turns his attention back to Master Chief Allen A. Larsen's medical record, where his improved health and the pomp of his sixth reenlistment warranted an around-the-world change of duty station. With a stiff warning from Commander E.J. Lundgren to "maintain a low sodium diet, take proper medication daily and get 15-minutes of light aerobic exercise three times per week," Master Chief Larsen departed from Greece in 1975 and steamed to Yokosuka, Japan.

Between America's bicentennial and 1980 Larsen received only prescriptions, annual checkups and another reenlistment physical.

Chris figured Larsen had been in the Navy for over 30 years at that point.

But living in the Far East proved to be too much for the forty-six year old master chief. Chris imagined the attack pilots he knew going to bed early, never raising a highball or a mug of black coffee to their ivy-league lips, eating bran cereal with skim milk and fresh fruit in the morning and reading historical novels before going to bed early at night, but not a thirty-year master chief. Even among career sailors, the thirty-year master chief is extraordinary.

To a sailor in the orient, a wink and a smile from a pretty girl in the doorway of a waterfront bar is almost irresistible. And the iniquity known to take place in the beds upstairs in those dark, smoky establishments can draw a sailor in with the force of an all-consuming whirlpool. In 1981, Larsen "suffered a coronary infarction." A nurse stapled EKG strips to the pages. At erratic intervals, a heart specialist had circled the jagged line's precipice and jotted medical symbols. These were indications of irreparable irregularities in the throbbing kernel of life inside Larsen's chest.

Early in 1982, Larsen saw Penny Brown at Tripler Army Hospital.

On the last few pages Chris deciphers the words "oxygen tent," "emphysema" and "lung cancer." In shock, he reads: "double leg amputation."

"Holy shit!" He realizes Larsen never left Tripler Army Hospital alive.

He wonders if Larsen could have been the guy he'd seen coming out of the elevator on the big bed with the nurse and orderly wheeling him into the Cardiology clinic.

He figures Larson would be about 46 years old, and that's ancient. He wonders what it would be like to be 50, but he can't imagine being so old. He wonders—a walker, a cane, adult diapers? Such an advanced age is unfathomable.

Chris slowly turns over the final page, Larsen's death certificate. Since he'd never seen one, he reads it with morbid curiosity and feels himself getting choked up.

He holds the stack of papers for a second, feeling the weight of it, the record of a sailor's life—a sailor's death.

Then the copier buzzes, and Chris shoves Larsen's stack of papers in the copier's chrome feed chute and presses the B-O-S-S.

He looks at the machine and notices each page of Larsen's record being sucked in, copied and spit out. One after another, he sees the pages duplicated with mechanical precision, and he realizes the irony of it.

He looks at the stacks of records piled around him, overflowing from cardboard boxes. "I'm a copy," he says and smiles. "My life is a copy of all you dead sailors."

Chapter 20: Baskin Robbins

After lifting weights and swimming laps together, Chris and Deirdre slide into the hot tub where a dozing man reclines in the scalding, bubbly water.

Deirdre says, "Hi, Afram. I'd like you to meet my friend, Chris."

"How are you?" Chris asks, as Afram's massive hand surfaces through the water.

Afram's brown skin has an olive under-tint. He has a big forehead and black hair parted in the middle. His hair is long and it grows straight over his shoulders.

"Chris wants to take your class because he's going to the Philippines when he leaves here," Deirdre says.

"The Philippines?" Afram says in awe. "With a scuba certification you can have some real adventures over there." Afram stands up and grips the lip of the tub in both hands. He flexes his muscular upper body and slides into a sitting position on the tub's padded edge. "Have you done any snorkeling or scuba diving?"

"No," Chris says, "but I'm a good swimmer."

"A lot of soldiers and sailors take my classes." He makes eye-contact with Chris. "Scuba gives them something exciting to do when they have time off."

"That's exactly what I need."

"I'd like to stay and talk." Afram glances at his enormous wristwatch. "But I've got a date." He swings his legs out of the tub. "See you tomorrow, the class starts at six. Deirdre can tell you all about it. I hear she's a wreck diver now."

Aboard the Enterprise, Chris had visited Subic Bay in the Philippines four times, once for a two-week stay, but he'd never driven a golf ball down any of the fairways on the Navy base's eighteen-hole golf course. Neither had he fired a rifle at the target range, nor taken a cruise aboard a glass bottom boat to behold the corals and colorful fish around Grande Island. But he'd seen the bars and the dance floors and the water stained ceilings in the little rooms upstairs at many of the clubs on the strip in Olongapo City outside the Navy base. He especially remembered one place called the Samurai Palace. It wasn't a real palace, just a dilapidated whorehouse behind a phony plywood façade of the Taj Mahal. He'd been to the Philippines four times, but never made it more than a few blocks from the base without ending up in a bar. He felt like a fool.

"Something exciting to do when I have time off." He smiles at Deirdre.

"Yeah." She's lying back with her eyes closed.

"Better diving than Hawaii! Imagine that," Chris says, now determined to get his basic scuba certification.

"So, are you going to do it?"

"Why not? I've been to the Philippines four times and—" he stops, not wanting to tell her about his barroom exploits and whorehouse antics.

After showering Chris and Deirdre swing by the rec' center's front desk to pick up the scuba class registration form.

Outside, Deirdre says, "I know a shortcut."

Chris follows her into a dark tangle of rhododendron.

"How am I going to get this physical signed off?" he asks as they emerge onto a baseball field.

"Fill it out and give it to me tomorrow, I'll have Lieutenant Ward sign it."

"She'll do that?"

"She signs anything I put in front of her."

They walk across second base and into center field. A ten-foot-high cobblestone wall forms a semicircle from one foul line to the other across the outfield.

Rising above the wall on the other side, the superstructures of several battleships moored at the Merry Point pier. A string of white bulbs sketches a delicate line from each ship's bow to the top of its superstructure and down to its stern. The white bulbs lend the battleships a pleasure-boat ambiance.

"Will she know she's signing off a physical?" Chris stops beside Deirdre in the wall's shadow in deep center field.

They toss their backpacks to the top of the wall.

Chris locks his fingers and Deirdre steps into the stirrup they make.

She puts her hands on his shoulders and says, "Of course not. She would never sign a release for scuba diving lessons for someone on medical hold."

Chris boosts her and she puts a foot on his shoulder and scrambles to the top of the wall.

He looks up at her and wonders how he's going to get up there.

"Climb up," she shouts.

So, he digs his fingertips into the cracks between the stones and gets enough of a toehold to drag himself up.

The thought of Deirdre surreptitiously getting her boss to sign the physical makes him apprehensive. Standing atop the wall beside her, he asks, "Are you sure it's safe?"

"Are you in good health?"

"Yes."

"Then don't worry about it," she says and leaps ten feet to the sidewalk below.

He looks after her; certain she'd broken both ankles.

"Come on, chicken," she yells.

He takes a flying leap, wanting her to explain the dangers of scuba diving, but she's absorbed in a reckless attempt to cross the street. Cars speed past on a blind curve where the street bends away in both directions. Chris stands on the curb watching her hair fly from side to side as she scans, wild eyed, for a break in the traffic. There's something untamed about her, and he realizes that his decision to take the class will be his own. Each time they start across, she grins as a burst of cars zoom around the curve and they jump back to the sidewalk.

Then it's quiet and they inch out, listening to the electric hum of a streetlamp overhead, daring each other with devilish grins, leaning out from the curb as far as they can to see if any cars are coming.

And then they bolt—

—a white convertible appears and a Toyota pickup, candy-apple red with oversized tires behind it, but the double yellow line flashes under their tennis shoes and they keep running, whooping in fear and excitement as brakes squeal and a pink face with a crew cut pokes from the pickup's passenger window and shouts an expletive. Horns blare on their heels as they vault to the curb on the opposite side of the street.

They laugh and catch their breath and realize they are holding hands.

Deirdre smirks.

They let go.

"Some short cut!" he says.

"It's better than going all the way around."

They climb the steps to a patio where chairs and tables are arranged outside Baskin Robbins.

After Deirdre orders a banana split with Very Strawberry, Pralines and Cream, Rocky Road, all the toppings, nuts and whipped cream, Chris orders the same thing with French Vanilla, Pistachio Almond Fudge and Rocky Road.

They sit at a table on the patio.

"I always get Rocky Road but switch up the other two," Chris confides.

"You're rad'," Deirdre quips, mashing her lips on a heaping spoonful of Very Strawberry and whipped cream but stops to confess, "I come here twice a week."

"Do you have a banana split every time?"

"No."

"I bet."

"Usually I get a cone."

"What's your favorite flavor?"

"Pralines and Cream."

"What'd you do before joining the Navy?"

"Dropped out of business school." She extends a spoonful of Pralines and Cream to him. "A secretarial program, it was my mom's idea."

"Joining the Navy wasn't your mom's idea?" He offers her some Pistachio Almond Fudge.

She rolls her eyes. "You'll love this," she says. "Ten times I explained to my mom that I was joining the Navy and I was guaranteed training in medical administration, but even after I left for boot camp she kept insisting I'd been drafted."

"Drafted?"

"Yes. She wrote a letter to a congressman while I was in boot camp and a naval investigator pulled me out of ranks one day."

"NIS?"

"Yes, my mom had started a freakin' congressional inquiry. They interrogated me for an hour and almost kicked me out, but I insisted on staying, so finally some admiral wrote her a letter and told my mom I volunteered and since I was nineteen there was nothing anyone could do."

"She must've been mad."

"My company commander made me call her every Sunday and write her twice a week. She chilled out a little after I got to San Diego, though."

"What happened then?"

"I saved some money and went to the Navy Exchange and ordered her a microwave and satin sheets and luxurious bath towels out of the catalog and had it all shipped to her."

"Change her mind?"

"Sort of, but she still doesn't understand the difference between the Navy and the Army."

"I have the same problem," Chris says. "I went home on leave and told my buddies I made a cruise to Japan and Africa and Australia on the USS Enterprise and they asked if I had to dig foxholes and sleep in a tent."

"Civilians, duh! They ask if I have to put camouflage on my face."

Chris eats a heaping spoonful of banana and Pistachio Almond Fudge. He stirs the melted mixture in the canoe-shaped dish and says, "I love ice cream."

"Me too." She tilts her dish and scrapes together the last melted spoonful.

"You're done already?"

She opened her mouth and stuck out her tongue to show him. "Want some water?"

"Sure."

He finishes his banana split and says, "Thanks," when she returns with two paper cups.

They look across at the ships tied to the piers. On the nearest, an officer and a sailor in tropical white uniforms are standing at the top of the gangway. Four sailors, dressed in jeans and T-shirts, emerge from a watertight door. They show their ID cards as the watch looks them over. The officer salutes and they walk down the gangway to the pier. The first cabbie in a line of taxis starts his engine as the sailors pile in.

"When I see sailors coming ashore," Deirdre says, "I feel like I'm not even in the Navy."

"What do you mean?"

"Living on a ship, cruising around the word, that's the Navy."

"You want to go on sea duty?" he asks.

"Well, I like having a car and an apartment. Pearl Harbor is pretty nice, but sometimes," her eyes get a faraway look and her voice goes dreamy, "when I see a ship pull in and a few days later it's gone, I think about what they say, you know, join the Navy and see the world."

Chris suppresses an impulse to tell her about the dread of being at sea for months at a time and the anxiety that comes from wanting to see the world but always ending up in waterfront bars.

"When your ship pulls into port," he tells her.

She turns an amused look at him.

"The strangest thing is not having any reservations."

"Reservations?" she asks.

"You don't arrive at the airport and pick up your rental car. You don't have a hotel reservation. The land just comes over the horizon one morning," he says, "and they drop the anchor and you climb down a ladder and onto a small boat that takes you to the pier. Then you pile into a cab with a bunch of friends and tell the driver to take you around or you go on foot and wander, looking for something to do."

"So what do you do?"

"Anything, go to the beach, a bar, a shopping mall, an amusement park, a zoo, you name it, a cemetery even. Once in Japan some friends and I were walking through what we thought was a park. We were on a big slate patio outside this cool building that looked like a temple, and all of a sudden a bell rang and bunches of little kids come swarming out, wearing uniforms. We were in a schoolyard and didn't even know it. Then we spent a half hour with a whole bunch of little kids writing our names in chalk and drawing pictures on the playground."

Deirdre laughs delightedly.

"Hong Kong is an amazing city" Chris says. "There's Victoria Harbor full of ships and junks and hydrofoils, and on one side is the Kowloon Peninsula which is mainland China, and on the other is Hong Kong, which is a British Crown Colony. There's skyscrapers a few blocks deep along the water and the backdrop is a dark green mountain range that goes up into the clouds."

"Very scenic," Deirdre says.

"My first time in Hong Kong I was nineteen and totally

overwhelmed. I ended up getting drunk for three days. But my second time I went out with my friend Larry. He and I found a classy restaurant where they made us take our shoes off and our table was in its own little dining room."

Deirdre nods approval.

"The walls were made out of waxy white paper, stretched between thin wooden slats, and we sat on cushions on the floor and ate with chopsticks at low tables. We couldn't read the menu so we pointed at different things. You would have screamed if you saw what the waiter brought us."

"What was it?"

"A bottle of rice wine with three dead lizards inside!"

"Lizards!"

"With their heads in the bottom and skinny tails looping around inside the neck of the bottle. The waiter showed us the label; he uncorked it and poured us each a taste."

"You drank it!"

"It tasted so good."

"No!" Deirdre squeals.

"Then three waiters came in, each wearing a fez and a white jacket, and they set the table, took lids off plates of food, they put our napkins in our laps and bowed and backed out, leaving us alone. Except for the rice and vegetables and a small rack of ribs we had no idea what we were eating. Ever had tofu?"

"Sure."

"Imagine a cube of tofu, except it's purple and semitransparent. As for the rest of the food, it could have been shark skin or seaweed or monkey meat."

Deirdre grimaces.

"It was high style cuisine," Chris says. "Like you knew there was a special chef whose only job is to arrange the food artistically on the fancy porcelain plates before the waiters bring it out."

"You should be a Navy recruiter."

"I'm not lying. Later that night, Larry and I found a little train called the Peak Tram, it's the coolest thing because you get on in downtown Hong Kong, there's busy streets and traffic lights and storefronts all lit up, and it takes you up a sheer mountainside. The skyscrapers fall away behind you, and there's only this little tram car on a narrow track being pulled on a cable up through the clouds. On the mountaintop there's a bar with big windows, and they have lookout balconies with gigantic binoculars you put a Hong Kong quarter in and you can see the city, and ships on the harbor and mainland China."

"You make me want to sign up for sea duty."

"You would love Hong Kong. Do you like to shop?" Chris asks as he slides forward on his seat and rests his forearms on the table.

"Some women love to browse," Deirdre says, "but I get too tense."

"What if you'd been locked away aboard a ship for six weeks and then one morning you got dressed up and someone gave you a thousand dollars and cut you loose in a Hong Kong bazaar?"

"Silk and porcelain?"

"Yeah, and samurai swords and cork carvings and those cool fold-out partitions with Oriental scenes painted on them, and tea sets with dozens of teas to choose from. And stereos…"

"And camera equipment?"

"Tons of camera equipment, and jewelry and jade figurines. Some guys even buy motorcycles if they can stow them on the ship."

"They should let women serve on battleships."

"You can go on a supply ship."

"I'd have to reenlist."

"And no apartment," Chris says.

"I don't think I want to reenlist." Deirdre leans in and rests her elbows on the table too.

"Me neither. What are you going to do when you get out?"

"I'm not sure, I've been thinking about getting a job at a dive shop and working my way through school. What about you?"

"I'm putting money in the college fund," Chris says.

Their knees touch under the table.

"I'm a little hesitant about going to college, though."

"Why's that?" he asks.

"My friends in college are studying history and art. And that's fine if your parents are paying for it."

"What do you want to study?"

"Probably business or premed."

"What did your friends think when you joined the Navy?" he asks.

"That's when I found out who my real friends are. Four of us have been best friends since kindergarten. Margret and Ally thought it was a great idea. Ally would have signed up with me if her parents hadn't been saving for her to go to college since she was born. And Margret came to see me here a few months ago. She couldn't believe that I have my own apartment and work nine to five."

"She thought you lived in a tent, huh?"

"Yeah, and did lots of pushups. That girl went wild, every time she came on base she met guys and made dates, I saw her the first night and that was it."

"Sailors and college women." Chris smiles.

"But then there's Elizabeth," Deirdre says as if placating a bratty child. "When she went away to art school in Boston, I was envious. And when I called to tell her I joined the Navy, she practically hung up on me."

"What a bitch."

"It bothered me, but now I'm diving every weekend and having such a good time."

"You're getting me psyched up for this class. We should go diving next weekend after I'm certified."

"I'll line up a charter for us."

Right then the lights over the patio go out.

"It's midnight," Deirdre says.

"It's been a long time since I talked with anyone like this." Chris is suddenly aware that they'd practically crept over the small table towards each other and now the seconds are expanding. He's acutely aware of a hollow spot in his stomach.

She'd been telling herself not to get anything started with this guy.

He knows he should take her hand or lean in and kiss her but can't quiet the nervous voice in his head. He wishes he could negotiate a kiss, but logic stops as heat flashes across his face.

She reminds herself that he's probably getting orders back to his ship in a week, but he smiles and she figures why not.

What if I try to kiss her and she doesn't want to, he frets.

He'll be going back to his ship soon, she reminds herself. But what could be more convenient, another voice in her head persuades.

Just kiss her he tells himself. And he can't deny the warm invitation in her eyes. The look arrests him. The negotiator in his head at last shuts up. He leans closer and she leans closer and their lips meet.

Chapter 21: USS Long Beach

Every time Chris glances across a page and sees a phrase like "malignant tumor," "fractured olecranon" or "cirrhotic liver," a morbid curiosity compels him to read the personal medical affairs of dead and dying sailors. But each record he reads to the final page, the story ends in either medical discharge or death in a hospital bed. Hard core cases follow a pattern of diagnostic testing, hospital stays and often admission to a ward where machines gather around the man on his death bed. Rubber hoses penetrate his stomach and anus. Drip tubes administering sedatives attached to a needle taped in the crook of his arm. Sometimes a tracheotomy in his throat blows oxygen to his lungs. Sometimes plumbing routes his heart's blood through an electric pump.

Chris continues reading the sloppy handwriting, file after file, but it wears on him, fails to flash the vivid pictures that Allen Larsen's medical history animated in his imagination.

Hospital death seems cowardly and Chris grows board with it, until suddenly the door opens and Deirdre leads Carlos Devlin into the room.

"Wingnut!" Carlos says.

Something is different about Carlos, and Chris realizes the cast has come off. "How's the leg, shipmate?" Chris asks, realizing that words like shipmate, and phrases like Navy chow and fine Navy day have crept into his vocabulary since meeting Carlos.

Carlos leans his crutches against the copier, unhitches his belt and drops his pants around his ankles. "Skin and bone is all that's left!"

Chris and Deirdre exchange an amused glance as they crouch to take a look.

Carlos's left leg is a healthy mocha-brown covered with curly black hairs, but his right leg is shriveled like a stick of beef jerky, mottled with wrinkles and scaly patches. A thick scar runs from mid-thigh to shin over the bulging prosthetic kneecap.

"How's it feel?" Chris asks.

"Stiff and achy." Carlos bends over to pull up his pants but he can't reach, so Deirdre and Chris hoist them to mid-thigh and Carlos takes it from there. As he tucks in his shirt and buckles his belt, he says, "It'll be six weeks until I know if I'm kicked out on a medical discharge or sent back to the fleet." His black eyebrows set in a look of grim determination.

"Stick to your therapy program," Deirdre tells him, then turns to Chris. "Carlos is going to learn how to operate the copier, so if you ship out we have someone to copy records."

"It's pretty complicated," Chris says. "I don't know if a bosun can figure it out."

When Carlos limps over and sits at the desk without making a retaliatory remark, Chris knows he must be seriously worried about getting kicked out of the Navy because of his bum knee.

"I can see that I don't need to introduce you guys," Deirdre says and shoots Chris a look as she walks out.

"What's a matter, Carlos?"

"Nothing."

"Come on, you should be happy about getting that cast off."

"It ain't that, Marlow." Carlos lights a cigarette.

Chris sits on a box of copy paper and pushes aside an urge to smoke even as he watches Carlos drawing a deep drag. "What's on your mind, Carlos?"

"You wouldn't understand." Carlos blows a cloud of gray-blue smoke toward the ceiling. "Everybody knows wingnuts hate the Navy."

"I don't hate the Navy."

"No offense Marlow, but you're a Navy-hating bellyacher."

Chris's is too amused to argue.

"I've been here for months," Carlos says. "I seen lots of guys with ulcers or just fucked up because of drinking too much and they blame the Navy, but it ain't the Navy's fault."

"What are you even talking about?" Chris asks.

"I love the Navy, Marlow."

"Oh, how sweet."

"Dude, I'm from South Central."

"Los Angeles?" Chris asks.

"Hell yeah, gangs, low riders, crazy ho's, drugs. I was a gangbanger in high school but when I enrolled at the junior college so I could get a career going I found out I was a minority, a Mexican, which is bullshit, man. My mom's people were on the west coast three-hundred years ago, before it was even part of Spain. My father's father is from Ireland. He crossed the Atlantic on a ship and then he crossed the continent on a horse. He was a sailor and a cowboy. But me, shit, between the gangs keeping me down and the Anglos keeping me out, I didn't want to be on the street and I sure as hell didn't want to work at In and Out Burger. I got nothing against people." Carlos smirks, "except wingnuts that is."

"Hate wingnuts!" Chris says.

"Seriously though, this is going to suck if they kick me out and send me back to LA."

"You got family there?"

"Yeah," Carlos says, "but there's nothing in LA for me, bro."

"You could go to college."

"Please, just stop. Okay," Carlos says. "When I started sailing aboard the Cushing, that dread I felt back in South Central, it went away. I was excited for the first time in my life. You probably think it's corny, Marlow, but I ain't ashamed to say I love this uniform and the hard work and travelling all over the world with my good shipmates!"

"That's how I felt when I first joined," Chris says.

"All you gotta do is chill out when you pull into port instead of drinking like a mad dog, Marlow, you'll be fine."

The copier buzzes and Chris unloads a warm stack of duplicates.

*   *   *

The next day they're walking to the chow hall for lunch.

"I got something to show you," Carlos says.

Chris follows across the street to a bus stop.

Carlos leans on his crutches and says, "There's a ship pulled in last night."

Chris is going to ask what ship, but the shuttle arrives and they climb aboard.

It drives out the Harbor Road, past the medical hold barracks. Through barbed wire topped fences, they see battleships towering above corrugated tin warehouses.

"There she is," Carlos says as they climb off the shuttle.

Sunlight gleams off the warehouses around them.

Carlos puts his hand on Chris's shoulder and points over the warehouse roof. "The USS Long Beach," he says. "She's a nuclear-powered guided-missile cruiser."

The ship's superstructure is a rectangular steel box the size of a barn sitting atop an armored pedestal of rocket launchers, phalanx cannons and gray fixtures. A row of thick, shockproof windows looks out from high in the top of the steel box. A colossal crucifix of metal pylons support radar domes, satellite dishes and signal flags flapping in the breeze high above the ship's main deck.

Carlos leads Chris toward a gate in the fence around the warehouse.

A lady marine stands inside a sentry booth nodding as Carlos explains that he has a friend in the shipyard, and since it's lunchtime, he wants to stop by and say hello.

They show their ID cards and the marine waves them in.

Carlos whispers, "Watch yourself, Marlow. You're in blackshoe country now."

They walk through an open door into the shade of a warehouse.

"Do you really know someone here?"

"No, I just want to show you around."

Steel I-beam rafters and winches for picking up heavy equipment loom overhead. Two workers in coveralls and hardhats hold a section of steel in gloved hands while another cuts through it with a white-tipped blowtorch. Dark goggles obscure their eyes, but the blowtorch illuminates their young grease-streaked faces. Another crew, each person working a rattling needle gun, strip the paint off a long section of steel bulwark. At the far end of the warehouse, beyond stinking vats of paint striper and molten zinc, they enter a corridor lit by red bulbs. They walk to the end and go through a door and out into the sunlight again, where they find themselves standing in front of a wall of gray steel, forty feet high and hundreds of feet long.

The smell of the sea is strong in their nostrils.

They're standing on a pier, and through narrow spaces between the rough-hewn timbers under their feet, Chris sees water lapping against barnacle-covered rocks. He hears two squawking gulls and looks up to see them circling overheard.

"Dry dock?" Chris asks.

"Yup." Carlos hobbles over and spins a wheel that undogs a watertight door. He steps through into a dimly lit ladderwell, and says, "Follow me, shipmate."

"You sure about this?" Chris asks as he steps through and closes the door. He follows Carlos as he makes slow progress climbing four steep ladders. At the top, Carlos spins a wheel, undogging a hatch above his head and climbs up.

"Wow!" Chris says as he emerges onto a catwalk. "Feels like I'm back on the flight deck."

From their perch atop the dry dock, they see far beyond the shipyard in every direction.

"Pearl Harbor is the largest naval command in the world," Carlos says, as they gaze out across the maze of roads, warehouses and buildings. Dozens of ships and submarines are tied to piers. In the distance, a fighter jet takes off from a runway, and beyond that, a grove of palm trees and a thin strip of white sand at the ocean's edge.

Immediately beyond the cable railing, the Long Beach, like a ship in a bottle, sits inside the gargantuan dry dock. A thin coat of green sea slime coats her black hull. Clutching the railing, Chris and Carlos walk toward the front of the ship. Her bow is fitted with a row of four Sea Sparrow rocket launchers, and her anchor chains stretch tight across her forecastle between capstans and hawseholes. They stop when they see the rip in her side. The jagged tear in the Long Beach's hull looks as if the churning sea tossed her onto a coral head, lifted her up and slammed her down again. Pipes and wires and twisted metal protrude from the crooked laceration.

"How'd that happen?"

"She went up on the rocks," Carlos says, scrutinizing the wound. "They worked their asses off to keep her from sinking. Flooded at least six compartments and were probably listing over when she came in."

"How long will it take to patch her?"

"If they were in a hurry they'd fix her in a few hours, but I bet she'll be here four or five days."

Chris shakes his head. "How often do they bang ships up like this?"

"Shit happens. It's a good thing they were only a few hours from Pearl. If they were far out in the South Pacific, they might have sunk. Coral reefs don't budge."

They lean on the rail side by side and assess the damage.

"Ever been on a ship had something like this happen?"

"No," Carlos replies, "but I fought a fire in the paint locker aboard the Cushing after some jackass was smoking dope in there."

"Damn."

"That guy died of smoke inhalation and then fire burned through three compartments."

"Where was the ship?"

"Arabian Sea."

"Were you scared?"

"Hell yeah, but it was exciting," Carlos says. "Alarms going off, lots of smoke and fire." He pauses. "Got decorated for dragging a man out."

"You saved a guy's life?"

"I did. But that's the Navy, though; if they can't convict someone, then they give out medals." Carlos laughs.

A work crew appears at the bottom of the dry dock—six men in dark blue coveralls, knee-high boots and hardhats. They are dragging a fire hose, laying it out beneath the ship's hull. They get in position, one behind the other and pick up the hose. They brace themselves as the water pressure turns on and the hose stiffens. It goes rigid and the men brace their legs and hold on. The guy at the front holding the nozzle sweeps the hose from side to side, working the powerful spray over the Long Beach's hull. They are blasting off sea slime that has grown like green hair all over the bottom of the hull.

"They won't be awarding any medals for this," Carlos says.

"Are you men authorized in this area?" a voice growls behind them.

They snap around and stand up straight at the sight of a chief petty officer scowling at them as he approaches in the narrow catwalk. He's wearing his khaki hat cocked to one side and his face is wrinkled like he's probably over forty—ancient.

"Well?" he demands.

Chris looks at Carlos.

"Actually, Chief," Carlos speaks up, "we heard about the Long Beach's accident and wanted to come over and take a look."

"Oh! You wanted to take a look huh?"

"Chief Surls," Chris reads the nametag over the chief's breast pocket, "we're here on medical hold, and, ah, all we do is pick up trash in the parking lot—"

"Honestly, Chief," Carlos cuts in, "we been picking up litter for weeks and it's boring."

"Yeah, it's boring—" Chris trails off.

The chief is still scowling.

"You miss the fleet," Chief Surls quips. Then he looks between them, into the dry dock at the hose crew blasting slime off the Long Beach's hull. "Do you men know your way to the exit, or do I have to kick your asses all the way down there?"

"We know the way, chief," Carlos says, nudging Chris toward the ladder.

They climb back down to the pier, but Chris can't shake the site of the men inside the dry dock—the sight of them bracing themselves and holding fast to the rigid hose. While walking through the noisy warehouse, Chris can still hear the water surging from that hose's nozzle, splattering against the gray steel.

"Can you hear that?" he asks Carlos.

"I hear all kinds of things."

"The hose," Chris says.

"What hose?" Carlos smirks.

But Chris can still hear it.

They walk past the marine guard and across the street to a bench where they sit side-by-side and wait for the shuttle.

Chris can't shake the sound of that hose spraying water and out of nowhere he suddenly remembers Larry being hit by the spinning propeller. The roar of pressurized water blasting from the brass nozzle fills his ears. In his mind he can see the water blasting the green slime from the battleship's black hull.

"So, you saved a guy's life, huh?" Chris asks trying to distract himself from the disturbing memory of his dead best friend.

"Sure did," Carlos says.

"What happened?"

"We were on the weather deck," Carlos continues telling his story, "and the fire was burning out of control in two compartments below us. As soon as we opened the hatch to let the first hose team climb down, black smoke poured up. The first hose team stuck a long high-pressure sprayer into the compartment and all four guys went in behind it. Boxes of plastic bags, gallons of paint and thinner and rubber wire insulation was burning and making black smoke. I was on the second hose team and had my OBA on. You know what that is?"

"Oxygen breathing apparatus," Chris replies. He'd been to firefighting school and knows how to don an OBA, load the oxygen canister.

"Right after they went," Carlos continues, "aerosol cans start popping and the water they were spraying hit a live electrical wire. The shock knocked them over and they lost control of the hose. You can't fight an electrical fire with water, so I grabbed a CO-2 bottle and followed my team leader down the hatch. All I could see in that smoke was orange flames and sparks where the wires were shorting out. The heat was so intense I thought my fireproof suit would melt."

"Hotter than hell, huh?"

"The devil's den, I shit you not. At the bottom of the ladder I stepped on Gunner Carlson, a live cable had hit him across his back and killed him. And a hull technician was crawling around in the water getting shocked, bawling like a cat with a broken tail. He had a broken arm because a cabinet full of paint cans fell on him and his OBA mask was melting to his face. I extinguished the fire. By the time they secured electrical power, my extinguisher was empty, so I snatched Logan, and he must weigh one seventy-five. I swear I never let go of the extinguisher, and I tossed Logan across my back and then charged up the ladder."

"Damn, Carlos, that's your true colors when you put someone else's life before your own." Chris puts a hand on his forehead and closes his eyes. He keeps thinking about Larry disintegrating in the blur of the spinning propeller, and at the same time he sees the work crew manning the fire hose in the bottom of the dry dock.

"Two men died in that fire but the captain still pinned medals on us," Carlos says. "You ever see a corpse? I don't mean all dressed up in a coffin at a funeral, I mean a real one."

Chis stares at the concrete curb at his feet with far away eyes and says, "My friend Larry Tynan walked into a propeller. There were four of us standing in the catwalk a few feet away but there was nothing we could do."

"Damn," Carlos whispers.

"Chief Hicks always told us that a spinning propeller—" The sight of the workers manning the hose in the dry dock persists in Chris's memory. He can't understand why the sight of them holding that fire hose stings behind his eyes. "Chief Hicks always told us that a spinning propeller—" Chris tries again but stops and looks nervously around.

Something is burning.

"Chief Hicks always told us," Chris says again. "'When the propeller is spinning it creates an optical illusion,' and he was right. It looked like you could walk next to the Hawkeye, between the fuselage and the engine. But that's where the propeller is and it spins so fast you can't see it."

"He walked into a propeller?" Carlos asks.

The smell of burned synthetic fiber fills Chris's nostrils and he looks across the street at the open warehouse door, expecting to see smoke drifting out, but there's no smoke so he exhales sharply to make the smell go away. But it doesn't go away, and he spits on the ground because now he tastes smoke in his mouth and ashes on his tongue.

"You okay, Marlow?"

Chris blinks hard, trying to clear his blurry vision. He rests his head in his hands and puts his elbows on his knees. "People get complacent when they do a dangerous job," Chris says. "The flight deck—" He stops because he can hear the water roaring from the end of the fire hose so loud it's as if he is holding the hose in his own hands. With his eyes closed he sees the shiny brass nozzle on the end of the hose. It's like a dream but he's awake.

"The flight deck is an accident waiting to happen," he says. "Larry just spaced out, you know. He tried to step back but it was too late."

Carlos says something, but to Chris it sounds like he's talking into a tin can.

Chris smells the burned flesh and the blood that went through the hot engine. Smoke is rising from a shredded piece of Larry's brown jersey.

Larry's insides are strewn across the deck.

"When they finally shut down the engine—" Chris keeps his eyes closed. "This is fucked up!"

"You okay, Marlow?"

"—what I remember is I climbed out of the catwalk with my chains over my shoulders and walked away like I was going to recover my plane and that's it. That's all I could remember." Chris lifts his head and looks at Carlos.

Chris's eyes look like ice cubes that are melting.

"—but what really happened is a flight deck director came over and yelled at us to man up. There was blood in the air like red fog. And this guy says into his headset, 'Send a corpsman up here with a plastic bag and a spatula because we got a messy fatality.'" Chris swallows but his mouth is dry and still tastes like burnt blood. "Then he ordered the four of us to take up a fire hose."

"Damn," Carlos smirks.

"The corpsmen came and they took away Larry's legs and a piece of his ribs. I can't believe I'm remembering this." A hot tear springs from Chris's eye and runs down his cheek. "We pressurized that hose and sprayed away the blood and the guts and the broken chain links. We washed down the scupper and the catwalk. It was like wet red paint. We washed what was left of him over the side."

"It's a dangerous job, Marlow, no getting around that."

"Washing a man's remains over the side?"

Right then the bus rounds the corner and they stand up.

"He was dead," Carlos says.

"Yeah, but—"

"But nothing." The shuttle's brakes squeal. "You joined the Navy to see the world and become a man, right?"

The doors fold open and the shipyard workers returning from lunch clamber out.

"Give me a break, Carlos."

They boarded the bus.

"I'm not kidding, Marlow. This is the fucking military. We're constantly pushing the envelope training to kill people, but sometimes the shit backfires and we get whacked."

They sit in the bench seats across from each other.

Chris remembers there was a chief snapping photos of the Hawkeye's blood-splattering fuselage and gore strewn across the nonskid deck. He remembers Martin Weary slinking away, so he didn't have to man up the hose. Angelo was in front, on the nozzle, but he let go and turned away to wretch. Chris stepped up and grabbed the nozzle and swept it side-to-side. A length of Larry's intestine was tangled around the Hawkeye's landing gear. A busted section of his spine washed up against the scupper and Chris pulled back on the handle on the nozzle to stop the flow of water while the corpsmen picked it up and put in the plastic bag.

Bloody shreds of Larry's brown vest and jersey were all over the deck.

Steven Oakes was mad as hell and he yelled at the chief, "Why are you taking pictures of this? Is that really necessary?"

The chief had what sailors call a shit-eating grin, and he said, "For the investigation."

Chris remembers sweeping the nozzle back and forth across the deck. Pressurized saltwater sprayed out and washed away the gore that had moments earlier been his best friend.

Saltwater sprayed from the hose and cleaned the deck, washing away what remained of Larry Tynan—washing him over the side and into the sea.

Chapter 22: Breathing Lessons

In a classroom adjacent to the rec' center's pool, Afram introduces Chris to the other three students who are taking the scuba course.

Chris shakes hands with Brian, George and Phil, three marines just out of boot camp, newly arrived at Pearl Harbor.

The marines are each about six-feet-tall with high-and-tight crew cuts and clean shaves. Each has a variation of the Marine Corps bulldog tattooed on his arm. Newly developed chest muscles bulge above their flat stomachs. They wear their Nikes laced to the top and they tuck their T-shirts into their jeans and wear belts—giving their casual attire a uniform look. They don't smoke, slouch, laugh or put their hands in their pockets. And they clip the words at the ends of their sentences as if with sharp scissors.

It's the first night of class and it's time to jump in the pool. All three marines change into identical red shorts.

Afram makes them swim twenty-five meters underwater, followed by three lengths of the pool using two different strokes. Next they tread water for fifteen minutes holding a five-pound block of black rubber, and then they have to dive from the surface down eighteen feet to retrieve the block off the bottom of the pool. The marines perform these skills without difficulty, but it takes Chris three tries to swim down and get the rubber block off the bottom.

Chris feels himself adopting the Marines' gung ho attitude—seeing everything in terms of the challenge it presents. The course becomes a mission, Afram their commander, their textbooks and dive tables are tactical plans. A scuba tank is more than a steel cylinder holding compressed air at three thousand pounds per square inch, because the marines handle the tanks as if they might explode at any moment, flinging sharp shards of steel that will tear off their limbs.

Chris and the marines go to a Honolulu dive shop to buy scuba masks, fins and snorkels. The shop owner, a red-bearded old Vietnam Veteran, admits that many of his customers are tourists, more interested in matching their swimsuits to the fins that come in lemon yellow, aqua-blue and hot pink. This simply won't do for the marines. Chris and his comrades choose standard black fins, because they are large and solid and the imaginary enemy can't spot them.

"Like Afram said," Brian reasons, "simple equipment is better. If we buy gear with gadgets on it, there's more chance of things going wrong."

"Affirmative!" George adds. "I want no problems with my gear when I'm diving."

They purchase standard Scuba Pro, low-volume, black rubber masks with oval tempered glass offering a wide field of vision. They choose the conventional J-shaped snorkels, no bright colors, pinstripes, purge valves or corrugated flexible tubing. It's that sober boot-camp mentality of function over fashion that makes them all choose the standard, high-quality gear.

The shop owner plays to their military bearing when he leads them to a glass display case that contains a selection of knives, compasses and gloves. Shunning the blades with bright colored handles and sheathes, red beard produces four oblong cardboard boxes from a drawer beneath the cabinet. "You men don't want any of that trendy fashion stuff." He waves a hand over the glass. "This is what you'll need, not only as a tool when you're down below, but as a weapon." Each box contains an eight-inch stainless steel knife, made with black, hard plastic handle, dull antireflective blade, serrated on one edge and scalpel-sharp on the other.

"Why's the finish so dull?" Phil asks. "I'd like to polish mine."

"Yeah!" Chris and the marines stop stabbing and slashing at the air.

Red Beard closes the deal when he looks slowly around at each fledgling diver and says, "Sharks are attracted to anything shiny, so if you pull out a shiny blade to defend yourself, it might bite your arm off, knife and all. That's why these dull-finish knives are issued to Navy Seals during their training on Blood Beach."

"Navy Seals?" Brain says, suddenly handling the knife like a loaded pistol.

"Seals are bad ass." Chris slides the knife into its black sheath.

All four men leave the shop with utter confidence in the quality of their new gear. If laid out among the items in their sea bags the new equipment will appear to be military issue.

Each night Afram lectures and quizzes them for an hour and a half. He covers depth, pressure, density and buoyancy, the effects on the body while breathing under water, the dive tables and corresponding equations.

He teaches them how to communicate underwater with hand signals. Follow me; Danger; I'm out of air; Let's descend; I'm cold; Let's ascend; and I'm okay—all communicated with simple hand signals.

On a long folding table, Afram displays the basic equipment which includes a depth gauge, a dive watch, spear gun and wet suit. Piece by piece he explains the use and care. He shows slides of coral and fish found in the local waters.

Every night after classroom instruction they go in the pool in buddy pairs. The first rule is 'never dive alone' and the second rule is 'keep an eye on your buddy.'

In the deep end they practice taking giant strides into the water, diving from the surface, equalizing the pressure in their ears, clearing water from inside their masks.

The hardest skill for Chris is ditching and donning. Ditching means stripping off the equipment on the bottom in the deep end, and that's easy. But donning, which means swimming back down and putting the equipment back on, seems impossible. He fails on his first two attempts.

The marines gather around him as he clings to the pool's concrete edge catching his breath. Brian hunkers down and squeezes Chris's shoulder, "Come on, sailor, we know you can do it!"

George and Phil rally him with bulldog barks and shouts of, "Just do it, squid!"

A powerful feeling of comradery sparks in his heart as he swims to the middle and treads water, then with a deep breath he dives. Pinching his nose and forcing air into his ears equalizes the pressure. He kicks toward the bottom. He closes his eyes against the stinging chlorine but again realizes that his descent has stopped. Though he claws the water he can't go any deeper. He opens his eyes and vaguely sees his equipment below. Just as he starts to panic and his lungs crave for air, he realizes it's the air in his lungs preventing him from descending any lower, so he exhales hard and descends rapidly. Now his lungs scream for oxygen, and he knows he must get to his regulator because the surface is too far above. He's afraid he'll pass out before surfacing if he turns back now. In the cloudy water, he can barely see his equipment. As he feels around for the valve and the regulator, he finds his self-confidence reaching a new height. Though his lungs ache and his thoughts want to fly into a panic, a cool self-assurance quells the fear. He finds the regulator, but doesn't stuff it in his mouth. Rather he follows the hose with his hand to the valve atop the tank. He turns the air on and clears water from the regulator, then calmly draws a breath. Methodically he dons the rest of the equipment.

*   *   *

After class, Chris and Deirdre soak in the hot tub.

Deirdre leans back on the padded edge and asks, "How's scuba?"

"Learning about the bends," Chris says languidly. "It seems kind of dangerous." Under the water, he put his hand on her thigh.

"That's nice," she says.

"Afram is a good teacher." Chris lifts his other hand out of the bubbling hot water and studies the prune-like wrinkles. He touches his neck and wonders when scales and gills will cleave his skin.

"You know something?" she asks.

"What?"

"I use to have no idea what it was like under water." Her tone dreamy. Steam rises from the bubbling tub.

Chris is about to say something but waits.

"Now I see coral gardens and caves and schools of fish, and something else. It's a mystery, though. You know what I mean?"

"What else?" he asks.

"You're a sailor. I figured you'd know. The mystery of the sea."

"King Neptune and all that?"

"Yeah," Deirdre says sliding one of her legs over his.

"Did you, like, see a mermaid or something?"

"I am a mermaid," she says.

"No you're not." He slides a hand up her thigh.

She giggles, pulls away. "I've logged over fifty dives."

"So, you're becoming a mermaid?"

"I think so. I'm getting weird notions about the ocean and the tides and the moon." She hasn't told anyone these thoughts and hopes Chris won't think she's nuts.

"What kind of notions?"

"More than two thirds of the earth is covered with water and our bodies are like ninety percent water, and the moon causes the tides to change," she glances at him through the steam. "The moon has a powerful influence on people, especially women."

"It does," he agrees.

"Life comes from the ocean. It's the womb of the planet. And the moon is constantly pushing and pulling at the ocean." She flashes her conspiratorial smile.

"Working nights on the ship sometimes they turn off all the lights and we lay outside and watch the sky, and the moon is so big you can see every pock mark on it and you can see a billion stars, so yeah I get what you're saying."

"I think the moon keeps the oceans in place," she says.

He listens.

"Gravity keeps things from floating away, right? That's basic."

He really likes that she's opening up to him, tell him her kooky ideas.

"Rocks and mountains," she says, "and cars and people and everything else stay put because of gravity, ok, I get it. No problem."

"Laws of physics," Chris says.

"Sure, but have you ever thought that it takes more than gravity to keep the oceans in place?"

"That's weird to think about," Chris says.

"Gravity exerts even pressure across the land, but how can it exert an even pressure on water? I mean, the Pacific Ocean is ten-thousand miles across."

Chris feels something in his mind moving outward.

"Gravity isn't enough to keep the oceans in place. It's the moon that prevents the oceans from peeling off the planet and floating off into space."

Chris imagines one of those pictures taken from outer space, sees the moon orbiting the earth, exerting it's push and pull on the oceans. "I think you're onto something."

"I know, right," Deirdre says. "The oceans are just a thin layer of liquid, and it just doesn't make sense to me that gravity is the only thing keeping it from floating away, peeling right off the surface of the planet and flowing off into space."

"Wow," Chris says, feeling kind of weird.

"So, obviously, the moon has to have a big effect on people because we're ninety percent water."

"Chris leans toward her with his chin an inch above the churning surface of the hot tub.

Steam rises like veils around them.

"It just makes me wonder how the moon influences people."

There's a warm invitation in both their eyes.

"The tides," Chris whispers as an irresistible force draws them together.

Chapter 23: Under the Waves

Afram's sleek speedboat is named the See Sea. Her flat bow
stretches forward from the cockpit. Down below there's a small berth,
galley and a head. A tinted windshield deflects the fast air gusting past
as the See Sea rockets across Oahu's calm coastal water.

Afram sits in the white vinyl captain's seat, the steering wheel in
one hand and the throttle in the other. A pair of Ray Bans hide his eyes,
and his long black hair blows like cracking whips in the wind.

Cliffs on Oahu's coast drop off behind them.

After a while, Afram slows the boat and shouts to the divers,
"Buddy up and do your final checks."

The boat slows and Afram climbs to the bow and drops the anchor.

Chris hoists the tank pack and buoyancy vest onto Brian's back, and
Brian does the same for him.

They double-check each other's hoses and straps.

They tighten their weight belts and slip on their fins.

Chris scans the water and glances across the cloudless sky.

The marines' rigorous behavior heightens his awareness. He
understands that the scuba class is more than learning to dive. It is
tempering his character.

The four apprentice divers sit on the speedboat's sides and Afram
shouts, "Put your regulators in, hold your mask firmly against your brow
and roll back."

Surrendering to gravity, Chris rolls backwards and water surges
over him, sliding along his spine beneath the tank. Instantly the blue-
green sea opens, engulfs him and seals smoothly over him.

The blizzard of bubbles clears and he sees the bottom not far below.
He flutters his fins and follows Brian under the hull to the anchor line.
It's a magical weightless sensation, gliding downward, like flying. He
squeezes his nose and forces air into his ears.

Soon his knees touch the sandy bottom. His depth gauge reads
thirty feet.

Afram makes the okay signal and the divers return it. Their smiles stretch around their black rubber mouthpieces, and their masks magnify their eyes to bugged-out proportions. The glass lens of Afram's depth gauge sways and sparkles in the shifting sunbeams that shine from the surface.

Chris turns his head, searching in every direction. Though he can see quite far in the gin-clear water, there's no coral or kelp or fish nearby.

One by one, Afram makes each student throw his regulator behind his back and remove his mask. Chris recovers the regulator, puts it in his mouth, clears it and takes a deep breath with no trouble. But salt water seeps into his eyes before he puts his mask on.

Next, Afram swims to the surface with each student on a simulated emergency ascent. When Chris pops above the surface, a breeze blows cool on the side of his head. Sunlight glares in his eyes and the choppy waves toss him about. When he goes back under, that few seconds of wind and sunshine above magnify the silent spaciousness of the undersea realm.

For over an hour, Afram works them through basic scuba skills.

Back on the See Sea, they do giant strides off the bow and backward rolls from the cockpit. Rooster tails of seawater splash the decks each time a diver plunges through the surface. And each time one removes his fins and climbs up the ladder, seawater sluices from his equipment-clad body and splashes the deck.

Afram gathers them around. "According to our dive tables," he explains, "we can do two dives to thirty-five feet repetitively and not have to decompress or spend more than a few minutes in the surface interval, but you should always take a rest between dives. So, while I move us to another site, you guys switch the gear over to your second tank."

*　　*　　*

With the boat anchored in at a new location, Afram quizzes them on their plan, their equipment and ways to conserve air.

"Always expect the unexpected." Afram's confident tone imparts years of experience. He hunkers on the deck, gathers them around and sees the raw ambition in their faces. "There are common hazards like sharp coral, sea urchin spines and stinging jellyfish. You might have a leaky hose or a strong current could separate you from your dive buddy. Don't panic." Afram pauses. "I can't possibly tell you about all the problems divers encounter, but I'll tell you two things that will greatly reduce the risks present on every dive. First, plan your dive according to the checklist in your book, and if too many problems occur, cancel the dive. And second, wherever you find a reputable dive charter so you can dive with people who know the area. Practice these two things and you'll be okay."

They make a second dive to 30-feet. They practice entries and exits, ascents and descents, neutral buoyancy, clearing their masks, recovering their regulators, ditching and donning and communicating with hand signals.

While resting on the boat during the surface interval they eat bananas, mangos, fresh rolls. They drink apple-cranberry juice. They set up their third tanks for their final training dive.

Throughout the day, Chris's self-confidence bounces higher than it ever has. When Afram asks him a question, he answers with a calm self-assurance that he has never felt before. He handles his equipment with knowledgeable poise and steady hands.

Afram fosters a professional and friendly environment aboard the See Sea. He tells stories about his boyhood on an island in the Philippines, learning to skin dive and spearfish with primitive equipment. When he was fifteen, his father moved the family to Manila. He learned wreck diving on the mangled steel hulks of Japanese destroyers in Manila Bay. When his father moved the family to Oahu, Afram earned his Master Diver Certification before he turned 21. For several years he hunted for lost shipwrecks around the Hawaiian Islands. Occasionally wealthy Australians, Americans and Chinese hired him to come aboard their yachts and lead them on expeditions to wrecks and caves between Hawaii and Midway.

Chris's mind swirls with images of millionaires on treasure hunting expeditions. He asks, "How'd you connect with people like that?"

"I took a photographer to a wreck I'd found and his pictures got some attention from National Geographic. Then he came back and chartered a three-month trip to photograph wrecks and reefs across the Pacific. He dropped my name a few times in his articles and word got around." Afram's smile beamed. "Well, the next thing I know, a

Frenchman calls up and says the Cousteau Society needs a local guide, they're shooting a documentary on undersea volcanoes."

How lucky, Chris thinks. But no, a new thought pushes across his mind. Afram's not lucky; he worked hard and prepared himself for an opportunity when it came along.

"Now we'll do a compass dive," Afram tells the guys, who dig into their bags and pull out their wristband compasses. "We'll start with two thousand five hundred PSI, so when we get to fifteen hundred we have to head back."

In pairs, the divers do giant strides off the bow and splash through the crystal-clear surface. When the frenzy of bubbles clears, they release air from their vests and descend along the anchor line. Afram pulls them together into a group near the ocean floor, where they set their compass bearings. Then they swim above the sandy bottom side-by-side.

A school of silver-gray sardines swims around them. Ahead, a coral reef appears. The reef is an oasis on the bottom of the sea. Purple lacework sea fans spread themselves against the subtle currents. The fans look fragile but Chris is surprised when he touches one and finds it as hard as bone.

The divers move along the reef. Every few feet a deep crack dashes the rock floor. Calcified pinecones, brittle to the touch, sprout from mauve-pigmented algae carpets. Tubers, fire coral and unidentifiable geometric skeletal structures grow from the chaos of rocks and ancient hardened lava. Tiny pores on the algae-coated rocks close as the divers swim over, changing the rocks from pink to rusty brown. Undulating tentacles of sea anemones cover the walls of deep narrow crevices.

Afram stops at a rock ledge and peers over as if expecting something special. Chris and the marines follow and there in a sandy dish a stingray hovers inches above the sand, quivering rhythmically like an idling magic carpet. When the divers creep over the ledge, the ray bolts, leaving them in a cloud of sand.

Their compass heading takes them along a rocky outcrop on the edge of the reef.

Something pinches Chris's calf and he turns around startled to find Brian pointing excitedly.

A school of giant grouper are swimming straight at them.

About a half dozen of the enormous fish, each several feet long and thick, are black around the eyes and mouth, and purple over the rest of their bodies. The closest one pokes at the bottom with thick black lips. It sucks a broken chunk of slime-covered coral into its mouth, puckers a few times and spits the coral out bone-white. The carefree way they keep coming closer, Chris wonders if they are unaware of the divers' presence. Then suddenly, when they are only a few feet away one of the fish faces the divers and freezes. A warning spreads through the school.

Fish and divers face off.

Gills undulate.

Divers inhale and exhale through mechanical regulators.

All at once, the big creatures turn and swim away, fading in the whitish-blue wash of watery sunbeams.

Afram moves in front, looks at his watch and goes around the group to check air supply. They're at about 1,500 PSI, so they head back.

Disappointed, Chris realizes that the bottle of air on his back allows for an all-too-brief visit below the waves.

*   *   *

At the marina, Chris rinses the gear with a hose on the dock and the marines load it into Afram's van.

"In about a month the diving school's headquarters in San Diego will mail you a laminated scuba diver ID card. You'll need it to fill tanks and rent gear," Afram says as the guys gather around. "Now you are certified for open water diving. Remember this is the most basic level and it qualifies you to dive under ideal conditions. While you're here on Oahu go diving with experienced charters and check out the beautiful dive sites."

Chris feels a powerful sense of achievement knowing that Afram has initiated him into the mysteries of the deep. And not only that, he's completed his mission along with three rugged young marines.

Chapter 24: The Shoreline

Deirdre pulls up at the marina in her blue Toyota Celica. The black tinted windows and chrome trim sparkle in the sun. Her driver's side window lowers with smooth precision.

"Hey, sailor, need a ride?" she asks.

He walks around to the passenger side and climbs in. The evening is off on a smooth note. They drive on a curvy road skirting Oahu's southwestern shore. Off on the horizon the orange sun is perched above the frothy tops of incoming waves.

Chris tells her about his encounter with the stingray and the giant grouper.

Her face beams with a knowing smile.

Her perfume reminds him of the first time he drank sangria at a house party in Visalia, California.

She pushes her hair back and he thinks maybe she has on a bit of makeup. She wears a loose cotton blouse, faded in the seams with onyx snaps undone at the neck to reveal a lacy white cotton bra with tiny, blue flowers. A braided brown leather belt circles through the loops on her white cotton Levis. She has a relaxed, summer-evening air about her that brings Chris's thoughts continuously back to that first pitcher of sangria.

A road sign says Pukano Point.

"You're going to like this place," she says, turning onto a dirt road.

*   *   *

The big house use to stand on Mabini Street in Manila until 1899 when its owner, a wealthy Spaniard who owned sugarcane plantations, had it dismantled and shipped to Honolulu and reconstructed for his wife on a lot downtown. It stood there for over forty years, until the morning of December 7, 1941 when the Japanese attacked Pearl Harbor. A seaman on the USS Maryland fired a deck-mounted antiaircraft gun at the Japanese planes, but several shells missed and fell on Honolulu.

One shell blasted most of the house to pieces. Eight bedrooms, the living room and the library burned to the ground, but the Honolulu Fire department saved the foyer and the kitchen. A few years later, what was left of the structure was purchased by an enterprising restaurateur who moved it yet again to a new location.

Now, propped on coral boulders, the Shoreline Restaurant looks to Chris like an ancient hull washed ashore in a storm. Hemp nets, cork floats and wooden oars nailed to the outside give the place a nautical ambience.

Stunted palms circle the lanai.

A staunch, bronze Hawaiian man plays his guitar in slack key style, strumming the loose strings with calloused fingers

Across the patio, Chris and Deirdre sit at a small table.

"Afram told me to wait until I get to the Philippines to buy diving equipment."

"Why?"

"Great prices on base over there."

"Probably no taxes."

The waitress sets a platter of kapu-weke (forbidden redfish over mango slices) on the table. Deirdre requests another set of strawberry daiquiris.

Chris serves the food onto their plates and says, "Since I met you, good things are happening."

"Really?" She sounds evasive.

"I went from the litter-pickup crew to scuba class."

"It's just island life."

"This fish is excellent."

"I know."

He savors a succulent slice of mango, swallows and says, "Forbidden redfish tonight and another diving adventure tomorrow."

The waitress delivers the daiquiris.

Deirdre lifts hers and says, "To another shitty day in paradise."

"I'll drink to that." Chris lifts his glass.

They drink.

"Where are we diving tomorrow?" he asks.

"It's a surprise."

"We're supposed to make a dive plan," Chris protests.

"All I'm telling you is we'll see a shipwreck at ninety-five feet and then we'll make a shallow dive on some lava tubes."

"Ninety-five feet?" He sips his drink. "Am I allowed to do that?" He's being serious but she isn't.

Her eyes, smiling over the goblet of slush, wipe away his worries.

"Nothing to it," she says. "We jump off the boat and go down. It's that simple.

"Yeah, but—"

"We're going with one of the best dive charters on the island and since you just finished Afram's class you're fresh on all the precautions."

"Okay, surprise me." He resigns himself to her plan.

"Doesn't diving make you hungry?" she asks.

"Yea, and what's that all about?"

"Your stomach compresses when you go down and then it expands when you come back up."

"When we got to the marina I was starving."

They finish their dinner listening to the mellow twangs of the guitar and order another round of daiquiris and vanilla ice cream with crushed Macadamia nuts and chocolate sauce.

Afterward, they dance a slow waltz, the only couple on the wide lanai.

On the drive back, Deirdre tells him about her underwater photography class. She says it starts in a week and she already purchased some of the equipment.

Knowing they will be leaving for the Honolulu Yacht Club early in the morning makes Chris want to invite himself to stay at her apartment, but he's too shy to say it. The problem with asking such a loaded question is it opens up the possibility of an awkward rejection. He wishes he could simply tell her he wants to sleep with her and, and— anxiety mounts in his stomach, making it difficult to figure out what to say. Part of him wants to go to her place and strip each other but he suspects they'd wake up feeling awkward. Another part of him wants to sleep alone at the barracks after a good night kiss, knowing they'll still be friends tomorrow.

"We have to get an early start," he says.

She stops at a red light as they enter Pearl City. "The boat leaves at eight," she says, wondering how he'll behave if she takes him home. She hates that she can't suggest that he stay at her place. It'll give him the idea that I want to have sex, she thinks, as she proceeds through the intersection. Maybe he's not even that attracted to me. Why is sex always the issue, she wonders, wouldn't it be nice to wake up and go diving after just sleeping together.

He wants to explain his conflicting thoughts, but tells himself, I have to be subtle and smooth. It'd be cool to sleep on her sofa. She's the smartest, most fun and daring and best looking woman I've ever met. Why ruin it because your damn hormones take over? "I'd like to stay at your place tonight," he blurts and instantly wished he could take it back. In an attempt to dress up the ugly thing he'd thoughtlessly uttered, he quickly adds, "But don't get the wrong idea." And instantly regrets having opened his mouth again. He places his hand on top of hers on the Celica's stick shift.

She rescues him from himself by saying, "I'd like you to stay over, Chris." She's tempted to say nothing more and just take him home and have sex. "But, don't get the wrong idea."

"Cool." His anxiety dissipates.

*   *   *

Dive textbooks and underwater photo equipment overflow from the coffee table onto the floor. Two scuba tanks, a buoyancy vest, fins, snorkel, driftwood, dried out corals are strewn across the living room carpet. A bright yellow wet suit sits in an upholstered chair with matching booties and gloves in its lap.

Chris sits on the couch.

Deirdre sits beside him and hands him a large, glossy photograph. "This was taken during a dive on the Mahi wreck." In the photo, Deirdre looks out through a big square hole cut in the minesweeper's hull. Her hair floats all around her, and her excited eyes contrast sharply with the wreck's black interior. "After the Mahi was scuttled, divers cut these square holes in the hull. They're great access for wreck divers and frames for underwater portraits."

"Nice. How deep are you?"

"Hundred and forty feet."

"And it's still so bright!"

"The sunlight shines all the way down. You can see two hundred feet in every direction even at this depth."

"Amazing," Chris says.

A carpet of blue-green algae, black mossy blotches and scaly reddish-brown rust covers the wreck.

"These are Moorish idols." Deirdre points to a constellation of yellow, black-banned fish shaped like spearheads hovering above her in the picture.

"There's so many colors that you've never seen on land."

"These are sea perch." She points to a group of fish shimmering in the camera's flash like blue-tinted tin foil.

"I didn't even notice them!"

"There's something in their scales that makes them change color according to the amount of light in the water around them." She puts the photo back into an envelope. "I borrowed all this stuff from the lady who teaches the photo class," she indicates the clear Plexiglas boxes on the table and the strobe. She picks up one of the boxes and unfastens the access panel. She shows Chris how the rubber gaskets make it watertight. The crazy daring that always glows like a neon halo about her dims. Her scheming eyes focus on the camera as she fits it snugly inside the Plexiglas box. Her voice takes on a serious tone as she explains how to operate the camera's shutter and film advance with the box's watertight control levers.

Glancing about the room, he sees all her gear and realizes these healthy adventurous activities can displace his drinking and smoking. He sits on the couch and runs a hand over the top of his head and feels sand and salt in his hair. Scenes from the afternoon's coral reef flicker in his mind. While he listens to Deirdre explain the basics of underwater photography, it occurs to him again that scuba has already started offsetting his addictions. Breathing easy, he relaxes there on the couch next to the girl.

*   *   *

Without turning on the lights, Deirdre strips off her clothes and slips under the sheet.

Chris pulls off his shirt and drops his jeans to the floor. It's cool next to her. He places a hand on her hip.

Her hand settles on his, and he feels her press it there, silently telling him not to move it. Then her hand grazes his forearm and rests on his shoulder.

Lust swarms inside him.

Their eyes adjust and they see each other in the dark.

"Good night, Chris," she says.

"Good night," he whispers.

She gives him a quick peck, half on the lips.

It's over before he realizes it happened. His lust spikes and then gradually subsides.

After a few minutes, her breathing falls into a steady rhythm.

Chapter 25: USS Brewster

The way they're carrying on about Singapore and Hong Kong, Chris figures the eight British divers have come east on holiday from England. They're a garrulous group with their highbrow accents and peals of laughter. Middle aged, the Brits stick to themselves with curt hellos and lots of inside jokes.

Roy and Betty from Arizona introduce themselves to Chris and Deirdre. They're on a second honeymoon.

A Samoan woman in white jeans and a bikini top buddies up with an elderly, white-haired man. They have net bags, spools of line and spotlights. The Samoan woman's jeans are ripped into fringes up to her knees and the strips are braided together.

After arranging their gear on the afterdeck, Chris and Deirdre climb forward by clinging to chrome bits mounted outboard on the boat's cabin and stepping along a narrow weather deck to the bow.

Once outside Honolulu's small harbor, the captain pushes the throttles forward and the bow rises out of the water. The boat rockets onto the open ocean.

It takes an hour to reach the dive site, motoring on the tranquil water, under a blue sky shot full of golden-white sunshine.

The water's surface reflects the sky like a flawless mirror.

The captain maneuvers the boat around and then sticks his head from the cabin and shouts to Chris, "Shipmate, lend a hand and toss the anchor over the side!"

Chris scrambles forward to where the captain pointed at a wooden crate on the bow. He lifts the lid and inside there's a crusty anchor and a length of chain. Grabbing it with both hands, he looks back over his shoulder.

"Toss her over!" the captain says.

Chris does and watches the anchor splash on the surface and disappear as the chain clatters from the crate.

The captain cuts the engines and climbs down to brief the divers. "We're directly over the shelf," he tells everyone gathered around. "There's a network of lava tubes at sixty-five feet. Don't go inside without lights and safety lines, and please don't break the corals. The bow of the Brewster lies out from the wall on the sandy bottom in ninety-five feet of water, and her twisted stern hangs over the bottomless shelf at a hundred and sixty-five. You should know but I'll tell you anyway, if you dive her stern you'll need to decompress before surfacing. Everyone keep an eye on your buddy."

Chris hits the water, the bubbles clear and he's paralyzed by the view. He feels like a bird perched on the highest part of the ceiling inside a massive opera house. His vision penetrates the crystal-clear water hundreds of feet in every direction before tapering out into murky blue-green. Thirty feet down the crest of a sheer cliff, and further below at ninety-five feet sits the coral-encrusted wreck of the USS Brewster. Rusted cables hang from her railings. Corroded anchor chains stretched tight across her forecastle and her anchors hang in the hawseholes on her bow. The deckhouse windows stare up at him like dark eyes from the deep. Her hull is split open amidships and her aft section lays twisted and dangling over a dark cliff.

The British divers descend like tiny toy action figures. Air bubbles quivering like beads of mercury ascending quickly, quietly as they exhale and descend further.

Roy and Betty come into view below. They hold hands and flutter their fins lazily as they descend toward the cliff.

Deirdre clasps his hand as she floats beside him. Her lips stretch around her regulator and her eyes glance this way and that. She holds up the okay signal.

Hastily he returns the sign and releases a hush of air from his vest. He pinches his nose and forces air into his ears.

They descend feet first.

The crest of the cliff glides past and there's Roy and Betty stopped to explore corals growing on the wall.

Chris feels the water pressing on him. His mask mushed against his face, and he has to concentrate to keep his breathing steady.

At sixty-five feet, the Samoan lady and the old man hover in the dark mouth of a lava tube. She swims gracefully, her movements fluid and relaxed. On the boat she appeared uncoordinated, almost clumsy when handling her equipment, but here in the gravity-defying atmosphere, the water holds her suspended and gives her a smooth gracefulness, a beauty she was robbed of in the air above. Her black hair drifts about her head and her white jeans ruffle and billow with the currents exiting the cave. Weightless and without effort she and the old man tie off their lines to protruding jags of rock and disappear behind beams of light shining from their powerful lamps.

Still forcing air into his ears, Chris looks at his depth gauge. The black needle on the dial moves slowly from seventy to eighty to ninety and stops as he and Deirdre's fins touch the bottom lightly at ninety-five feet.

They exchange okay signals and she points toward the ship.

They push off with their knees, flutter their fins and fly up to the cable railing along the main deck. Deirdre suddenly grabs his wrist and Chris feels a tremor of fear. Her free hand points to the ship's dark cabin.

A dozen yellow fish dart out of the big empty window frames followed by several startled, much larger, silver fish. Then a shark appears in the window. It effortlessly chomps one of the silver fish in half, the head flopping end over end to the deck.

The gray shark, a giant beast, slides from the cabin, out through one of the window frames. It hovers there chewing its prey, oblivious to the cloud of chum around its mouth. With a flick of its tail and a torque of its sandpaper-skinned body, it darts over the rail and descends below the line of the hull and is gone.

Unable to communicate their excitement, they look into each other's masks and see amazement magnified in each other's eyes.

For several minutes, neither of them strays far from the rail. They examine the rust-crusted anchors and marvel at how the moss-like growth on the ship's steel deck changes color when their shadows fall on it. Chris waves his arms and watches it change from gold to brown and back to gold again.

After a short time exploring the forward deck and peeking in the windows where the shark had come from, Deirdre indicates her watch and signals that they should ascend. They kick their fins, fly over the sandy bottom and slowly rise along the coral-covered wall. They see vibrant magenta, flame and white anemones. Black urchins and nameless scaly swags of sea life cling in the rocky crags. Loner fish patrol close inside the crevices, protecting their nooks, investigating everything that floats by. Sand and bits of broken shell rest in balcony-size ledges that jut from the ancient wall.

A fish the size of a pineapple swims slowly past. It's all black including its eyes, but blue gems embedded in the tips of its quarter-sized scales twinkle as if a neon light glows inside. The fish winks its onyx eye as it swims past.

Several starfish cling to the pocked conglomerate.

In a deep gash, where the wall splits open and grows dense with colorful corals, Chris glimpses a huge open clamshell and a pink wad of flesh inside before it clicks shut with smooth precision. He knows clams don't have eyes, but he's sure it has detected him because of the way it clicks shut the instant he sees it.

Moments slipped by and Chris relaxes in the soft watery lulls that rub the monolithic seascape. As alien as this subterranean world seems, his aqualung equipment imparts a primal feeling, a certainty that his life began millions of years ago in the sea.

The Samoan woman appears in her flowing beauty from the lava tube. She and the old man have nets full of crustaceans, probably an island delicacy.

Chris and Deirdre follow them upward into the bright sunlight at the top of the wall. The hull of the boat with the ladder descending behind it floats above. They wait while the woman and the old man climb aboard.

Deirdre grabs the bottom rung of the ladder with one hand and yanks off her fins with the other. Chris does the same. As he clears the surface, he takes the regulator from his mouth and says, "Do you believe the size of that shark?" Salt water streams off them and their equipment. They sit on the bench seats and swing their tanks into the racks, unbuckle their weights and packs, unclip their vests and look at each other wide eyed.

"It could have bit you in half!" Deirdre says.

"It made a snack of that fish. Do you think it saw us?"

"I don't know. Their eyesight isn't too good."

"That was scary," Chris says.

"We played it cool, though," Deirdre says as if they just got back from a walk in the park.

They take their sack lunches and climb forward to the bow where they rub Bain de Soleil on each other's shoulders.

Deirdre pulls a big wedge of Edam and a banana from her bag. Chris sips cranberry juice and opens a strawberry yogurt.

The boat cruises slowly on the calm water. Several long thin clouds float in the sky. The sun sends intense heat in clear white rays.

*   *   *

From the deck, they see the reef 40-feet below. The Brits are jumping in two at a time. Holding hands, Deirdre and Chris take the giant stride together.

She flies a few feet above the reef with her hands at her sides and legs kicking gracefully. He follows into a wide coral trench and flies above her as they chase a school of sea perch. The silvery fish swim forward, freeze, swim forward and freeze again.

Deirdre exhales bubbles that grow quickly to the size of basketballs and explode against Chris's face and neck. They sizzle into thousands of tiny bubbles and race around his mask and his ears as they rise to the surface. He gazes on her strong shoulders and her waist.

She's so brassy the way she leads him into this adventure, he realizes, the way she gravitates towards danger. The way she takes what she wants from life.

At the end of the trench, the coral opens into a wide canyon. Above them, near the ridge, three silver barracuda hover ominously. The largest has several painful-looking fishhooks stuck in its jaw.

Sunlight streams through a crack in the coral cliff. They cross the deepest part, keeping an eye on the barracuda. They swim through a hole in the wall and come out in a patch of maroon sea fans. Deirdre points to small fish darting out from nooks and crannies, nibbling at debris stuck in the fans.

Chris follows her into a lava tube. Off in the darkness he thinks he can see man-eating sea monsters and bottomless caverns descending into black, airless graves.

Deirdre stops.

Chris sidles up beside her and sees in the dim light the head of a dark green moray eel protruding from a gnarled crack. It slithers out of the darkness, wiggling through the water like a snake slithering across the ground. Its vulture-like beak and white eyes scare Chris, but he stays still. Afram had told him morays are friendly and they only eat what is already dead. The eel comes right up to him, and Chris shudders as it darts into the opening in the front of his vest. Before he knows it, the serpent slips under his arm and around his back. The slimy skin wiggling beneath his air tank nearly sends Chris bolting to the surface, but he doesn't dare move for fear that he'll spook the damn thing and cause it to bite him. It coils itself around him and pops its head out from under his arm. It looks from side to side, its jaw slowly opening and closing as if smiling. It's obviously enjoying itself. Deirdre gives Chris an enthusiastic okay sign, which he does not return because he wants the creature to go back to its crack in the wall. Gently, Chris flutters his fins and slowly moves away, trying not to squeeze the eel or arouse its fighting instincts. It must sense Chris's departure, because it slithers out from between the nylon straps, uncoiling itself from around his torso, and returns to its home in the rocks.

They exit the lava tube where the reef abruptly ends. The sandy bottom spreads away like a flooded desert. The surface above looks like a zillion shifting, rippling, blue and white chips of precious stone. The sunrays refract in a helter-skelter kaleidoscope of broken light beams and the sandy bottom is an ever-changing array of laser-white scribbles.

Deirdre hovers above Chris as he leads them back across the reef. His square shoulders and triceps stand out against the multicolored corals below. She likes his narrow waist and compact buns and giggles at the sight of tendons stretching the skin on the backs of his bony knees. He stops here and there to study a fish or coral formation.

Chris hovers below the boat as Deirdre ascends to the ladder. From across the reef he sees a queer looking fish approach. It stops a few feet away. Initially, he feels sorry for it because it has hideous yellow-green flesh stretched painfully over a hammer-claw bulge protruding from its brow. Bony knobs like stunted horns sprout from the sides of its head. Its body tapers back to a tail that bends upwards in a complete U-turn that makes it look like a deep-sea saxophone. Chris cannot detect eyes in the fish's head only a rash of black dots speckling its yellow-green skin. Tiny fins like frantically flapping hummingbird wings stir from its white underbelly. His sympathy goes out to the fish because he feels certain that it is a freak of nature. It will never be the gourmet centerpiece, filleted on a plate next to a serving of saffron rice. He wants to pet it, to comfort it somehow. As if the fish detects Chris's friendly intentions, it advances to within inches of his face. He looks at the poor creature and feels it trying to connect with him, perhaps befriend him, when suddenly the whole of its hammer-claw face retracts to reveal dozens of spiny, toothpick-sized teeth. Menacingly the creature opens it jaw slowly. Every muscle in Chris's body tightens. He inhales a huge breath through the scuba regulator, as the creature's stirring hummingbird fins move it closer until he feels it disturbing the water near his neck. He exhales violently and kicks toward the surface, afraid the damn thing is about to bite him.

As Deirdre helps him off with his tank, he says, "I was just threatened by a fish!"

"What happened?"

They rinse their gear and lay it out on the bench. As he describes the creature, she giggles. He tries to remain serious, but Deirdre has stripped off all but her bikini, and seeing her now on the boat in the sunlight, his tension vanishes. She whips her hair back straight from her smooth brow and her casual sexiness relaxes him.

They climb to the privacy of the bow and lean against the hot cabin windows as the captain accelerates toward shore.

They hold hands as the boat careens across the water's cool blue surface.

Chapter 26: Shark Steak

Deirdre pulls over and they climb out of the car.

Standing on the side of the road, they gaze across a pineapple plantation sloping downhill toward the sea while the sunset lights the sky in the shades of a ripe peach.

After contented sighs and a kiss, they hop in the car and drive to the North Shore. It's dark when they park in front of the Belly Buster. The beach is deserted. A man jogs by with two golden retrievers trotting beside him.

"It's up this way," Chris says.

They cross the street and walk up the dirt road as a crowd of people descend towards them, several carrying flaming Tiki-torches. Others have wicker baskets, jugs of wine, guitars and bongo drums.

"Is that Chris?"

"Jack," Chris says.

Several women have hibiscus flowers in their hair. A few of the guys wear leis.

"This is my friend Deirdre," Chris says.

"Aloha!" Jack says with a welcoming smile.

"Aloha," Deirdre says.

"Aloha," several members of the group greet them.

"Big Chief!" Jack says to Chris, "You're just in time for a shark bake luau on the beach." Jack passes one of his baskets to Chris, and the parade continues.

"Hi Chris," Marsha says.

"Aloha," Chris says, "this is my friend Deirdre."

"Aloha," the ladies greet each other.

"We were wondering when we would see you again," Marsha says. "You've got perfect timing."

"A shark, huh?" Deirdre asks.

"A six-footer," Marsha says. "It's been baking for three hours."

"Imagine," Deirdre gnashes her teeth at Chris, "baked shark for dinner."

The procession continues down the dirt road and stops as an old pickup truck drives by on the deserted blacktop road.

On the beach, Jack and Marsha rake the sand away from a long mound ringed with rocks.

Someone lights a bonfire. Others stake the torches around.

Two guys tune their guitars.

Under the sand, a layer of steaming palm fronds. Jack and Marsha peel back the big leaves to reveal a baked shark on hot bricks and smoldering coals. A tall man with a big brown belly, straight black hair and dark eyes, sets a large pot of mashed sweet potatoes in the coals. The big man brandishes a knife and cuts a deep gash along the shark's back. The flanks separate with a smooth melting motion to reveal long shark steaks. Paper plates and plastic forks and knives are passed around. A bowl of juicy sliced pineapples appears. Each person takes a scoop of sweet potatoes, a slab of shark steak, a few slices of pineapple. Jugs of white wine follow a sleeve of paper cups. Everyone sits in a big circle around the fire.

Deirdre sits close beside Chris. "This is wonderful," she whispers, and he notices she has a hibiscus blossom tucked behind her ear.

After a minute, Jack stands up and says in a loud voice, "Not everyone here knows each other, and many of you visiting from the mainland need to meet your Hawaiian brothers and sisters. So, here goes. You all know Marsha, my wife, and," Jack takes a deep breath and proceeds by pointing an open hand at each person around the fire, "our friends Ray and Dotty are from Big Sur. Marko, Lee and Terry are my neighbors. Marko caught tonight's shark with Teri on the boat today. Thanks guys." There's a cheer and appreciative hand clapping from all. "Chris and Deirdre our friends from Pearl Harbor, we're happy to have crashing the luau, and Doug and John from Florida who have come to ride some large waves, Sara and," Jack rolls his eyes toward the sky as if the next woman's forgotten name is written in the stars, "Jessica, from Colorado. Liz, Tina, and Al from Maui. Ben, Hannah and Nathan our friends from Portland, Oregon, and Peggy and Tom from Marsha's new job!" Jack takes a bow then sits, as everyone around the fire greets each other.

Then for a few moments, only the sound of crashing waves and crackling fire as everyone digs into their food.

More people arrive with wine and logs that are immediately stacked on the fire. A golden glow flickers across the sand. A big dude with a pair of bongos falls in beside the guitar players and the rhythms take on a tribal bounce. People are up and milling around.

"Congratulations on your new job," Chris says to Marsha.

"It's nice to see you enjoying island life," Marsha says.

He tells her about the scuba lesson and describes the encounter with the school of giant grouper.

"What does the Navy call this special assignment you're on?" Marsha asks.

"Medical hold," Deirdre buts in, "if you can believe that."

"First surfing, now scuba and luaus," Marsha teases.

"What next, Chris?" Deirdre asks. "Outrigger canoe racing?"

"I'll try anything," he quips.

"Did he tell you about surfing the big waves?" Marsha asks.

"He said he took lessons from your husband," Deirdre says.

"I thought he'd be too embarrassed to tell anyone."

"Embarrassed?" Deirdre gives Chris a look.

"I'm not embarrassed." He restrains a smile.

"He rode the big waves," Marsha says.

"I should tell the guys on medical hold about this," Deirdre says.

Chris crosses his arms on his chest and feels stupid thinking about the little hernia Major Burkham found on his stomach.

"To be fair," Marsha says, "Chris did good on the first one until it started to break and toss him over the falls as they say."

"Over the falls," Deirdre laughs.

"Instead of diving off the back as it curled over, Chris rode up to the crest." Marsha waves her hands over her head to animate the catastrophe. "It's like going over a waterfall."

"Wow." Deirdre is impressed.

"He tumbled inside the breaker."

Both girls laugh at Chris's expense.

Jack walks over and sees Chris is the only one not laughing, so he starts right in. "You have to give him credit for going back out there," Jack says.

Chris smirks, leery of this false praise.

Marsha's laughter gains a second wind when Deirdre, quite impressed, says, "You tried again?"

"More than once," Chris says proudly.

Jack recounts Chris's second pummeling by the big waves.

"Then I started getting the hang of it!"

"Did you surf one all the way in?"

"I figured out how not to go over the falls," he admits.

"How's that?"

"Either burrow like a mole through to the back of the wave," Jack says as he pours Deirdre some more wine. Chris declines the jug. "Or if you're at the top when the wave starts to break, you dive off the back."

When Deirdre and Marsha drift into conversation with some other people, Jack says, "You know Chris, I feel bad about laying that pollution rap on you."

Chris is amazed when he realizes Jack is concerned about him, because it's unusual for anyone to be concerned about him.

"Don't get in trouble with the Navy," Jack says. "I'm sure they have cruel punishment for a sailor with a bad attitude."

"You made me realize I'm completely out of touch with the ocean and that's no good for a sailor."

"Yeah, but now you're into surfing and scuba, huh?"

"I took a class and made some dives."

"You gonna stay on the island for a while?"

"I don't know. My doctor'll send me packing soon."

"Where you going?" Jack asks.

"Philippines probably."

"There's a country with excellent aquatics. You'll love it. Be sure to stop by before you take off, okay."

"I will," Chris says.

Chris and Deirdre split another shark steak and a juicy slice of pineapple. They sit by the fire eating and talking with all sorts of people who mingle around the luau.

They dance to a few songs, Chris holding her around the waist, her hands on his shoulders. They sway as the guitarist strums a tune, backed by bongos and crashing waves.

The fire burns low, but moonlight and twinkling stars glow on the edges of the clouds and reflect on the expansive ocean.

A light breeze blowing in from the sea, sand strains through Chris and Deirdre's toes as they sway slowly to the music.

A while later they walk along the beach in ankle-deep surf, the fire and the luau fading into darkness behind.

Deirdre suddenly runs and Chris runs after her. Laughing, she dives into a crashing wave.

The water is warm.

They swim out beyond the breakers to where their toes can barely touch the sandy bottom.

Chris plunges under, grabs Deirdre's ankle.

She dives under and grabs his wrist.

They surface in an embrace and kiss while the waves carry them in to where they can stand.

Their mouths are salty.

They hold each other close.

Chris snaps the clasp on the back of her bikini top.

She pulls the string loose on his trunks.

They run their hands over each other.

He lifts her and she wraps her legs around, welcoming him.

Embraced by gentle waves in silver moonlight.

Chapter 27: USS Arizona

After the zero eight hundred muster on Monday morning, Christopher Marlow and Carlos Devlin sign out and leave the annex, but they don't hop on the shuttle bus bound for Tripler Army Hospital. Instead, they start walking across the base.

"I'm crazy for letting you talk me into this," Carlos complains, as he hobbles on his new cane. "Damn MAA is gonna bust us!"

"Everyone gives slack to us guys on medical hold," Chris says.

"They probably won't let us out there in working uniforms."

"Well, we gotta at least try. I've never been out there."

"Never?" Carlos can't believe him. "And you been to Pearl how many times?"

"Lots," Chris says. "But you been out there plenty of times, so you can give me a guided tour."

"Damn wingnuts!"

They wait at a bus stop for fifteen minutes and Carlos is biting his nails the whole time. "Bus probably don't even run this early." Cars carrying sailors and marines to work drive past. Carlos feels every officer staring at him with suspicious eyes. "If somebody stops and asks what we're up to, we're gonna be in deep shit."

"We'll play dumb, like we just got off a boat and we're looking for the medial annex," Chris says.

After half an hour, no bus arrives.

"Hell with this," Carlos says. "Let's walk."

They make their way slowly along a road that skirts the warehouses of Pearl's fleet supply division. They pass the empty pier where the Enterprise and the Sacramento had tied up two weeks earlier. They show their identification to a marine guard at the gate and walk off base.

They walk along the Kamehameha Highway until they come to the entrance for the USS Arizona Memorial. Outside the museum, they read plaques bolted to rusted Japanese torpedoes and gray painted anchors arranged on the lawn.

A few minutes before nine, a bus pulls up and tourists with cameras hanging from their necks get out and congregate around a woman who is obviously their tour guide.

Chris and Carlos linger near the group and listen as the guide directs their attention to the mountains behind her. "That is the Waianae Range and high up there between the peaks there is a notch known as Kolekole Pass," she explains. "Hawaiian legend tells us about a goddess who stands in the pass to guard against intruders, but on the morning of Sunday, December 7, 1941, the goddess must have been asleep as were most of the sailors aboard the ninety-six ships tied up here in Pearl Harbor. The first main assault wave of Japanese bombers flew through the Kolekole Pass on their sneak attack at approximately seven fifty-five AM. Two hours later two thousand four hundred men were dead, eighteen ships sunk and one hundred and eighty-eight airplanes destroyed."

The guide rattles off facts and anecdotes, while Chris and Carlos lean on a railing overlooking the channel. The gleaming marble memorial erected on the sunken hull of the USS Arizona is just a little ways off across the water.

Carlos lights a cigarette.

Chris enjoys the morning sun on his face.

When the museum opens, they go inside and watch a documentary that tells the entire story from surprise attack to national monument. Then they climb into a small boat and motor out across the water to the Arizona Memorial.

Everyone climbs out of the boat, onto a dock outside the white memorial. Inside, Chris doesn't know what to make of the clean white lines with openings along the sides, but he likes it. The roof sags in the middle, making it look tall and strong at both ends. His thoughts settle on the idea that it's a tombstone and people can walk inside.

A breeze blows through the openings and natural light fills the clean, white space.

They walk through the church-like hall, pausing to stick their heads outside the openings and take in the view. Chris looks into the water at the rusted remains of the Arizona's smokestacks, the outlines of her hull visible a few feet below the surface.

A thin film of oil from a leak somewhere below makes a rainbow in the sunlight on the water's surface.

At the sight of tourists dropping flower petals on the water, his heart squeezes with a new emotion. It's warm like a shot of whiskey going down his throat—a concoction made of nostalgia and respect for this hallowed place. His heart stirs. Under the flower petals he imagines compartments flooding and men drowning in the dark while thunderous explosions rock the steel around them. And they're still trapped there now, just a few feet below the soles of his boots. Wet skeletons that had once been hearty men like himself and Carlos, now piled at the bottom of a ladder, picked clean by salt-water critters. Some compartments must have been sealed watertight and could still be dry. There must've been men who were badly wounded, Chris figured, and they lay on the deck or in their bunk dying and now they're in the dark, their fates sealed as tight as the welded steel around them.

Scenes from the movie he and Carlos watched in the museum, play across the sky before Chris's eyes. The massive gray and black dreadnaughts sit silent at anchor, tied side-by-side together on Battleship Row, quiet in the Sunday morning calm. The buzz of Japanese aircraft suddenly streaking across the sky, dropping torpedoes and strafing the metal decks with gunfire. Explosions and orange flames and black smoke erupting skyward. Men shouting in anger ... and pain.

"Check this out." Carlos tugs Chris's sleeve and they walk back to the inner chamber.

There on a marble wall, Chris sees the names of over a thousand fallen sailors listed alphabetically in small brass letters. Their epitaph reads:

TO THE MEMORY OF THE GALLANT MEN
HERE ENTOMBED AND THEIR SHIPMATES
WHO GAVE THEIR LIVES IN ACTION
ON DECEMBER, 7 1941 ON THE USS ARIZONA

"You got a cousin buried down there, Marlow."
"No shit!"
"He was a coxswain!
"A cock what?"
"A coxswain, handles small boats. A real blackshoe. Look up there."

Chris scans the alphabetical listing of names until he finds US H. Marlow. He wonders if old H was a distant cousin and feels certain he must be.

There they are, the names of the dead men below, not organized by rank or occupation, not separated into groups of enlisted or officer, sailors or marines, blackshoes or wingnuts. They are all equal in death, their names listed on the wall.

Chris wonders about the decision to seal the hull and leave the bodies of the dead inside. Did they want to be locked in their death chamber for all eternity? He's certain some of those old souls still long to feel grass between their toes.

Outside, Chris and Carlos sit on a bench on the dock and wait for the small boat to come pick them up. High on a flagpole, the stars and stripes flutter against the blue sky. Chris tries to imagine what it was like that morning just over forty years ago.

He looks up at the green mountain ridges far back above Pearl City and imagines two squadrons, maybe twenty prop planes, like a swarm of bees swooping down from the morning sky.

Where the white memorial now sits before him, he sees the dreadnought's colossal steel towers rising from their mighty gray hulls. Batteries of silent antiaircraft guns sleep in the morning calm.

Japanese Zeros, their engines growling as they swoop in and drop aerial torpedoes and rattle off bursts of armor piercing bullets. Torpedoes hit the ship's hull below the waterline and explosions tear the steel. Sailors awake with dread in their hearts; guys like Larry, Carlos and Weatherbee, leaping out of their bunks, elbows bumping each other as they scramble to pull their pants and boots on. Air raid sirens are wailing. The ship is jolted so hard muddy water pours in through rips in her hull. Some men, still in their underwear run to their guns, cursing their attackers. High velocity, large caliber bullets ricochet like driven hail off the bulkheads and metal fixtures. In less than ten minutes, the Arizona's magazine erupts, spewing flames and smoke into the Sunday morning sky. Topside, on the burning ship's deck, men desperately attempt to load their guns, but a big explosion and a fireball consumes them—fusing their flesh and blood to the hot, warped steel forever. The ship sinks and her hull presses into the mud on the bottom of Pearl Harbor. Flames scratch the sky.

"I'd give anything to be in a battle like that," Carlos says.

"Back then I would have."

"I don't actually want a disaster to happen," Carlos says. "But if the shit goes down I'm there!"

"You'd put your life at risk?" Chris feels the warm grip of

patriotism in his chest again, hears the flag snap in the breeze.

"Fuck yeah, that's the Navy adventure," Carlos says.

"You know," Chris says, "if we get in a war with Iraq or Iran we'll be fighting against guys we trained. Christ, they'll be shooting at us with guns we sold to them, Carlos."

"That's bullshit."

"No, it's not," Chris says.

"Then why'd you join, anyway?" Carlos demands.

"To sow my wild oats," Chris mutters but there's a quiver along his nerves as he imagines the skeletons of his shipmates in their tomb below. He knows better now and can't deny it. "I just wanted to save money for college," he says, but knows he's gotten himself into a lot more than that.

Above them, the stars and stripes snap in the breeze.

"You're fucking lying," Carlos speaks for the dead. "After you graduated from high school you laid on the couch all morning scratching your nuts watching TV and you were bored shitless."

Chris knows it's true.

"You're in the fucking military because you want to belong to something bigger than yourself."

Chris can't disagree. He likes the way his dungaree pants fit, the Dixie cup hat on his head.

He's been bored since leaving the ship. He misses the adrenaline scraping insides his veins while working on the flight deck of the USS Enterprise.

But he also knows, there was a time, not too long ago, when he wanted all the adventure, all the blood and guts he could get. But now he knows better. Now he knows firsthand about blood and guts and he knows that even water blasting from a fire hose can't wash those nightmares away.

But now, in this place, if only for a minute, he's at peace with the war inside his heart.

Chapter 28: Girl in Every Port

"Major Burkham will see you in a few minutes," the Army corpsman says.

"Thank you," Chris replies. "I'll wait on the balcony."

He sits on one of the lounge chairs, closes his eyes and wonders about the cardiology results. It would be just his shitty luck to have finally quit smoking only to discover he has a defective heart valve. He glances at the tin can on the floor, the same one he pitched a cigarette butt in two weeks earlier. In the filters snuffed in the sand there, he sees traces of his old life.

Smoking, he thinks, what a disgusting habit.

He takes a deep breath of clean air. His thoughts are calm with a self-assured contentment, but then he thinks about Deirdre and a pang of sadness fills his heart. They had talked until late in the night, and they knew there was nothing either of them could do. She knows he can't hide out on medical hold, and he knows there are thousands of dollars to be earned out on the Persian Gulf—money he needs to deposit into the Navy College Fund.

They had promised to write.

He goes inside and sits on the bench outside Major Burkham's office.

A moment later her door opens and she says, "Come in, Marlow."

His medical record is open on her desk. "How do you feel, Airman?"

"Fine, Ma'am." He stands at ease.

"That's good. I have some reassuring news for you." She glances at the new top page in his record. "Cardiology reports your heart is within normal limits. The valve size, seating and timing are all normal with no sign of heart disease."

"That is reassuring, Ma'am."

"Now, if you eat right and give yourself time to digest before lying down to sleep at night, you'll be okay. But you must understand that if you gorge yourself at mealtime your hiatal hernia can cause a great deal of pain that can make it hard to breath and cause anxiety." Now she looks him in the eyes. He respects her because she tells it to him straight. "You must not smoke and you must not drink alcohol to excess, is that clear?"

"Yes, ma'am."

"Just so you are aware, there is a surgical procedure for the hiatal hernia, but I do not recommend it in your condition because you have no sign of ulceration and very low probability of it becoming strangulated. Nevertheless, you must adapt your life style to prevent this condition from bothering you."

"Yes, Ma'am," he says as the words ulceration and strangulation start knocking around in his head.

"I want to send you back to the fleet, Airman Marlow, and I want you to be fully assured as to the quality of your health." She picks up a pen and signs the top page in his record. She closes the folder and hands it to him.

"Thank you, Major Burkham."

"You are welcome, Airman, good luck to you."

*   *   *

With a clean bill of health, he returns to Pearl Harbor. At the travel office, he receives a one-way ticket on TWA to Tokyo with a connecting flight to Manila. He glances at the price on the ticket, $837, and feels special because the Navy is paying to send him a third of the way around the planet. At the dispersing office, they give him a three hundred dollar cash advance, and he instantly wants to head into Honolulu for a night on the town, but his new self-confidence stifles that thought.

But even then a faint idea—that he'll have a few nights to go out on the town in the Philippines before the Enterprise arrives—emerges like a shadow in the back of his mind.

He's walking across the Navy base to the medical annex and the ninety-five degree heat draws perspiration from his skin like a fiery vacuum. He wonders how Deirdre will react to the farewell, when suddenly he notices the USS Long Beach is out of dry dock and now tied to the pier at Merry Point.

He touches his ribs on the left side of his chest and thinks about the jagged rip in the Long Beach's hull. "I'm patched up too," he whispers.

*   *   *

In the annex's air-conditioned lobby the thought crosses his mind that she's known from the start that his stay is temporary. He'll write, and if things work out he'll be back in a few months.

He sees her in the reception area and she looks up as he enters.

"How'd it go?" She glances at the medical record in his hand and she knows he's leaving.

"You're the coolest girl I've ever met," he says as his heart breaks inside his chest.

"When are you leaving?" She doesn't blink. Her eyes don't tear up. She doesn't grope for a chair to collapse in.

He wants to go to a bar and drink her off his mind. "I'll miss you," he says, trying to provoke her emotions.

"I'll miss you too." She swallows hard, betraying her nonchalance. "Let's spare the farewell crap." She ices up.

His eyes race down the pearly buttons on the front of her blouse. He knows there's a zipper on the side of her skirt.

He extends a handshake.

She glances out at the lobby and he looks too.

There's nobody around.

His hand goes to her hip.

She throws her arms around his neck, knocking his Dixie cup hat to the floor.

Their bodies press together and their lips meet.

She's as sweet as honey.

Then it's over.

She walks away into the offices behind the reception area, leaving him to pick up his hat and papers off the floor.

Chapter 29: Anchors Aweigh

"I'm scheduled for an explanatory surgery next week," Weatherbee says.

"Explanatory?" Chris asks.

"Yeah, explanatory," Weatherbee insists.

"Where they cutting this time?" Carlos asks.

They're sitting in the barracks TV lounge.

"The doctors been monitoring my blood and suspects my kidney, you know 'cause it filters the blood and all, there's lots of toxic waste in the kidney, so much that if it broke, then all the waste would go into the blood and kill me."

"In your kidney?" Chris asks.

"Yeah, my kidney."

"Your one kidney?" Carlos holds up a finger.

Weatherbee shifts in the overstuffed chair, flashes a perplexed look. "Yes." he sniffles. "Toxic waste in my kidney. What's a matter with you guys, can't you hear?" His brow furrows, lips purse.

"It's all good, Weatherbee." Chris sits back on the coach.

"Just ask your doctor how many kidneys you got," Carlos advises. "If he says one, don't let him operate."

Weatherbee shakes his head and sighs.

"How's your therapy going?" Chris asks Carlos.

"Shit, watch this!" Carlos stands up and drops his pants around his ankles. He squats slowly. The muscles in both legs strain. The scar across his knee shines where the prosthetic kneecap bulges. The hairs on his thigh that were flattened after months in the cast have returned to their curly softness and the skin has regained its brownish hue.

"Awesome," Chris says.

Carlos pulls up his pants. "And no limp," he says as he paces back and forth on the carpet. "I ain't limping, am I?"

"No, you sure ain't limping, Carlos," Weatherbee says.

"I don't see a limp at all," Chris says.

Carlos does a lap around the TV lounge. "What about you, wingnut, where's the Enterprise?"

"Probably the Sea of Japan by now. I'll get over to the Philippines before they arrive."

"Got your condoms?"

"Yeah, but I ain't gonna be whoring around. I'm going scuba diving."

"Shit, you'll go muff diving," Carlos snaps and Weatherbee snorts.

"Whatever," Chris says. "My scuba instructor told me there's Japanese barges sunk during World War II that have grown into amazing coral reefs."

"I went snorkeling there one time," Weatherbee says. "Saw a school of the prettiest little fishes."

Carlos sits back on the sofa. "How much longer you gonna be in the Navy, Marlow?"

"Less than a year," Chris says.

"You should reenlist," Carlos says.

"I'm getting out and going to college," Chris says.

"I'm staying in if this damn knee doesn't get me kicked out."

Weatherbee's eyes flutter and his head pitches to the side.

They look at him and Carlos chuckles.

"That knee won't keep you out," Chris says, as he stands up. "Well, Carlos, I gotta go upstairs and pack. You take it easy."

They shake hands.

"You too, shipmate—I mean wingnut," Carlos says. "Smooth sailing, my friend."

*   *   *

His sea bag has gained a few pounds with the new scuba gear, and it feels good strapped on his back as he steps onto the barrack's porch at five AM.

He stands out by the road and waits for a cab to take him to the airport. It's quiet and cool and he looks through the trees and across the harbor. He sees a battleship setting out to sea so he drops his seabag on the grass in front of the barracks and walks across the road. He climbs onto the boulders and scrambles out a little ways onto the jetty where he can see it's the USS Long Beach getting underway.

There are sailors in dress whites standing along the rails.

The breeze picks up and Chris's black neckerchief flutters across his chest. The bellbottom cuffs of his dress white pants ruffle. With one hand, he holds his white hat on his head so it wouldn't blow away.

He stands on the black boulders watching the mighty battleship plow through the water as it crosses the harbor. Through the cool morning air he hears the voice of an officer on the ship order, "Hand salute!" Chris watches sailors snap to attention, each bringing his right hand up to his brow as they pass the Arizona Memorial.

With her hull patched and painted, Christopher Marlow knows that the Long Beach is going to be just fine out on the open sea.

The End

Dear Reader,

If you enjoyed SAILORS DELIGHT, please post a review at the online bookseller where you found it. A review can be as simple as a few short comments.

As an independent author I rely heavily on your purchases and positive reviews. For more information about my nautical novels and sea stories please go to: **www.malcolmtorres.com**

Sincerely,
Malcolm Torres

Acknowledgements

During the time I was writing SAILORS DELIGHT, I received support and encouragement from many people. Thank you to family, friends and fellow writers who read early revisions and graciously provided suggestions for improvement, especially Thomas Eugene Fleck, Tira Gene Plumondore, Erick Fleck, Thais Carlucci, Joseph Carlucci Sr., Teresa Lynn Willard and Scott Driver. To all the good people at World Cup Coffee in Portland, Oregon, thank you for the caffeine. Last but not least, I owe a special debt of gratitude to all the sailors with whom I served in the US Navy aboard the USS Enterprise (CVN-65).

Please turn the page for a free preview of

SAILORS TAKE WARNING
A Mystery Thriller
By Malcolm Torres

MALCOLM TORRES

SAILORS TAKE WARNING

A Mystery Thriller
By Malcolm Torres

PART I

ABOARD THE USS NIMITZ

Chapter One – Day 1

Kate Conrad leaned out the pharmacy's dispensing window and handed the man a tube of medicated cream. She was about to tell him to apply it twice daily to the affected area, when the alarm bell rang.

At twenty, Kate was tall with short-clipped sandy hair and blue eyes. Second thoughts about leaving the University of California at San Diego to join the Navy still haunted her, but as a member of the ship's Flying Squad, she never thought twice when that alarm bell rang.

"Follow the directions on the label," she said hurriedly while locking the pharmacy. She ran from the medical department, calling back over her shoulder, "And don't scratch no matter how itchy it gets!"

In the main deck passageway, Kate waited and listened to the bell's incessant clangor.

It rang from waterproof speakers throughout the ship—a bone-rattling metallic din, threatening to perforate eardrums.

Thousands of sailors looked away from computer screens, set aside power tools and paused conversations. Throughout the multilevel maze, eyes turned toward speakers mounted on bulkheads. Those asleep in narrow bunks under white sheets and scratchy wool blankets startled awake—eyes suddenly open in air-conditioned darkness.

A squeal of feedback squashed the clanging bell, and a computer-generated female voice announced, "AWAY THE FLYING SQUAD. THIS IS NOT A DRILL. FLAMMABLE SPILL ON THE AFT HANGAR DECK, FRAME TWO FOUR FIVE. AWAY THE FLYING SQUAD, AWAY." The bell resumed its urgent call to action, reverberating against every bulkhead.

Kate Conrad ran aft inside the main deck passageway, shouting at sailors walking ahead of her, "Gangway! Coming through!" After weeks of endless boredom, Kate relished the adrenaline shot as she ran to the accident scene.

The eight-foot-wide corridor was the Nimitz's main drag compared to so many other narrow passageways, but sailors crammed in, walking two and three abreast. Fluorescent lights glared off the polished green Formica. Bundles of cable, ventilation ducts and myriad pipes carrying water, jet fuel and sewage crammed into the low overhead. Bulkheads marked with weld scars and rows of rivet heads. Fire hoses stowed in compact racks. Watertight doors, battle lanterns and fire extinguishers flew past in Kate's peripheral vision.

They were the shipboard equivalents of ambulances screaming along crowded boulevards. In passageways throughout the ship, sailors squeezed behind pipes and doors, flattened themselves against bulkheads, like cars pulling to the curb, as Flying Squad members ran past, their black boots booming on the steel, their cries of "Gangway!" and "Make a hole!" punctuating the boredom of shipboard routine.

Frequent drills tested her ability to locate damage control lockers and emergency medical stations hidden away inside the Nimitz's 1,000-foot-long and 17-deck-high hive of compartments and passageways. She'd studied 3-D schematics of the ship and proved she could find any location blindfolded during blackout and smoke drills.

Jet fuel mist swirled down around a ladder angling at 45-degrees through an open hatch in the deck above. The smell seared her nose; Kate pulled a gas mask tight against her face and exhaled hard to clear it.

Fire Marshall O'Malley emerged from the jet fuel fog. A human tree trunk with the bark peeled off, he shouted orders at sailors distributing extinguishers, mops and buckets in a disciplined frenzy. O'Malley's fierce eyes stared out through his face shield. "You and you," he roared, pointing a thick finger at two boatswain mates. "Grab

2

oxygen bottles and a stretcher. Follow EMT Conrad!" O'Malley stared at Kate and shouted, "There's one serious injury and several overcome by fumes on the fantail. Move it."

She grabbed her bulky EMT kit from the damage control locker and a fresh shot of adrenaline pulsed into her limbs as she climbed the ladder into the mist. At the top, in the aircraft hangar, she came face to face with the cause of the current emergency.

Jet engine shipping containers—steel cans, each the size and weight of a minivan—were normally stacked three-high and chained to the deck in this area. As best Kate could tell, one container had fallen over and landed on several wooden crates, reducing them to splinters. A second shipping container had fallen over, rolled across the deck and smashed a pipe against the bulkhead.

A fountain of fuel—creating an asphyxiation, fire and explosion hazard—squirted in multiple directions across the hangar, splashed on several cargo containers and misted in the air. Kate saw the cloud of vapor billowing through the open space packed with jet aircraft and aviation support equipment.

Sailors scrambled about dropping bails of rags and tearing open bags of absorbent granules, dropping them on a growing puddle of fuel that sloshed this way and that as the ship rolled on erratic ocean swells.

A jet mechanic in blue coveralls and a scuffed yellow hardhat shouted, "Over here," hailing Kate and the boatswains.

They splashed through the jet fuel puddle, and followed the mechanic through a shop crowded with partially assembled jet engines. "A shipping container fell on the poor guy," the mechanic explained. He swung open a big metal door and led the way out onto the fantail, an open deck on the aft end of the ship where sailors throw trash overboard, go fishing and occasionally bury a shipmate at sea.

Passing from the ship's air-conditioned interior to the scorching humidity, here a few degrees north of the equator, Kate broke a sweat instantly. She pulled off her gas mask and took a deep breath. The oppressive claustrophobia of the ship's cramped interior fell away. Blue ocean and boundless sky expanded to the horizon.

A crowd stood gawking at the accident victims.

"Give us room here," one of the boatswains ordered in a thick Boston accent.

"Let's go, move it," the other boatswain shouted as the crowd shuffled toward the far side of the fantail.

Kate went directly to the injured man lying on the deck, while the boatswains administered oxygen to several sailors who were soaked with jet fuel and overcome by fumes.

She knelt and placed her hand on his shoulder and saw his grease-streaked brown jersey soaked with jet fuel and blood. She opened her kit and noted his head cocked at an odd angle and his eyes open in a dead-ahead stare. Between baby-fat cheeks, his lips twisted in a grotesque kiss.

She found no pulse at his wrists or neck. She pulled on a pair of Nitrile gloves and a facemask, stuck two fingers between his teeth and pulled his jaw down to reveal a mouth filled with blood. She grabbed a pair of surgical scissors, and in one smooth motion cut his brown turtleneck jersey from collar to hem and pealed back the wet fabric.

Blunt force trauma had crushed the entire left side of his chest. A malicious purple bruise covered his smashed torso. Blood flowed from punctures where fractured ribs pierced skin. Kate pictured the shipping container tumbling over, knocking him down and crushing him—causing massive thoracic trauma. Flail chest—she remembered from training—when ribs are broken in so many places that the shattered sections detach from the ribcage and play havoc with the diaphragm, making it impossible to breath. Fuck, she realized, he's already dead!

Examining his neck, she found it wasn't broken. She turned his head to the side. She grabbed a suction device from her kit and tried to clear his airway, but too much blood flowed from his mouth. She dropped the suction device, grabbed a tracheal tube, inserted it in his mouth and pushed it down into his lungs.

"Oh-two," she shouted.

The kid from Boston connected an oxygen bottle to the tracheal tube and let it flow.

The victim's chest raised a little.

Kate thought maybe, held her breath for a few seconds hoping, but his busted chest contorted and collapsed. Blood flowed from the torn skin where his broken ribs protruded.

"Gentle pressure," she whispered.

The kid from Boston grabbed a towel from the kit. He pressed it against the guy's chest, trying to hold the ribs in place, so Kate could get him breathing, but his torso was all Jell-O and broken bones.

Oxygen filled the victim's lungs and contorted his ribs. A large blood-blister bulged through the skin on his shattered breastbone.

Flail chest with hematoma. Kate knelt on the steel, helpless with her first responder kit. He needs a team of specialists and a thoracic surgery suite, Kate thought, as air and blood gurgled out of him.

The mechanic squatted beside her. "A shipping can weighs over two tons," he whispered. "It took eight of us to lift the corner of it just so we could pull him out."

Kate closed the dead man's eyes. She gazed across the ocean and noticed a ship cruising a ways off. It looked strange riding in the Nimitz's wake. It had spinning satellite dishes and high towers with long antennas. She wondered if the people on that ship could see the Nimitz.

* * *

In the medical department, the sheet came off the second the dead body hit the examination table.

"Owwww!" Gutierrez groaned when she pealed back his jersey and eyed bone splintering through bruised-black flesh. Her brilliant white teeth bit her lower lip.

Kate snipped the dead man's laces and pulled off a boot.

Gutierrez bucked up and began snipping his pants.

Kate tugged at a silver Navy ring on the dead man's left hand but his fingers were pudgy and it wouldn't budge.

"Try this." Gutierrez handed her a tube of petroleum jelly.

The chief medical officer, Commander Sternz, entered the room. A stout woman with a freckly, olive complexion and dark eyes, Sternz wore her black hair in a bun so tight it looked painful. A smile rarely stretched her lips and never reached her eyes.

Kate tugged at the ring and said, "A shipping container fell on him, ma'am. He died from internal bleeding before I got there."

Sternz glanced at the caved-in chest and said, "Finish stripping this cadaver and lock it in the morgue. Meet me back here at nineteen hundred for an autopsy." She glanced mechanically from Kate to Gutierrez. "This gives us a training opportunity," she said. "We'll explore his thoracic interior." Then Sternz left the compartment, oblivious of the door banging shut behind her.

"She's colder than this guy," Gutierrez said.

Kate dropped the Navy ring into a Ziploc bag along with the dead man's wallet. They slid a thick, black plastic body bag under him, folded his arms and legs inside and zipped it shut.

Kate rolled the gurney across the hall to the morgue. She typed the combination on a keypad lock. She held the door with her foot as she maneuvered the gurney into the small space.

Vertigo wiggled behind her eyeballs and her knees wobbled. She stepped forward to prevent herself from stumbling. Wondering if a rogue wave had hit the ship, she glanced at the rows of shiny stainless steel drawers.

She thought about Donna Grogan with a broken spine, fractured skull and covered with sticky maple syrup. Grogan went into the morgue, but then where'd she go, Kate wondered. And Larry Burns, the cook who died of a heart attack while pulling a tray of dinner rolls from an oven in the bakery. Somebody put him in here, just like Grogan, but where'd his body go? Kate glanced at the drawers, wondering which ones Grogan and Burns had occupied.

She positioned the gurney and prepared to put this guy, whose name she didn't know yet, into cold storage.

* * *

Kate grew up on the beach in Ventura, California. Muscles rippled on her long arms and legs. In high school, she was fiercely competitive in volleyball and track, so dragging a 170-pound corpse from a gurney to a morgue drawer wasn't a problem.

She grabbed the body bag, braced her legs and out of nowhere a shadow of doubt flitted across her mind: What am I doing? I should be in college!

After months at sea, these thoughts intruded several times a day. I'm filling penicillin prescriptions for sailors with the clap, when I should be in a pre-med program or at least at a Friday night keg party with friends!

"Okay, cool it," she reminded herself that the University of California at San Diego volleyball scholarship had only covered one-third of her tuition bill. She remembered the start of every semester, standing at the financial aid window signing a student loan promissory note. She still felt the anxiety and depression that swelled in her chest after several terms; after she did the math and calculated her growing mountain of student loan debt.

One night at the library, cramming for an Anatomy exam, a panic attack hit. Owing so much to Bank of America, she feared, would prevent her from ever buying a car, a house, or having kids. Shoving the textbook aside, she tallied what she'd owe by the time she earned a medical degree. The six-figure number gnawed at her during lectures and labs. She awoke in her dorm room in the middle of the night with such dread it was difficult to breathe. I'm too young for this kind of debt, she told herself as she sank back into a troubled sleep.

A few days later, with sunlight streaming through the library windows, she was surfing the web and saw, under a banner ad for Clearasil, a picture of a female sailor dispensing a prescription over a pharmacy counter.

The next day, she rode her bike off campus to meet with a Navy recruiter.

* * *

With fists that spiked their way to a high school volleyball championship and a UC San Diego scholarship, Kate dragged the body bag onto the cold drawer.

Outside the morgue, she double-checked the lock.

In the records office, she dropped into a chair, touched color-coded menu options on a screen to open a fatality report. Reaching into the Ziploc for the dead guy's wallet, the ring slipped around her finger. She pulled it out, examined the blue gem and read his name, Stanley Comello, inscribed inside. Her mind flashed on his chubby knuckles and out of nowhere, tears brimmed on her lower eyelids. She dropped the ring back into the bag, and opened her eyes wide and inhaled deeply through her nose to make the tears go away. In Comello's wallet, she found his ID and glanced at his picture. At 19, he hadn't burned off the baby fat. His chubby cheeks and toothy smile gave him a slow moving, good-natured look.

She swiped his ID and his record started downloading.

She glanced at a whiteboard where they kept track of the number of days they'd been at sea. Across the top, someone had written "DAYS ON AN INVISIBLE SHIP . . ." and below that, a big number 93 in the middle of a dark smudge where someone erased and updated the number every morning.

She remembered the ship cruising behind the Nimitz and wondered if it was the Hayward. Had it finally found them?

She filled in the fatality report and clicked save.

Before meeting Terrance McDaniels for dinner, Kate checked the lock on the morgue one last time.

#

SAILORS TAKE WARNING is available in paperback and eBook format at all online book sellers. To find out more about Malcolm Torres's other exciting nautical novels and sea stories, his twice-annual newsletter and the upcoming podcast, please go to:

www.malcolmtorres.com

Made in the USA
Las Vegas, NV
14 January 2022

41347310R00132